THE HORSEMAN'S LAST CALL

THE HORSEMAN'S LAST CALL

Bill Gallaher

TouchWood
Editions

TouchWood Editions
touchwoodeditions.com

LIBRARY AND ARCHIVES CANADA CATALOGUING IN PUBLICATION
Gallaher, Bill
    The horseman's last call / Bill Gallaher.

"A wild Jack Strong story".
Issued also in electronic formats.
ISBN 978-1-927129-00-5

    I. Title.

PS8563.A424H67 2012   C813'.6   C2011-907346-3

Editor: Marlyn Horsdal
Proofreader: Sarah Weber
Cover image: Glenbow Archives NC-6-12955B
Author photo: Jaye Gallagher

We gratefully acknowledge the financial support for our publishing activities
from the Government of Canada through the Canada Book Fund, Canada
Council for the Arts, and the province of British Columbia through the
British Columbia Arts Council and the Book Publishing Tax Credit.

The interior pages of this book have been printed on 100% post-consumer
recycled paper, processed chlorine free, and printed with vegetable-based inks.

1 2 3 4 5 16 15 14 13 12

PRINTED IN CANADA

For Denise and Cheryl, dear friends down the years.

CONTENTS

Background

IN VOLUME ONE, *The Frog Lake Massacre*, Jack Strong, born Caleb Caine, was involved in the massacre and joined Sam Steele in the hunt for Big Bear. In Volume Two, *The Luck of the Horseman*, a personal tragedy turned Jack's life upside down, after which he went to South Africa with Steele and the Lord Strathcona's Horse to fight the Boers. Wounded and nursed by a farm wife, Jack fell in love with her but because she was married, he returned to Canada. When he realized his mistake, he hurried back to South Africa with the newly formed constabulary to find her. Volume Three opens with Jack back in Canada with his new bride, reunited with his good friend Jim Spencer.

ONE

The Little Karoo

THE FIRST STARS BEGAN to grace the cloudless sky and from out on the placid lake came the haunting yodel of a loon. We sat on our front porch in contented silence, Jim and Maggie Spencer, their infant son, Peter, and Ree and I.

The spring and summer had flown by at dizzying speed, as we built our house, a barn, and a corral. Pine trees grew as straight as taut ropes on the property, and we cut and peeled them and built our house in a long rectangular shape. We brought boards from a mill in Kamloops for the roof and to partition off two bedrooms at one end, one for Ree and me and the other for the children we hoped to have. The house faced a small lake and stood next to a grove of trembling aspens, for Ree loved the sound of the wind in their leaves. Besides Jim and Maggie, who lived a mile down the road, neighbours had come from all around to help with the construction and it had gone quickly. It was hard work, but each log and board that went into the house was a step toward a home of our own, and we fell into our bedrolls each night exhausted but content. Once the house was habitable and we could move out of the tent we'd been living in, Ree painted a sign that I hung from the porch eaves. It read, "The Little Karoo," in honour of the land on which we had met.

With the house finished, we threw a party. Jim and I took a wagon into town and bought a pig dressed for roasting and a cask of whisky. We cooked the pig on a spit over a fire in the front yard and invited everyone who had worked on the house for a meal and drinks. There were enough musicians among the crowd to form an ad hoc band and we danced and sang the afternoon and early evening into the past. Ree got to hear Jim's incredible voice for the first time, and like everyone else who heard it, she could only shake her head in amazement that he had chosen to be a cattle rancher over a professional singer. But that was Jim.

Now the party was done and everyone but Jim and Maggie had gone home. The pre-dusk sky reflected off the lake; Jim and I sipped whisky while the women had tea. Peter lay sound asleep in his bassinet. We sat there as quiet as the settling night, all sublimely happy to be back in each others' lives.

I was fortunate to have such good friends, particularly Jim. If you were in a jam, you couldn't do better than to have him on your side. Though he wasn't easily riled, a wise man would not push him to that point. He stood above my six feet in height and had the strength of a circus strongman—I had once seen him topple a pompous British sergeant-major on a horse. His dark hair, sideburns and moustache complemented

a handsome faced weathered by the outdoor life of a cowboy.
We had shared more than most men—a hunt for a murder-
ing Indian, a cattle drive to the Klondike and a year in South
Africa fighting the Boers—and we owed each other our lives.
He had saved mine in the Yukon and I had saved his during
the war. Then, after our return to Canada, he had married
Maggie in Ottawa and they went off on their honeymoon. We
were supposed to meet in Calgary and buy some land together,
but I had not told him about Ree. She had been my temporary
nurse after I was wounded on her farm at the edge of the Great
Karoo, and I had fallen in love with her. That she was already
married was the reason I never told anybody. I had foolishly
thought I could forget her but when that proved impossible, I
left Jim in the lurch and returned to South Africa to find her.

He had no idea where I had gone and I had no means of
letting him know, but he never truly doubted that I would
return and had purchased enough land for both of us. He had
not been able to find anything in the Alberta foothills, our
first choice, but came across this wonderful property south
of Kamloops, in British Columbia, and had been overly fair
in splitting it. He had offered me half, as we had originally
planned, but I didn't need that much. All I wanted to do
was break and harness-train horses, so I took a third, 300
acres, and left Jim with the rest for a cattle herd that fluctuated between 250 and 300 head. That we could share this
evening together, on this land, despite the two years between
our farewells in Ottawa and our reunion, made it that much
more sublime.

The loon yodelled again. "I don't think I'll ever grow
tired of that sound," Maggie said. "Someone should make a

phonograph recording of it so that people in the cities could enjoy it too."

Maggie was a generous soul and it was like her to want to share. A sturdy, no-nonsense woman with long, raven-dark hair, she seemed the perfect match for Jim. She was pretty but not spectacularly so, yet the warmth and charm generated from her core made her very attractive. And having been raised with eight brothers, she understood men better than most of her gender did.

I couldn't have agreed more with her comment and said, "And without the two of you, we wouldn't be sitting here enjoying it." I raised my glass. "Here's to you, Jim, and to you, Maggie. 'Thank you' seems a sorry way of expressing how we really feel, but thank you anyway."

Jim, who had an enviable knack for accepting things as they came, raised his glass in return. "There's no other way it could have happened."

"I'm so glad," Ree added. "I can't tell you how happy you've made me."

Indeed, after several years of struggling in South Africa to get a sheep ranch established and then having to contend with a war that took her first husband, she had found her place in the world. This land was peaceful and she loved its pine forests, stands of aspen, lush meadows and the small lake that provided fresh water.

Jim hitched up their wagon and he and Maggie left with Peter before it got too dark. Ree and I sat for a while longer, holding hands, listening to the night. Scarcely a day went by that I didn't inwardly celebrate my decision to return to South Africa to look for her. I have always been blessed with my fair share of luck and it was luck as much as determination that led me to her. I loved everything about her—her well-proportioned, slender frame, her long, chestnut hair that framed a pretty face accentuated by a full mouth, and especially the grace with which she approached life. Then I lit a lamp and we went inside and prepared for bed in our first home.

Yet there was still much to do. We now had to acquire horses to be broken, some for riding and others for pulling wagons and sleighs, which would entail harness-training and teaching them to work in pairs. They would fetch a good price in any urban centre where horses still provided a cheap source of transportation. Our emphasis would be on quality rather than quantity and we hoped the stock would eventually include Clydesdales and Shires. There was enough grass in a nearby meadow for grazing in summer and we fenced it off, saving other meadows on the property for hay. Then Jim and I rode down into the Nicola Valley where a rancher had a dozen horses for sale. I picked eight of the sturdiest and we herded them home.

By late fall, we had the operation under way. The work kept me around the main part of the ranch, which meant that Ree wasn't left alone too often. Whenever I went off on horse-buying excursions or trips into town for supplies or to ship horses by train to buyers on the coast—our biggest market—she had the option of accompanying me. More often than not, she chose to stay at home. She was content there and hated to leave.

Life was showing its good side; nevertheless, any still pond is bound to experience ripples from time to time. Ree wanted a family but our efforts since our marriage had proved fruitless.

She was extremely disappointed and blamed herself. If she had not able been to produce children with her first husband, Oliver, or with me, and I had fathered a child in my first marriage, then it clearly must be her fault. She needed comforting during those times, as she thought she was failing me. All I could do was provide reassurance that I would gladly spend my life with her, whether children entered the picture or not. Even so, a child would have filled her life with joy, which in turn would have pleased me immensely. Later that fall, when Maggie announced that she was pregnant again, Ree was excited for her and Jim but deep down, I think she felt no small degree of envy.

Winter came and with it Christmas, and snow lay knee-deep across the hills and in the valleys, and the lake froze. It was a special, unrepeatable event in that it was our first celebration together in our own home. That we could share it with Jim and Maggie was a bonus and for the first time in years, I felt connected to something valuable and worthwhile. I had conspired with Maggie to order a dress for Ree through the Sears Roebuck catalogue and she loved it. As it turned out, Ree had a conspiracy of her own going and had the present she had bought for me kept at Jim and Maggie's so that I would not be able to guess what it was. When I saw the length of it and felt its weight, I could see why. I tore off the tissue paper and exposed a box containing a Browning A5, a 12-gauge, semi-automatic shotgun that could hold five cartridges in its chamber. A nicer fowling piece had yet to be made and it was a fine companion to my Browning-designed Winchester hunting rifle.

They were weapons designed to put food on the table and not for war, and for that, a man had to be thankful. I had been wounded twice and had the scars to prove it—one on my right cheek that was a souvenir of Riel's rebellion and another on my right chest that I had received in South Africa—and I wasn't eager to try for a third. It is never a good idea for a man to push his luck, so I hoped never to find myself on a battlefield again. And sitting there in front of a warm fire with the woman I loved and good friends, and all the things in life I cherished and desired, I never imagined that I would.

THE NEW year of 1904 saw the horse-training business steadily improve and while we were not likely to get rich, I was my own boss and doing what I wanted to do. Both were valid substitutes for pockets full of money. Life hummed along smoothly until it brought some surprises that had nothing to do with the ranch.

In March, a cable arrived from Vancouver. Eleanor McRae, my former mother-in-law, had died from a gynecologic cancer. Ree and I hurried to the funeral, where the weather was as sombre as the service. Alexander McRae was beside himself with grief, having lost a wife and companion of 35 years. He laid her to rest beside her daughter and granddaughter—my first wife and our child—Charity and Becky, the first two great loves of my life who had been taken from me in a tragic accident. Eleanor had faced her inevitable demise, McRae said, "with great courage."

My old friend Joe Fortes attended the funeral and we visited with him for a while in his new home on English Bay. His passion for swimming hadn't dwindled by an atom and he still earned an income by offering swimming lessons to the public. In a world of rapid change, Joe was an anchor of stability and you never spent time with him without feeling grounded.

Spring broke, warmer than usual according to the old-timers, and the snow disappeared rapidly. At the end of June, Maggie gave birth to another son, James Jr., and there was much celebrating in the Spencer household. Jim was proud of his boys and made a point of being the father to them that his own abusive father had never been to him, which is to say he spoiled them rotten. For Ree and me, it was easy to be slightly envious over their burgeoning family, but change often arrives swiftly at one's door and it is astonishing how the misfortunes of some can result in good fortune for others. That was how Davey O'Farrell came into our lives and though we knew the general circumstances, it wasn't until later that Davey was able to fill in the details.

HE WAS a shy boy, tall and thin, with fair hair and blue eyes. His features were plain but when he smiled, it was as if someone had turned the sun up a notch or two. He was 10 years old and the only child of Irish immigrant parents who lived in a ramshackle, two-bedroom, wood-frame house on the outskirts of Kamloops.

His father was a labourer for the Canadian Pacific Railway on the section of tracks west of town. On Saturday nights, after a long week's toil, he would go to the saloon and come home just in time for dinner. Sometimes he'd be late and come home in his cups. Davey didn't mind though; he liked it when his father drank because the two of them had more fun then. Davey also liked the smell of whisky on his father's breath, mingled with the smell of sweat from an honest day's work and the sweet aroma of pipe smoke. They were the smells of a real man, Davey thought. And it always amazed him how his father could snap a match into flame with a flick of his thumb, then draw in an immense volume of smoke and expel it from his nose like a fire-breathing dragon. When he blew smoke rings, Davey would poke his finger through the holes and tear the rings into ragged clouds.

"That's just like life, Davey," his father once said. "Ye're travellin' along mindin' yer own business and God jabs his finger and tears yer life into wee bits."

When his ma was busy, he and his dad would play cribbage. Once Davey had learned how to play and was dealing the first hand in their first real game, his father had solemnly proclaimed, "Ye realize, lad, that ye're pitted against the champion of the world and no mortal soul has ever beaten me?"

Such an assertion did not surprise Davey, yet somehow he won nearly every game. The next time they played, his father declared once again that he was the world's cribbage champion. Davey asked, "Dad, how come you're still champion of the world when I win all the time? Shouldn't I be champion?"

"That's a fair question Davey," his father had replied. "And I'm sure yer ma'd be up to answerin' it, if ye'd care to ask her."

"How come she needs to answer it? Why don't you?"

"Well, the fact is, Davey, I am. Maybe not directly, but I'm sendin' ye to the right place to get an answer, and that's just as important. Yer ma has an answer for everything."

His ma had tittered and said, "Hush, Declan. You mustn't be tormenting the boy like that!"

"Do ye call this torment, Mary?" his father asked, fishing a stick of candy from his pocket and offering it to Davey, who suddenly forgot the question.

It had not been unusual for his dad to bring a gift for Davey when he came home from the saloon. If it wasn't candy, it might be a small toy. One night he had brought a pocketknife, with a shiny blade and deer-antler grips. His father had said, "Ye're 10 years old now, Davey. It's time ye had a good knife of yer own. Tomorrow, I'll show ye how to keep it sharp."

His father would often make promises like that and forget about them the next day. It didn't matter. Some fathers never even bothered to make promises, so Davey loved him anyway.

He loved his mother too, of course—loved the way she always took care of her family, loved how she always had an excuse for his dad when he stayed out drinking. She'd say, "Yer father works hard to put a roof over our heads and food on our table, Davey, and wouldn't we be ungrateful in the eyes of God if we complained because he stumbled once in a while? There's no point in layin' blame; it's just the way men are."

She would help her husband to bed if he needed it, and be silent about it in the morning. Davey was not old enough to understand how much of his love for his father was inspired by his caring mother.

On occasion, his dad would bring home a bottle of whisky and he and his ma would stay up late drinking, laughing and having a merry old time. Sure, they argued, but it seldom lasted and was never spiteful or disrespectful. If Davey was still awake when they went to bed, he'd sometimes hear his father grunting and his mother moaning, sounds that he didn't quite know what to make of other than that they seemed to be enjoying themselves.

The night his father had brought home the knife, he had also brought some whisky. It was a lovely, warm summer evening and the three of them had played cards until late, laughing themselves silly. Then his ma sent him off to bed. He was tired but stayed awake for the longest time, excited about the knife. He kept opening and closing it, revelling in the feel of the wonderful thing in the dark, and how the blade locked into place. It was a fine knife, not cheap like the knives of some of the older boys he knew. In time, he grew tired and placed the knife on his bedside table. He fell asleep to the good sounds emanating from his parents' bedroom.

In the middle of the night, he dreamed that someone was choking him and awoke to find his room filling with smoke. He was frightened and confused, and for a moment didn't know what to do. Instinctively, he grabbed his knife from the table and hurried to the bedroom door. He flung it open. Thick, hot smoke billowed in, nearly overwhelming him. He was terrified but had the presence of mind to run to his window, throw it open and climb out into the night air. He ran to the nearest house and pounded on the door with his small fists, screaming, "My house is on fire! They're burning! My ma and dad are burning!" He looked at his house and could see that flames had filled the interior and smoke was rising thickly from his open bedroom window and from beneath the eaves.

Mr. Garvin, whom Davey knew as a grumpy old man, opened the door angrily, pulling the suspenders of his trousers over his undershirt, but when he saw the house on fire, he went into action. He didn't even stop to put on his shoes. He ran to rouse the fire brigade, which someone else had already alerted, but by the time it arrived with the water wagon, it was too late. Davey's house was lost, fully engulfed in flames that roared and crackled high into the sky. All that remained in the wake of the fire was a smouldering skeleton. The Garvins would not let Davey see the awful blackness that was his parents' bed and the grotesque forms that lay upon it. Even so, he knew that he was now alone and that whatever happy times he had enjoyed before were gone forever. He clutched his knife and cried, and trembled so hard that those about him thought he might shake into small pieces. His father had been right. God had jabbed His finger and had torn Davey's life to bits. Mrs. Garvin took him into her arms and gave him comfort.

IT DIDN'T take long for word of the fire and the loss of two lives to spread through the valleys around Kamloops and along with it, talk of a boy who was without parents and a home. Davey had no recollection of aunts and uncles or grandmothers and grandfathers. His family had had no need of any of those; they'd had themselves. The authorities tried to find a relative but came up with nothing. The Garvins looked after Davey with the understanding that it was only until a decent home could be for him.

Several people knew that Ree and I were childless and might be willing to take Davey as our own, and a rider came to our ranch with a note from the local judge. I rigged the democrat immediately and we drove to town with as much speed as we could manage without spilling over.

TWO

Davey

THOSE FIRST FEW WEEKS with us were difficult for Davey. He spoke hardly at all, and smiles, when they came, were only half-hearted. His knife was always somewhere close, if not in his pocket, then by his bedside. It was his way of staying connected to his parents, especially his father. He had nightmares, crying out in his sleep, nonsensical but terror-laden sounds, and he blamed himself for not saving his parents from the fire. He should have gone into their room and awakened them, pulled them out with his thin little arms, but instead he ran to save himself. It was unforgivable.

It was a great burden for a child to carry and Ree took him in her arms, her eyes wet with tears. "It was too late to save them, Davey. There was nothing you or anyone else could do. If you had gone into their room you would never have come out."

"At least I'd be with them," he sobbed.

"Be with us, Davey," Ree urged. "We want you to be with us."

Davey was what Ree had wished for most of her married life, a child to care for and to love, and even though he had trouble warming to us, he brought her great pleasure. I admit to having doubts at first but there is something about a child's presence in a home that both authenticates it and lends it grace.

At first, Davey called us Mr. and Mrs. Strong but Ree thought that was too formal. She would have loved it if he had called us "Mum" and "Dad" or variations of those words, but felt they would be sacred to Davey. She suggested Aunt Ree and Uncle Jack but he could not bring himself to use even those. Although other children had talked about their aunts and uncles, he had never had any that he knew of and was unaccustomed to using such titles. So when he referred to Ree in my company, it was always "she" or "her." When he spoke to Ree about me, it was "he" or "him." It was quite clever how his 10-year-old mind was able to get around not addressing us the way we would have liked. And if he was not able work it out, he simply remained silent.

"You know, Davey," I said to him one day, "if you want to call us Mum and Dad, or even Aunt and Uncle, we would feel honoured, although we understand how hard it might be for you. But as hard as it is, you have to call us something, son. We deserve at least that much."

He nodded. "I know," he agreed, meekly.

In the end, it wasn't anything that Ree or I said that brought us together as a family; it was two horses. Two horses taught Davey it was okay to love something beyond his parents and that, in turn, it was okay to love us.

It was one of those glorious days that made a man glad, not only to be alive, but to be alive in such a grand place. I was in the corral, working with a stubborn bay that had decided it didn't need training, and Ree was giving Davey an arithmetic lesson in the house when three strangers rode up, trailing a packhorse laden with mining equipment. One was an elderly man, tall and thin, with a kind face, who sat his horse as if he were extremely proud of it. His handlebar mustache was white and I guessed him to be in his sixties. The other two men were perhaps half his age. One was dark-haired with sunken cheeks above a triangular chin, also sporting a handlebar mustache; the other was a pleasant-faced chap with reddish hair and a short goatee. He wore a Derby hat while the other two men wore Stetsons. I would have wagered that he thought of himself as a bit of a ladies' man.

The older man touched the brim of his hat. "Afternoon. I wonder if we might get a drink of water." He had a slight southern drawl and spoke softly but well. A gentleman, I thought, and he confirmed it when he doffed his hat as Ree and Davey joined us.

"How do you do, ma'am," he said. The others removed their hats as well but I thought that they would not have done so if their companion had not.

"The pump's over there," I said, nodding toward it, though it was obvious to anyone but a blind man. "It isn't the best water in the world but it hasn't killed us, so far."

"Thank you. Much appreciated."

The three men dismounted. The old fellow stuck out his hand. "I'm George Edwards and these are my partners, Louis Colquhoun and Shorty Dunn."

I shook everyone's hand and as I grasped Edwards's I noticed a small figure of a dancing girl tattooed at the base of his thumb. I thought it an odd place for a tattoo until he showed Davey how he could make the girl dance by wiggling his thumb. I could see Davey's young mind working, perhaps thinking how much he could impress others if only he had a tattoo like that.

I had heard of Edwards. Despite his drawl, I knew that he lived down Princeton way, about seventy miles to the south, where his generous spirit had won him many friends, especially among the children of the town. His horse did tricks and he often gave the kids rides. They loved to see him make the girl at the base of his thumb dance, and he had even built a small skating rink for them. He played a fine fiddle, too, and was always in demand at parties. It appeared that the entire community was fond of Edwards.

I hadn't heard of the others. Colquhoun, the red-headed man, was of medium build and seemed gregarious while Dunn was small in stature and didn't appear to have much to say. I couldn't put my finger on it, but his gaunt features made me think that he might have a bit of a mean streak.

Edwards said that he had been helping on his brother's ranch for the past few years, but he was really a prospector at heart. When Dunn and Colquhoun had shown up and encouraged him to resume his previous occupation, saying that they would join him, the three decided to investigate some of the feeder creeks of the North Thompson River.

"This here's Pat, by the way," he said, referring to his horse, a grey male with a few years in its hide, and so calm it must have been gelded. "Say," he said to Pat, "what time do you reckon it is?"

Pat nickered, tossed his head and stamped his foot twice. I checked my pocket watch. "Pretty close," I said. "It's 2:15."

"Pat's still working on those quarter hours," Edwards chuckled.

Davey was astonished. "How did he know that?"

Edwards shrugged and grinned. "Pat is wise beyond his years. What's your name son?"

"Davey."

"How old are . . . Wait a minute. Tell you what, Davey. You whisper how old you are in my ear, so Pat can't hear, and we'll see if he can guess."

Edwards bent over and Davey, tentative at first, whispered into his ear. The old man straightened in mock amazement. "Why, I'm not sure Pat can count that high. But let's see. Maybe I'm wrong." He turned to Pat and, resting his hand on the horse's withers, said, "I know it's asking a lot, but how old is Davey?"

Pat neighed and stomped his hoof 10 times. Davey was speechless for a moment, and then he repeated his first question. "But how did he know that?"

"It wouldn't be fair to say, Davey," Edwards said. "Pat gets real annoyed when I talk out of turn. Ain't that right, old friend?"

Pat shook his head up and down, as if to confirm what Edwards had said. It was easy to see what Edwards was doing but Davey was young enough to believe that horses could fly, that magic and all of its affiliations were still afoot in the world. It would not have been right to spoil it.

Edwards and his friends stayed for lunch before moving on. He loved to tell stories, most of which sounded like tall tales, but he had such a pleasant manner and easy way of telling them that the truth was not paramount. And he certainly kept Davey entertained.

Afterward, he wanted to leave a small remuneration in return for our kindness. "Feeding three unexpected mouths is a huge demand on the larder."

"Nonsense!" Ree exclaimed. "It was our pleasure, indeed. It's always nice to have company drop by. I do wish you'd brought your fiddle, though. I would have made you play for your dinner!"

Edwards laughed. "And I would have happily done so. But it's too fine an instrument to be packing around these hills."

After Edwards and his friends had departed, it was clear that the old man and, especially, his horse had enthralled Davey. "It'd sure be neat to have a horse like that," he declared and I was pleased to hear the life in his voice, which until then had been mostly flat. "Do you think they'll come again? I hope so!"

"Well, you heard me tell him that he was welcome anytime. But who knows? If Mr. Edwards strikes it rich, he may have bigger and better things to do." I grinned and clapped his shoulder. "I know it's hard to believe, but I've heard that there are more interesting places in the world than this ranch."

Davey and Ree returned to their arithmetic lesson and I went back to work with the bay, whose temperament had not improved at all with the respite. It snorted and shook its head, as if to say it would rather be doing something else more pleasurable for the remainder of the afternoon. Yet my mind was only half on it. I wondered about our guests and if they knew what they were doing. As I understood it, all of the creeks in the bottom half of the province had been worked and reworked until they had nothing left to yield, if they'd had anything in the first place.

That evening, in bed, Ree and I talked about Davey. He'd not had an easy time settling into his arithmetic lesson after his meeting with Pat and we discussed whether a horse of his own might be the beacon he needed to find a way out of his grief. It was hard to say, because since his arrival at the ranch he had displayed little interest in our horses, either to look after or to ride. Living in town, he had had little to do with animals of any description; in fact, his father had used a bicycle to get around. But Pat had ignited a spark inside him and we thought that perhaps a young filly or colt he could grow with and we could train together—especially to do some of the tricks that Pat did—might be just what Davey needed. None of our stock was suitable, so we decided to put the word out to see what we could find. We also decided not to tell Davey but to let events develop slowly and naturally.

JIM CAME over a couple of days later, seeking my help. A rancher about 35 miles east of Kamloops, on the south branch of the Thompson River, wanted to shed a couple of dozen cows and Jim thought it would be worth looking at them. If they met his standards, he would need my help trailing them home. We could take in the horse races in town first, stay overnight and get a fresh start up the South Thompson the day after. I was eager to go because it would also provide an opportunity to look for a good horse for Davey.

We set out for Kamloops the following morning, along the Brigade Trail, the old Hudson's Bay Company fur-trading route that had become the main wagon road. In town, we liveried our horses, took rooms at the Montreal Hotel and went directly to the races. We left more money in the track's coffers than I would care to admit, considering both Jim and I were self-proclaimed good judges of horses. As it turned out, we could not judge anything right and the best I could do was a third-place finish in the second race and Jim a third in the fourth. But it was money well spent. Win or lose, there are few things more exciting than watching several tons of horse-flesh thunder down the homestretch, the dust or mud flying, depending on the weather, and the spectators noisily urging their favourites to the finish line.

In the evening, I checked out the few horses that were for sale in town but found nothing suitable. We turned in early and I vaguely recall the hotel vibrating as a train rumbled through town about midnight, then another, two or three hours later. At dawn, a loud pounding on my door awakened me. I opened it to see the desk clerk who said, excitedly and with much animation, that someone had robbed the train and Wallis Fernie, the local Provincial Police constable, was forming a posse to go after the bandits and needed help. I had known Fernie, as had Jim, since South Africa, when we all belonged to Lord Strathcona's Horse. Having met us at the racetrack, he was aware that we were in town and I figured that he would be keen to draw on our experience. The clerk went off to rouse Jim while I dressed hurriedly.

Fernie had just come into the lobby as Jim and I arrived downstairs. An earnest, serious man with a reputation for being fair, he was also one of the best trackers around. He looked tired, as if he had been up most of the night, which was undoubtedly the case. He filled us in on the details.

Bandits had robbed the Canadian Pacific Railway train about 11:30 the previous night, shortly after it left Ducks station, about 15 miles east of Kamloops. While it was stopped at the station, two men had climbed into the coal tender and hidden there until the train got under way again, at which point they stormed the cab and accosted the engineer. Both men brandished revolvers and wore handkerchiefs tied across their faces. One man also wore goggles; a mile or so down the line, he ordered the engineer to stop.

As the train squealed to a halt, another man came out of the dark and boarded it. He wore a cap and had the collar of his sweater pulled up over his mouth and nose; he was carrying a package of dynamite under one arm, ostensibly to blow open a safe if need be. He ordered the fireman to come with him and together they uncoupled the rest of the train from the first railcar behind the coal tender. The bandit presumed it was the express car. The two men then returned to the engine and ordered the engineer to move the shortened train forward some 300 yards. While one outlaw guarded the trainmen, the other two went to the railcar and commanded the two clerks there to hand over the registered mail for San Francisco and anything else of value.

A clerk gave them a bag with eleven letters in it but said there was nothing on the train for San Francisco, nor was there any gold. The reason he gave, which was the truth, was that it was the first day of their summer schedule and the train had been broken into two sections to accommodate the increase in passengers. This was not the express car, it was the baggage car—the express car was on the other train some distance behind. Cursing, the gunmen took the registered mail and some liver pills, ignoring several innocent-looking packages that contained $40,000 in cash. They told the engineer to pull the train some distance farther along the tracks and stop; then they jumped off and fled into the night.

One of the clerks had recognized the thief who had used his sweater as a mask when it inadvertently slipped down. It was Bill Miner, he was sure, the very man who had robbed his train two years before in the Fraser Valley and escaped with $7,000. This time he got away with only $15, but the amount was of no consequence. The CPR was a sacred institution; sometimes it was hard to tell where the company stopped and the government began. Robbing it for pennies or for millions was the same intolerable slap in the face to both.

I remembered reading about that first robbery and about Bill Miner. He had had quite a checkered past, which included train and stagecoach robberies in the United States, invariably followed by stiff prison sentences. It seemed Bill wasn't bad at the robbing part but his getaway skills needed honing. The trainmen had said he was a real gentleman, though, and local citizens, none too happy about the money the government spent subsidizing the railway, insisted at the time, "Hell, Bill Miner's only robbed the CPR once. The CPR robs us every day!"

Fernie finished his tale, saying, "I know you've got more important things on your mind, boys, but I could sure use your help. I don't expect it'll take long and you'll be about your business before you know it."

Given Miner's reputation, I didn't think it would take long either. Jim sent word to the rancher we had planned to visit, asking him to hold the cows for a while, and we both sent messages to Maggie and Ree that duty called and to expect us home when we got there.

THREE

After the Fox

WE RODE UP THE valley, a half dozen of us, along the road
that parallelled the tracks. The fine weather we had been
enjoying for the past few days was about to end. The morning
was gloomy and overcast, and it looked as if it would be wet
later on. A forest fire was raging in the hills on the north side
of the river, so rain would be welcome. Beneath the clouds
hung a pall of smoke, and the smell of it was sharp and acrid.

While the robbery had occurred at Mile Post 116 on the
railway—measured from Craigellachie where the last spike had
been driven and the eastern component of the railway met
the western—the outlaws had fled from the train between Mile
Posts 119 and 120. There we found a package of dynamite
wrapped in a Kamloops newspaper, and human footprints
leading to the south, ascending the steep side of an embankment and heading deeper into the trees. The footprints were

distinct. Two of the bandits wore hobnailed boots while the third might have been those of a woman, for they were slender and smooth.

We urged our horses up the embankment. The trail gave out, but not far in among the trees, we came upon an abandoned campsite that was well established. Though it did not offer an unobstructed view, the railway tracks were clearly visible, so the thieves had most likely used it as an observation post to watch the comings and goings of the trains. There were no obvious tracks leading away from the camp, but there was only one logical direction for the robbers' escape, and that was south into the hills. To the west was Kamloops, to the east was Monte Creek and to the north was a swift-flowing river with a forest fire on the far side.

We fanned out, searching for tracks, and much farther up the hill found some in softer ground. They led to the main campsite. A quick investigation proved that Miner was living up to his reputation for being less than brilliant on the getaway. It was clear that he and his cohorts had ridden into the camp on horseback, but had departed on foot. The hoofprints and footprints went off in different directions, the horses west toward Kamloops and the humans south toward the international boundary. That the horses had left riderless was apparent from the depth of the hoofprints coming and going.

"I'll wager that in their excitement they didn't hobble their horses properly and the animals wandered off during the robbery. Or maybe the train spooked them," said Fernie.

"Seems that way," I agreed. "And I'll bet they didn't waste any time looking for them, either. It would have been too dark and there'd be no telling how far those horses had gone."

Fernie sent two men in pursuit of the animals and the rest of us pushed southward. He said, grimly, "Let's hope these men are not as dangerous as they are stupid."

We worked our way slowly across the hilly, heavily wooded and sometimes rocky landscape. Here and there, tiny lakes had turned black, reflecting the dark overcast. On hard terrain, the tracks would disappear and we had to spread out until we came upon them again on a more yielding surface. Though it was not always easy to find them, they invariably trended south and it became clear that the outlaws were not trying to throw us off the trail. They were probably making haste for the border, nearly a hundred miles away.

About eight miles on, we came to a broad meadow, split in two by a well-used east-west trail, and found another camp on the far side. Our quarry had lightened their load and had left a large quantity of food behind. Other things littered the site: a mucous-crusted handkerchief, a small piece of candle, and some scraps of paper. One was part of a letter that offered little information and the other was a page from the *Manitoba Free Press*, dated April 10, with advertisements that were probably of no significance.

It began to rain hard enough that we pulled our slickers from our saddlebags and donned them. We let the horses eat some grass and then moved in among the pines, out of the worst of the rain. Night came faster in the forest than in the open and it soon grew so dark that continuing was pointless. We hobbled the horses, set up a primitive camp and after some beef jerky, hard biscuits and tea, waited out the long, tedious night.

In the morning, two riders arrived from the west, one a police constable, the other a rancher keen to join the hunt. "Good of you to come," Fernie told them. "You can never have too much help in a situation like this."

Bloodhounds were on their way by train from the coast, the constable said, with a contingent of the Mounted Police, who would try to intersect our course, perhaps at the Douglas Lake Ranch, which lay several miles to the south.

The weather had not improved much, which did not make tracking any easier, but with perseverance we always found signs of passage. Nevertheless, we had to pay close attention; otherwise, it was easy to believe that no human had ever passed this way before. The timber was thick in most places and while it kept the bulk of the rain off us, it slowed our progress substantially. Many deadfalls made it impossible to ride in a straight line. I doubted that we were making any better time than the bandits were—six or seven miles from dawn until dusk, if we were lucky. We saw nothing. All that broke the monotony was the tawny side of a deer as it went crashing off among the trees, and when something spooked our horses, it was most likely the scent of a bear.

As the days wore on, I began to worry about Ree and Davey. I knew they could manage quite well without me but a man likes to think he's indispensable. Jim was feeling the same way, and he had children to be concerned about. Knowing Ree, she would ride over with Davey to help make Maggie's life less hectic, and the two women would enjoy not having men in their lives for a while.

We'd come nearly 30 miles through heavily timbered country and then it opened up. We knew that we were nearing the Douglas Lake Ranch, one of the biggest cattle outfits in the province. If we did not have Miner by then, we told Fernie, he would have to go on without us. It was time we were getting home.

"I understand," he said. "I'm sure the ranch'll have some men to spare. I appreciate your sticking it out this far. It's been downright miserable."

It had rained on and off most of the way and the sky remained overcast, the air chilly for the season.

The terrain was hilly, with isolated thickets and small ponds, and the tracks ended in a shallow grassy valley running generally east to west. We knew it would be impossible to find them in the grass, so Fernie split the posse in two. He sent half, with the other constable, to follow the valley east in case Miner changed course toward the Okanagan. The rest of us carried on south and soon came to a treed gully where we got lucky. We found more tracks and they were fresh.

It appeared to Fernie that the outlaws had decided not to risk exposure in the open areas and instead were staying among the trees. He predicted that they were making their way toward Quilchena, a dozen miles to the west, in the Nicola Valley.

We rode on for 15 or 20 minutes and suddenly came upon a trio of men. They were sitting on the ground in a small glade, each of them leaning against a tree, eating lunch. While we were surprised to encounter them, they could not have helped hear our approach, yet they had not fled. Instead, they smiled and waved hello as if they hadn't a care in the world. I recognized them immediately. It was George Edwards, Louis Colquhoun and Shorty Dunn.

Good God, I thought, *we've been trailing the wrong men.* All this time we had presumed that we were following bandits but we had actually been following prospectors. Yet the tracks that had led us to them were the same ones that had led away from the site of the robbery.

Fernie pulled out his pistol. "Who are you men?" he demanded. Edwards stood and amiably introduced himself and his companions.

"What's your business here?" Fernie's voice was gruff, and icy with suspicion.

"I might ask you the same thing." Edwards looked bemused and I could not blame him for answering a question with a question. Fernie was dressed in civilian clothes and there was nothing about him, other than his attitude, to indicate that he was a police officer.

"I'm Constable Fernie of the Provincial Police."

I interjected. "I know these men, Wallis, and they are who they say they are. They stopped by my ranch a while ago with an outfit. They said they were heading out to prospect for gold."

"That's right." Edwards suddenly recognized me behind several days' growth of beard and my hat brim, which was pulled low across my face. "We've been prospecting up Monte Creek way and now we're headed home to Princeton. Had no luck at all."

"Right," said Fernie, dismounting. "And it's getting worse. You're under arrest for train robbery."

Edwards laughed, so spontaneously and without guile that Fernie's accusation seemed outrageous. He reminded me of some child's favourite grandfather. He said, kindly and very respectfully, spreading his arms out in appeal, "Surely,

Constable, we don't look like train robbers to you. If we were, we would have run. We heard you coming from a long way off."

Just then, Shorty Dunn leapt to his feet and shouted, "Look out, boys! It's all up!" He pulled out a revolver that he had hidden behind him and shot at Fernie. The bullet whizzed by the policeman's head, sailed over Jim and me, and thudded into a tree somewhere behind us. We reached for our rifles as Dunn tore off, up a gentle slope and deeper into the trees. Fernie fired his pistol at him and got off a lucky shot. The bullet caught the fleeing man in the leg and he went sprawling onto the ground. "I'm shot!" he screamed.

Fernie went after Dunn, while Jim and I had Edwards and Colquhoun covered, although it was probably unnecessary. They were too stunned by the turn of events to try anything. Edwards's eyes filled with disbelief and Colquhoun's mouth flew open. Fernie reached Dunn and relieved him of his weapon, plus another smaller one concealed in his jacket pocket. He forced the man onto his wounded leg and made him hobble the few yards back to the glade.

Edwards continued to insist that they had not held up any trains, that Fernie's civilian clothes had confused Dunn who thought we were villains set to rob them.

"You can tell that story to a judge in Kamloops," Fernie snorted, pushing Colquhoun against Edwards. "Tie these men!" he ordered and while he held his pistol on them, Jim and I took some rope and bound their wrists behind them. Once the three men were secure, we searched them. On Edwards, we found a pair of goggles and a bunch of liver pills.

"Where did you get these?" I asked, recalling that one of

the bandits had worn goggles and that liver pills were among the loot they'd taken.

"Found them a few miles back," Edwards replied. He looked me unflinchingly in the eye. "Surely you believe me, Mr. Strong. I'm no thief."

"We'll see, George," I said.

Expanding the search into the trees around the campsite, we found more weapons, including a rifle. It appeared to me that they had heard us coming and, tired of running, decided to see if they could bluff their way out. Yet even though the evidence was incriminating, Edwards maintained his facade. He spoke convincingly. "You have arrested innocent men while the real culprits are getting away. Your superiors will not be pleased."

He was such a likeable man that I might have given him the benefit of the doubt, but Fernie was in charge here and it was his mistake to make. I helped Dunn onto my horse, because he was not able to walk, and, at gunpoint, we marched Edwards and Colquhoun only a short distance before we were out of the trees. Just then, Joe Greaves, one of the ranch owners, came loping up to us on a dun stallion, reins in one hand and a rifle in the other. He had heard the gunshots and come to investigate. He was surprised to see George Edwards, for he knew him well; he also knew Shorty Dunn. He too was sceptical.

"You sure you got the right men here, Wallis?"

"I haven't the slightest doubt," the constable answered, as adamant about his position as Edwards had been about his own.

We took our three captives to the ranch house where Greaves loaned us a buckboard to transport them down into the Nicola Valley and then north to Kamloops. Along the road that snaked into the valley, we encountered a contingent of North-West Mounted Police with two bloodhounds, led by a burly, no-nonsense corporal. After he introduced himself, Fernie smiled and asked jokingly, "You looking for these men?"

The corporal rode alongside the buckboard, leaned over, pushed Edwards forward and grabbed his hands. The man winced in pain. When the Mountie saw the dancing girl tattoo at the base of his thumb, the slimmest of smiles cracked his stern face. "Not anymore." Then to Edwards, he said, "Hello, Bill."

The heavy clouds that had plagued us during the search still sagged over the surrounding hilltops, and the rain came and went in drizzles and downpours as Jim and I headed home. We rode out ahead of Fernie, the Mounties and their prisoners, but I told the constable before we left that in case Miner's horse, Pat, happened to show up, I would not mind having dibs on him if he were available. I told him how smitten Davey was with the animal.

"I'll see what I can do," Fernie had said. "God knows you've earned it."

BILL MINER, alias George Edwards, alias William Anderson, alias William Morgan was taken, along with his cohorts, to the Kamloops jail. They rode past our front yard, and Miner wore a blanket over his head like a shawl, too embarrassed to face us. Davey wanted to run to the gate to see him, still not quite able to comprehend that the man he had so admired was also a notorious train robber.

"We shouldn't gape, son," I said. "He'll have enough of that until they get him into a cell."

"But where's Pat?"

I told him that when the thieves had improperly hobbled their horses, they had wandered off. "My guess is that Pat was too smart to get involved."

Davey nodded knowingly. "Yeah."

When the weather cleared, Jim and I finished the job we had embarked upon before the train robbery and rode up the South Thompson to look at the cattle he was hoping to buy. He wondered if we might be too late but the rancher had heard that we had joined the posse and held onto the animals, when he could easily have sold them. He explained to Jim, "A man shouldn't lose out on a good opportunity just because he's got a well-developed sense of duty." Jim bought and paid for 24 head of fine stock and we trailed them to his ranch.

I had not been home for more than two or three days when Fernie sent word that I should come into town, that there was a piece of horseflesh waiting for me. It had to be Pat, Miner's horse, and I was excited for Davey. But just in case it wasn't, I said nothing, only that I was riding into Kamloops on business.

FOUR

Raven

"HE'S LONG IN THE tooth," Fernie said of Pat. "But he's a gentle beast and if he's for that boy of yours, why, he'll do just fine for a while."

I passed much of the time during the ride home wondering what Davey's reaction would be when he saw Pat. He still did not feel comfortable enough with Ree and me to divulge his feelings but we both believed that the horse had lit a spark in him. As I led Pat into the yard, Davey came out of the house with Ree behind him, an apprehensive smile on her face. Davey looked slightly bewildered.

"Is that Pat?" he asked, incredulously.

"None other than, Davey."

"Why is he here? How did you get him?"

I dismounted and took Pat over to him, telling him how we had come to be the proud owners of a famous bandit's horse. As I spoke, Davey stroked Pat's neck, still not sure what to make of the situation. I said to Pat, "Do you remember Davey, old friend?" Right on cue, Pat nodded. Davey was flabbergasted. Then I put my hand on Pat's withers and asked, "Do you remember Davey's age?" He dutifully began stomping his hoof and when he reached 10, I lifted my fingers and he stopped. Davey was beside himself.

"Would you like him for your own?" I asked.

"Yes!" he exclaimed and there was a trembling in his voice, a nervousness, but a flame flickered in his eyes.

"Do you think you can look after him if I showed you how to do it?"

He did not hesitate. "Yes."

"You can even ride him around, Davey, after you have a few lessons. What do you think of that?"

"I think it's good," he said, his head bobbing up and down.

"Great!" I said. "We just have to remember that Pat is getting old, so we won't run him too much."

"That's okay. I'll just walk him."

We gave Pat a stall in the barn and it became Davey's responsibility to maintain it. I showed him how to currycomb and brush him, how to trim his hoofs and pick them free of debris and, most important, how to keep the stall clean. "Mucking out a stall is one of the true tests of a man's love for his horse," I said. "Grooming it is another. You brush and comb Pat every day and it'll be one more reason for him to love you in return."

I never had to show Davey those things again nor remind him of his responsibilities. Pat became an important part of his life and he would arise early in the morning and be out to the barn, cleaning the stall before breakfast. That's the way it is when you love an animal.

Within the week, word came from a rancher down in the Nicola Valley that he just might have the horse I had asked about before the train robbery. That evening, over some jumble cake—baked rings of flour, sugar, cinnamon and almonds that was Davey's favourite dessert—I said off-handedly, as if the idea had just occurred to me, "What do you think about getting a younger horse for you that we can train to be just like Pat?"

He actually smiled for the first time, not a wide-open, happy smile but a smile nonetheless. "I think that would be great."

In the morning, Davey and I saddled Red, a strawberry roan that I had taken a liking to, and Pat, and we pointed them south toward the valley and the ranch. I had given Davey some riding lessons and he sat the horse well. He and Pat were on good terms, so Davey rode him with confidence.

The horse the rancher had for sale was a fine little filly, nicely disposed, jet black with white stockings and a small white diamond on her forehead. Davey was tentative with her at first but she nuzzled him and he began stroking her neck, softly at first, then with greater self-assuredness.

"I think she likes you, Davey and she's also getting to know your smell, getting to know that you're friendly. She'll always recognize you now, and if you'll let her, she'll come to know that you're one of the good things in her life. How do you like her?" I asked.

"She's a beauty," he responded, so caught in the moment that I think it had given him a reprieve, if only temporarily, from the tremendous burden of grief and guilt he carried.

"Can we give her the home and care she deserves?"

"Yes, and I promise to look after her as good as I look after Pat."

"Then that's just fine by me." I turned to the rancher. "It looks like you've sold her."

Reports of Davey's situation had spread, and the rancher knew, beforehand, whom the horse was for. "Tell you what. The boy and the horse look like they were made for each other and it don't seem right to take any money for somethin' so natural."

I opened my mouth to protest but he held up his hand. "No more needs to be said."

It was a generous gesture, and if that weren't enough, he heaped on more kindness by inviting Davey and me to stay the night, with a promise of beefsteak and mashed potatoes for supper, and bacon and eggs for breakfast. But I had to beg off. Ree would worry because I hadn't told her we'd be gone overnight and there was no way of getting word to her. All I could do was tug on my hat, look the man in the eye and say, "Thank you very much." I believe anything more would have embarrassed him.

As we rode at a walk up the valley, I asked Davey, "What sort of name do you think she should have? Since she's yours, you can give her any name you like."

I could see behind his eyes that his mind had sprung into action but he was quiet for a long while. "I'll call her Blacky. No, not that. That's too plain. Raven. I want to call her Raven." The enthusiasm in his voice warmed my heart.

"Perfect," I agreed. "I couldn't think of a better name."

DAVEY AND I embarked on a course of training that consisted of him helping me as I worked with my stock, and learning more about horses and riding, some of which took place on a hunting trip deep into the hills where he not only proved himself a very skilful rider but a worthy marksman as well. Then we turned our attention to Raven.

"You and Raven don't speak the same language, Davey," I told him. "But that doesn't mean you can't understand each other enough to be friends. You just have to remember that while it's possible to be friends, you are not equals. One of you has to be boss and better it's you than Raven. That's the way it is with horses. With most animals, actually."

"But how can I be boss when she's bigger than me?"

"She might be bigger than you in body but you're bigger here," I replied, tapping my temple with my index finger. "So what we have to do is lay down the rules for her so that she knows how to behave, in fact, so that she *wants* to behave. But always keep in mind that she would rather be with her own kind, where she feels safer. The only way she'll feel safe is if she knows you won't harm her. It's a trust you have to earn."

We introduced Raven to a halter and then a saddle, and got her used to carrying a load. Soon, Davey was able to stand with one foot in the stirrup, fighting his impatience to throw the other leg over and straddle her. Once Raven was comfortable with him in the saddle, we began teaching her to respond to his leg pressure to get her moving. This is easier than it sounds because horses are sensitive to touch, and when the alternative is spurs it usually does not take long for them to get the message.

I taught Davey about other ways horses communicate: how

they will flare their nostrils, flatten their ears against their heads and pull their tails in tight against their rumps if they are frightened or feeling aggressive. How they will snort if they sense danger and maybe squeal if they are going to fight one another. "Neighing is good, though. It's the way they announce their presence. Nickering is even better. If they do that, you can count yourself in as a friend."

Davey and I worked together with patience and firmness, rewarding Raven's good responses with a rub on the withers and a kind word. She understood and slowly turned into the horse we wanted.

It was a busy time for Davey, not only training Raven with me, but also doing his chores and schoolwork. And he never forgot Pat, his first love, and tended to the old grey faithfully. No doubt the regimen was good for him because Ree remarked that he seemed more attentive and happier.

He was keen to go off alone on Raven but I rode alongside him at first just to make sure both were doing the job expected of them. He sat her comfortably and she responded well, but then both had been exceptional students. Davey was also eager to let her run full out and I could not see any reason to stop him. We tried some short sprints down the road, races really, and Raven proved to be sure-footed and fast. One day, when we had returned to the ranch after a short ride to the meadow where our stock grazed, I decided it was time to let him go on his own. He did not need much prompting. He turned Raven, urging her forward, and she fairly flew out of the gate and onto the road, with Davey whooping in delight. It was hard to tell where the boy ended and the horse began. They disappeared, which sent my heart into my throat. I waited anxiously, until

I heard Raven's hoofs pounding out their return. They came into the yard and Davey reined up in a cloud of dust, grinning like a fool. He dismounted in one swift movement as if it were the most natural thing in the world.

"She's perfect, Dad! I love her! She does everything I want her to do!"

I was so excited for him that it took a few moments to realize what he had called me. *Dad*. Just like that. With that single word, something shifted, moved forward and hummed along more smoothly.

That evening, after he had turned in for the night, I went into his room and sat on the edge of his bed. I talked about his accomplishments, of how proud Ree and I were of him. He remained quiet as I spoke but I could tell that he was feeling good about himself. Moreover, his face had a softer, happier cast to it. "I think it's time we taught Raven some of those tricks that Pat knows. Is that okay with you?"

"Can we start tomorrow?" he asked, eagerly.

"You bet." I could see that he might have trouble getting to sleep contemplating that prospect, but it was by far a better reason than the thoughts that had kept him awake before. I squeezed his arm. "First though, we'll go for a ride, maybe have a race, so you better get some rest. You and Raven will have to be in top form to beat me and Red. Goodnight, son. Sleep well."

"G'night, Dad."

The word was as sweet as one of Jim's songs.

Ree and I sat at the kitchen table with coffee and talked. She reached over, placing her hand on mine. "I think Davey has finally found a home."

I sighed. "Yes. This has been a remarkable day."

Earlier, Ree had been astonished when Davey charged into the house, on fire, and called her "Mum." She could scarcely believe her ears. It was like the first rainfall after a long drought and we were both amazed at how easily the boy had slipped into calling us the names we most wanted to hear. For Ree it was doubly thrilling. Since the nearest schoolhouse was in Kamloops, she had taken on the added task of teaching Davey the three Rs, as well as a solid foundation in horticulture, egg gathering and firewood hauling. (He did well in most areas, although arithmetic was not his strong suit, and in that way he might have been my natural son.) The best of it was that Ree was able to spend time with him, one on one, which at first had made her feel nervous because it held the possibility of either destroying their relationship or strengthening it. That it prospered was testimony to her patience and understanding, and the basic goodness that was innate in Davey.

Next morning, after we had completed our chores, Davey and I raced to a nearby meadow and back. He and Raven won easily, without any help from me. During our absence, Ree went into Davey's room to tidy it. Lying on the bedside table was his knife. He had never left it behind before. She picked it up and turned it over, gingerly, for she knew that she held a treasure. She could not stop the tears of gratitude that slid down her cheeks.

FIVE

Intimations of War

THE YEARS ARRIVED IN a hurry and left even faster. The ranch had its difficulties but mostly provided us with a respectable income and independence. Ree took on Jim and Maggie's two oldest boys—they eventually had three—as pupils, as well as a couple of girls in the area, and essentially ran her own private school. She was a born teacher, just as she was a born mother, although the second-oldest Spencer boy tested her patience with his overabundant energy.

Soon after his memorable ride with Raven, Davey was able to speak of his parents and the night he had lost them. By then he had truly become our son, and to make it official we adopted him. We did not insist that he change his last name because it was still important to him. Besides, it was best that way; his name was real whereas mine was fiction, and I did not intend to revert to my father's name. Other than Jim, Ree was the only other person I ever told that I had changed it as a youngster, so she understood.

We had not only gained ourselves a fine son but also added a top hand around the ranch. He filled out and grew into a tall young man who, to his dismay, looked much younger than his age. Yet he possessed the quiet confidence of more mature men. A stubborn streak ran through him that would not allow him to leave a job half done, and he had a way with horses that even I envied at times.

The ease with which Davey dealt with horses, however, deserted him utterly when it came to members of the opposite sex. He was bashful and tongue-tied around them, sometimes painfully so. He had fallen in love with a girl who had been one of Ree's pupils, and she with him, but if she had not taken the initiative at a dance one Saturday night, they might never have got together. Her name was Nora Crawford; she was a delightful, pretty girl whose hair was as black as Raven's. We kidded Davey about that being the main reason why he liked her so much. They were a good match and planned to be married when the time was right.

Jim and Maggie became the aunt and uncle that Davey never had. Ree and I were godparents to their three boys, and a visit to the Spencer household always left us grateful that our friends enjoyed good health and that unless something unforeseen happened, it was unlikely that we would have to fulfill those duties. The boys were a handful and if there was trouble around to get into, they could sniff it out like bloodhounds. They would eventually grow into successful men in their own right, but how they ever survived childhood was one of life's great mysteries.

The Bar JM was prospering, for Jim and Maggie raised high-quality beef, running a herd that fluctuated between 250 and 300 head. It had earned itself a solid reputation throughout the southern part of the province, as well as a decent living for the Spencers, and they had even been able to hire an extra hand to look after the cattle on their winter range.

Gilbert "Gibby" Gibson was perfect for the job. He was a shaggy, grey-haired curmudgeon who walked with a limp because he had been born with his right leg turned in. He loved cattle but harboured a powerful distrust of human beings, bathtubs and most other things that kept a body clean. Jim and I built a cabin next to a small lake in one of the ranch's larger meadows where the cows wintered, and there Gibby lived, making sure they had feed and that the ice was broken along the lake's edge so they could drink. Jim kept him well supplied with food and tobacco, and Gibby drew his water from the lake. It is hard to find someone willing to take on such a lonely life and Jim knew he was lucky to have the old man.

Meanwhile, my relationship with Jim continued to flourish, for it was the best of all possible worlds. Few things can drive friends apart faster than money or vying for the same woman, but we were lucky that neither of those complicated our lives. Often we would ride together to check out cattle and horses for sale in the surrounding area or just head into town for the races and a break from the ranch. We both recognized our good fortune to have fine families, but a man needs some diversion in his life every now and then, and that is what my trips with Jim provided. We were easy in each other's company, he and I, with plenty of talk when talk was wanted and a comfortable silence when it was not. Indeed, it was on one of those trips that I had at last told him about Charity and Becky; the subject had always been too painful to bring up. But Ree was my confidante and telling her had made it easier to tell Jim. When I finally did, I wondered how he would respond. He was quiet for a moment. "You kept that piece of information to yourself for a long time, partner."

I nodded. "Well, I believed it was my fault, so it wasn't an easy thing to talk about."

"I expect it never will be. You know, Maggie always insisted that something serious was eatin' at your soul, but I thought it was just you, and maybe the trouble you'd had with your old man. She said, 'No, it's more than that.' It's funny how women are able to pick up on those things."

That Jim remained a friend and a neighbour was one of the many good things in my life.

In 1913 and 1914, the economy dipped and sales dropped off. A mechanized world seemed to be preparing to render the horse obsolete as a means of transportation. We had a healthy bank account and were not hurt much by it, but we knew that we would probably have to rethink our uses of the ranch or get out of the business altogether. Even so, we had no complaints and paid scant attention on that lovely summer day, in late June of 1914, when the newspaper reported the assassination of an obscure archduke in an even more obscure eastern European city.

It was not until August, when the guns of war rent the air in Europe, that we sat up and took notice. In Kamloops, as in every city and town across the country, war was soon on everyone's lips. All along the valley, you could scarcely pass anyone who did not have something to say about it, an opinion, usually, passed on as if it were a universal truth. Canada was raising a contingent of troops to send overseas, but the speculation was that the war would be over before they stepped onto the battlefield. At worst, it would be just a cleanup operation. In the meantime, it increased the demand for horses, and business began to escalate until I had as much work as Davey and I could handle.

Part of me wanted to jump into the fight immediately, but my older, more cautious side said that if it was going to be that simple, it might prove to be a great adventure for younger men with endless reserves of energy. One war in a man's lifetime was plenty for me and what's more, I had Ree, Davey and a business to think about. As far as Davey was concerned, his focus was more on Nora than on war, and he did not appear anxious to go anywhere that would separate them.

Life went on and the war played in the background like static on a radio. Two days before Christmas, Pete Spencer arrived at the ranch early in the morning. His dad was ill with a miserable cold and he was wondering if I would run some provisions up to Gibby on the winter range.

"You bet, Pete," I said. "Tell your dad that Davey and I will do it, and to take it easy."

Davey and I hitched two recently trained Clydesdales to our hay sledge and headed over to Jim's. It was a crisp, clear morning and the horses were happy to step out and stretch their muscles. The pair worked well together and would fetch a good price on the coast.

When we arrived at the Bar JM, Jim was outside opening the barn. His eyes were red and rheumy and his nose ran constantly. He coughed from deep within in his chest, a rattling noise that didn't sound good at all.

"Mornin', Jack," he said, hoarsely. "How are you, Davey? Thanks for comin'. Didn't feel much like doin' this on my own."

"You should be in bed, Jim," I said. "Davey and I will look after this."

"I think I'll take your advice, Doc. I thought the fresh air might perk me up some but it doesn't seem to be workin'. Maggie and the kids are coughin' their lungs out, too, so we can all hack and snort together. Anyway, it goes without sayin' that I really appreciate your help." He pointed toward the house. "Those boxes on the porch are for Gibby. Wish the old bugger a Merry Christmas for us. Tell him there'll be turkey served here on Christmas Day if he's interested. I know he won't come down—he never does—but invite him anyway."

I laughed. Gibby's lack of sanitary habits made him a difficult man to be around. "You're a braver man than I am, Jim, and that's no lie."

"My stuffed-up nose'll help a lot. And at least it isn't fly season." Jim sighed. "Well, I'll see you boys later. Thanks again."

He went inside the house as Davey and I pitchforked hay into the sledge and loaded the boxes. Once we had everything secured, we climbed on board and set off through the snow, the bells on the harnesses jingling loudly in the still air. The old man would hear them from far off and know we were coming, but more importantly, so would the cattle. Anything sudden could startle them and cause a stampede, and if they headed onto the lake, they would crash through the ice. A rancher on the other side of the valley had lost 60 head that way, and he never startled his herds again.

We drove along in silence, listening to the bells, the tramping of the horses' hoofs and the sledge hissing through the snow. The Clydes were performing beautifully, following the trail that cut through the jack pine and fir forest without difficulty, across small meadows and over frozen bogs. Whenever I glanced at Davey, he was lost in thought and I wondered if something was bothering him.

"Anything eating at you, Davey?"

"Ah, not much. Just been thinking."

"About anything in particular? You and Nora doing all right?"

"Oh, yeah. We're doing just fine."

"Glad to hear it. She's a lovely girl. Your mother and I think the world of her."

He was silent for a while. Then he said, "Dad? When do you think the war is going to be over? They said it'd be over by Christmas, but now the papers say they need more men."

"I wish I had a crystal ball so I could tell you, but I somehow doubt it will end any time soon. Wars have a nasty habit of lasting longer than everyone expects."

"I didn't think so, either. So when I was in Kamloops the other day I got some information on enlisting."

My heart flipped over. "You did?"

"I think I should enlist, Dad. I don't want to be a slacker. According to the paper, fellas my age are enlisting all the time."

I had half expected this and felt more proud than apprehensive over the possibility of Davey's going overseas. I would never have forced him to enlist and the fact that he wanted to do it entirely on his own, especially in light of his feelings for Nora, said much about his sense of duty and responsibility. "My guess is that I'm the first person you've told about this."

"You're right. I tried to tell Nora yesterday but I got cold feet. She's not gonna to be very happy. I don't suppose Mum's gonna like it much either."

In fact, Ree would be devastated. Dead set against either of us getting involved, she had said so several times. I was certain that she would make every effort to try to stop him.

"Well, Davey, if you're man enough to go off to a foreign land to fight a war, then you've got to be man enough to face her with the truth."

Davey knew as well as anybody that no man, regardless of his age, could enlist without the permission of his wife or mother. He made a face. "Something tells me that fighting in a war might be easier than facing Mum."

"You could be right. Tell you what, though. I think the war effort can do without you until the new year, so it might be a good idea to wait until then to talk about it. I'll do what I can to support you but don't be surprised if your mum tries to rein you in."

We came out of the trees and entered the broad meadow that was the winter range for Jim's cattle, which I could see spread out around one side of the small lake. We did not see Gibby anywhere and, as it was lunchtime, assumed that he was in the cabin making a bite to eat. I was hungry enough to join him, though I doubted that there was a clean plate in the cabin and few places to sit that wouldn't leave a person with an itch.

I "helloed" the place but if Gibby was in there, he was not paying attention. It was possible that one of the cows was in trouble and he had gone to tend to it. If so, I thought it likely that he would have banked up the stove before he left, but I had not seen any smoke coming from the chimney as we approached.

In fact I hadn't seen any heat rising and should have noticed that straight off, but I was still trying to digest Davey's news. There had also been a recent snowfall and though we could see depressions that were clearly footprints around the cabin, the new snow was undisturbed.

"Wait here," I said to Davey and jumped from the sledge. The cabin door was closed but unlocked. It did not have a lock or a bar because Gibby had not thought it necessary. I pushed it open. I should have felt a wave of warmth on my face but there was just a strong, stale smell. There wasn't a fire in the wood stove and the cabin's interior was gloomy and frigid. I could see my breath. By anyone's standards, except perhaps Gibby's, the place was filthy. Over in the far corner was his bed, empty and unmade. I shivered.

I went outside to Davey. "Gibby's not in there and it doesn't look as if he's been there for some time. Let's take a look around."

The well-used path to the privy was still visible beneath the new snow. Similarly, there were tracks, many of them, along the lake's edge, going to and coming from where the cattle were. We followed them to the herd where they disappeared in much-trampled snow. We searched along the tree line around the meadow, just in case the old man had somehow lost his senses and wandered into the forest. We called out his name several times but heard nothing in response. I had not noticed any human tracks on the trail that we came in on, but Davey and I went to double-check I was right. It seemed that Gibby had · simply disappeared.

We walked back to the cabin. I looked at the privy again and thought, *Oh no, surely he's not in there.* "Maybe you better wait here,"

I suggested to Davey, and walked down the path to the outhouse. I pulled the door open and there was Gibby, crumpled in the corner, dead as last autumn's leaves, his pants down around his ankles and the trapdoor of his long johns unbuttoned. His face had a purple cast but considering the circumstances, he looked reasonably peaceful. My guess was that something inside the old codger had killed him, probably a bad heart. I thought it had probably taken him fast.

I called to Davey. "Well, I found him." I poked my thumb behind me. "He's in here. And the only way he's coming out is if we carry him."

Davey came over and peered in, his eyes wide. "He's dead?"

I nodded. "For a day or two, at least. Maybe more."

There was nothing we could do for Gibby, but the cattle needed tending. We put the feed out for them and broke the ice at the edge of the lake so they could drink. It had refrozen, solid, although not as thick as the older ice farther out. It was another indication that Gibby had been dead for a while. Then we put the boxes of food into the cabin. Jim was going to have to find a replacement caretaker and whoever it was would need them. The next task was to bring the body out of the privy and load it on the sledge. Davey looked squeamish about it but I told him, "If you can't do this, son, you've got no business even thinking about going to war, and I can't support you. You'll see a lot worse over there, guaranteed."

He hesitated. I didn't think it was because Gibby's death reminded him of his own mortality—he was too young to give that much thought—it was more likely that he did not want to be reminded of his parents' demise. To his credit, though, he said with resolve, "I can do it, Dad," and led the way to the outhouse.

Gibby was as solid as ice and some of his clothing had frozen to the wall and floor. Davey sucked in air audibly, entered and tugged at the corpse until he was finally able to get it out the door. The crumpled shape in which the old man was frozen had turned him into a grotesque figure that only barely resembled anything human. "Grab his legs, Dad," Davey muttered, gripping Gibby beneath the armpits.

I grasped the legs and together we carried him to the sledge and laid him on it. He hardly weighed anything at all. I went into the cabin, pulled a blanket off the bed, shook some of the stiffness out of it and returned outside. I covered Gibby with the blanket and said, "Come to think of it, maybe we'd better throw the mattress and the rest of the bedding on too."

It would have been pointless to leave it behind because no one would want to use it. It was best to burn it all at Jim's. God knows what sort of bugs could have been hibernating in it.

On the way back to the Bar JM, Davey kept glancing behind at the blanket-covered mound as if he could not quite believe that a dead human being lay under it. It was a timely lesson, I thought. And if it prepared him even a little for what might lie ahead should he enlist, then I had an unwashed, smelly old man whose time had come to thank for it. Still, Davey and I had never talked about war—we'd had no reason to until now—and I had never told him about my experiences in Africa during the Boer War.

Davey's thoughts seemed tuned to mine. "You fought in the Boer War, Dad," he said, "but you never talk about it. How come?"

"I always figured there were better things to talk about. Men being shot or blown up is not exactly a pleasant subject."

"Can you tell me about it?"

I hated dredging up those memories, but I thought that if Davey was considering going to war, then he ought to know something about what he would be getting himself into. "Well, to be honest, there are parts of it that I've never been able to put behind me." I told him of seeing men having the life shot out of them and being blown into bloody fragments; I told him of lynchings and looting, and of burning the farms of innocent people and later seeing them, gaunt-faced and starving, in concentration camps. "It's nothing like anything you've ever read about, Davey. Men are capable of doing horrible things to each other at the best of times, and war can make them even worse. It's the world gone completely mad. It's mankind gone completely mad."

He took it all in, unflinchingly. "Maybe it's everything you say, but isn't it a man's duty to fight for his country? That's what you did and that's what the papers say we ought to do."

"They're right. The two most important things in life are love and loyalty. Without them, we can hardly call ourselves human beings. They not only apply to men and their families, they also apply to men and their country. Look, Davey, it would be a sad day for me to see you go, but I also have to say that I would be very proud. I believe it's the right thing to do and if you are really committed to doing it, then I'll back you when you talk to Mum. But don't expect that it's going to be easy."

"Thanks, Dad." He was quiet during the rest of the trip and I hoped for Ree's sake that he was rethinking his position. Yet even dragging a dead man behind us, I knew it was nearly impossible to convince a youngster that Death lurked at the side of the trail for everyone, young and old alike, always willing to stick out a foot to trip a man up and spirit him away.

I hated to bother Jim when we reached his place but as it turned out, he had heard us coming and came out to greet us. He spied the mattress and bedding, and did not have to look under the blanket to know what the rest of the cargo was.

"Shit," he said. "What happened?"

"I think his heart gave out on him," I answered. "We should let the authorities in Kamloops know. I'll ride in first thing tomorrow morning."

Davey and I accompanied Jim into the house where Maggie poured us a hot cup of tea and brought us biscuits. It was uncharacteristically quiet in the house, as the kids were sick in bed. Maggie did not appear to be faring well either.

"You look like you ought to be in bed, too," I said to her.

She managed a smile. "It would be a shame to miss this peace and quiet."

Afterward, Davey and I put Gibby in a shed. I told Jim that we'd take turns checking on his herd and taking feed to it until he was feeling better and able to find a replacement. Then we went home in the gathering dusk.

Ree went pale when we informed her about Gibby. "Oh, the poor man!" she mourned. "Dying all alone like that."

"Well, for whatever reasons, it was a life he chose," I said. "But if he'd had any choice about where he wanted to die, I'm not sure he would have picked a privy."

The following morning Davey and I rode to the Bar JM where I left him to help Jim with his chores while I went to town to fetch the constable. Back at the ranch, the law officer examined Gibby to make sure there was no evidence of foul play, and then said that we could bury him ourselves or he could take the body back to town, whichever we preferred. Jim shook his head. "I don't think Gibby would like bein' among all those townsfolk. It'll be better if we bury him on the hill behind the house. He took good care of our stock and he deserves at least that much."

Together, Davey and I built a rough coffin out of pine planks, more square than rectangular, then hitched a horse to a small toboggan, put the coffin on it and went over to the shed. The blankets on top of Gibby came off as stiff as boards.

"Leave 'em beside the shed," Jim said, sniffing. "I'll burn 'em later."

We carried the old cowherd out and placed him in the coffin. He was as rigid as the blankets. We nailed the lid on and loaded the pickaxes we would need to break through the frozen ground, and a couple of shovels, then went up the hill behind the house. We produced a good sweat getting that hole dug, Davey and I doing most of the work because Jim was too fatigued. He had a small flask of brandy on him and took several pulls on it to ward off the frigid air. Maggie did not attend the brief ceremony because she could not leave the children, so there were just the three of us: more people than Gibby probably would have liked at his funeral anyway. Jim coughed loudly to remove some of the phlegm caught in his throat and over the grave, he said, "I didn't know you well, Gibby, but well enough to know that you were a good, reliable man. If there's a god in his heaven, I'm sure he knows it too."

It is a hard thing to do, to cover a man over with earth. Beyond signalling the end of his life, every shovelful is a reminder that there is a number to your own days as well. I hoped Davey was getting the message.

SIX

A Man's Duty

I THOUGHT REE WAS going to faint when Davey told her what he wanted do. There was a slight tremor in his voice, probably because he knew that what he had to say would hurt her when it wasn't in his nature to hurt anyone, especially his mother. Ree's mouth started to move as if she wanted to say something but the words would not come out. Tears showed in the corners of her eyes. Finally, she gasped, "Oh, Davey, I so hoped you wouldn't want to! What about Nora? What about your plans?"

Davey stood his ground firmly. "She'll just have to understand, Mum," he said, and added hurriedly, "and Dad supports me on this."

Ree looked at me, shocked. "Please tell me that this isn't your doing, Jack. Surely, you of all people ought to know better."

"It's not my doing, Ree," I said. "He did it without any prompting from me. But I have to be honest—I do fully support him."

"But he's only 19, Jack. He's still a boy!"

"I was only 16 when I went off to fight the Indians. Besides, he's not a boy. He's a young man and if he feels his country needs him, he ought to go."

Davey interjected. "I need to go, Mum, and I need your permission."

"How can I be expected to send you to a place that might prove to be the death of you? It seems like you just came into our lives and the thought that you might leave us is horrifying. Please, Davey. I beg of you. Don't ask me to do something I might regret."

"I have to, Mum," Davey pleaded. "Other fellas my age are enlisting and there's no reason why I shouldn't, too."

Ree shook her head. "No! I won't let you. You need someone to help you make better decisions, and I guess it's up to me because it appears your father's usual good sense has deserted him."

Davey was angry but held it in, begging Ree to let him go, but she would not give her permission. He stomped into his room and slammed the door.

I disliked Ree's cutting remark but she was clearly distressed, and an argument from me would only make things worse. Nevertheless, I felt compelled to point out that there had been talk in the newspapers recently about striking the law requiring parental or spousal consent off the books. "You know that if they do that, he'll go no matter how much you protest."

"Maybe so. But in the meantime it's my decision and while it is, I say no!"

I left it there. It was pointless to go any further; Ree was not about to change her mind. Later Davey came out of his room and apologized for his behaviour. We dropped the subject for the time being and our lives slowly returned to a semblance of normal. But I knew Davey was merely biding his time.

AS THE winter of 1914–1915 slid by, thousands were dying on the battlefields of Europe. At Ypres, in Flanders, during the fall, more than 24,000 men had been lost. That number was incomprehensible and many thought it was a printing error. But it wasn't. It was the reality of modern warfare. Yet it did little to quash the notion many young men held about the glory of war. All they knew of it was what they had read in fiction and poetry, suffused with gallantry and heroism.

The numbers did not deter Davey in the least. When the government rescinded the law that gave Ree the power to prevent him from enlisting, he apologized to her and hastened to Kamloops the next day. Offered his choice of regiments at the recruiting office, he chose Lord Strathcona's Horse, the cavalry unit I had fought with in South Africa.

I was proud of him. Ree, however, was heartsick and silent on the matter. A part of the foundation of her world had collapsed and there was nothing she could do but accept it. With great effort, she did. As the day of his departure loomed closer, she grew manifestly more accustomed to the idea. She wasn't enthusiastic, but she had at least come around to the reality of it. Still, on the day that Davey left, she gathered him into her arms and wept.

"I'm sorry, Mum," he said, tenderly. "It was never my intention to hurt you. But I have to do this."

"I know, Davey. I know. But I don't need to tell you how important you are to our lives, so please come home to us."

"I will. I promise."

"I'm proud of you, son," I said as I hugged him. I didn't dare say anything more and all Davey could get out was, "Thanks, Dad."

WITHIN TWO weeks, Davey was in training and by mid-summer, he was in England, wallowing in the rain and mud of Salisbury Plain with his fellow soldiers. In a letter, he wrote that, much to his disgust, the Horse had been reassigned as an infantry regiment and he had no clear idea when they would be crossing the Channel. At present, their biggest foe was an epidemic of lice. Ree did not mind that sort of enemy.

With Davey overseas and so many men dying, I began to feel guilty about being ensconced on the ranch and considered talking to Jim about it. It wasn't as if we'd never talked about the war—that was unavoidable—but we'd never mentioned enlisting, perhaps each of us subconsciously unwilling to put any ideas in the other's head. This was more important for Jim than it was for me. He had not only a wife to consider; he had three children who needed a father. However, my son had thrown his hand in and as time passed, I found myself with fewer and fewer excuses not to do the same.

Summer that year burst suddenly and early over the land, and the hot, dusty days melded into each other into weeks that turned as rapidly into months. Business was booming, and we could scarcely keep ahead of the demand for horses.

It was easy money, as the government decreed that a horse ridden only three times was a horse broken and fit to belong to the army. I did not think it was anywhere near enough, but the need for fresh horses, or remounts, for the cavalry was too high for me to be overly critical. Even so, I felt distracted and unable to give the job my full concentration. Half my mind was on the war and Davey, and I considered myself one of the slackers he refused to be.

It ate at me until one day, under the pretext that I was riding over to Jim's, I went into the hills, thinking about what I should do, trying to reach a decision. In the end, it boiled down to this simple fact: my obligation to my country was greater than my obligation to Ree. In turn, she had an obligation to provide support for me. This was the duty of every man and every woman in time of war. My mind made up, I rode home to tell her.

She was in the kitchen preparing supper when I walked in.

"How are Maggie and Jim?"

"I didn't go there. I went for a ride instead. I had some things that needed working out."

I could see her shoulders stiffen. She knew exactly what I was talking about and became visibly distraught.

"I knew this day would come," she said flatly.

"I'm sorry, Ree, but I can't stay here and feel good about myself, especially with Davey over there."

"So not only do I face the possibility of losing a son, I now stand to lose a husband as well. Do you have any idea how much the two of you mean to me? That I could not stand to lose even one of you, never mind both of you?"

"Of course I do."

"I don't think you do. If you did you would stay at home where you're needed." She stopped for a moment to collect herself, for she was on the verge of tears. "Did we not come here, Jack, because we knew it would be far removed from other people's wars?"

"Yes, we did. But I can't be held accountable because the situation has changed."

"But you *can* be held accountable for the decisions you make as a result of those changes, and this is not a good decision. And what about Davey, if he comes home and you don't? You are his father now and he idolizes you—I sometimes think he only went because he wanted you to be proud of him. Is it fair to expect him to cope with losing two fathers in a lifetime when one loss is too many for any child?"

"Ree, don't do this to me, make me feel guilty. I can't not go. I can't hide here on this ranch while Davey and other men go out and put their lives on the line for the Empire."

"The Empire?" She was incredulous. "Surely the Empire's issues are no concern of yours. Besides, what has the Empire ever done for you except almost get you killed!"

"The Empire gave me Canada and a life I enjoy. The Empire gave me you. Other than love, Ree," I said, repeating what I had told Davey, "loyalty is all we have to give meaning to our lives. Without those two things, what are we? Creatures marking time between when we are born and when we die, and not much more."

"But what about your loyalty to me?"

"My loyalty to you has to be contingent upon everything else being in order."

Ree walked over to the front window where we kept an

ancient arrowhead that we had found over a dozen years before in the hills above False Bay in South Africa. She picked up the artifact, turning it over in her fingers. "Do you remember when we found this?" she asked softly. "You speculated that it belonged to a hunter and I said maybe it was a warrior. I think I was right. And nothing's changed except that the ways men kill each other are more sophisticated. And remember the octopus that pulled the baboon into the water?"

She was referring to an incident during our hike back to the bay when we had encountered baboons that had learned to forage for oysters along the rocky shoreline. A small male had reached into the water to pull one from a rock when a huge octopus grabbed its arm and pulled it in. "That's what war does to men, Jack. It wraps its tentacles around them and pulls them to their death."

"Not always," I protested. "And men are not baboons."

"Really?" A pause, then, "I'm sorry, Jack. That wasn't fair." She closed her eyes for a moment. "What about Jim, then? Has he said anything about going?"

"Jim and I have never talked about enlisting, so I don't know what he has in mind. Whatever the case, I can't live my life according to what he does or doesn't do. Look, Ree, I learned some time ago from men far greater than me that it's my duty to stand and be counted if my country needs me. It needs me now. And you know as well as I do that some women have been giving white feathers to able-bodied men who won't volunteer. Every time I go into town, I expect to get one."

"So you're more afraid of a white feather than you are of death."

"Yes. I don't know what comes with death, but I do know what comes with a white feather and I couldn't live with it. I know this upsets you and I'm sorry, but dealing with it has to be your part of the war effort." I spoke much too sharply and immediately regretted it. She didn't deserve my anger.

"It's too much effort. I've played this scene before, Jack, and I don't like the ending. I'm simply not staying here while you go off and get yourself killed for some silly patriotic notion. It's South Africa all over again. Oliver lost his life in the service of his country and he barely got a decent burial. They gave him a wooden cross and I got a letter saying the government sends its regrets but your husband is dead. A letter, Jack! A life for a letter! Flesh and blood leaves and a piece of paper comes back in its place. What kind of an exchange is that? Now you're asking me to do the same thing all over again. What do I do when a piece of paper replaces you or Davey? Save it beside Oliver's? Is that how this will end? It's a terrible thing you're asking of me, Jack, especially when you don't need to go. You're 45, for goodness sake! I wouldn't suggest for a moment that you're old, but you are much too old for this kind of nonsense, and they won't take you if you don't let them."

"They'll take almost any fit man now. Besides," I added, "Sam Steele is 65 and I read in the paper that he's in the thick of it. It isn't just a young man's war; it's every man's war."

"Yes, it *is* men who fight wars, isn't it?" she said sorrowfully. "I suppose that's because it's men who start them."

"You're right," I agreed, adding lamely, "so it's men who have to finish them."

"Then if you must go, you might as well sell the ranch to

Jim or someone else because I'll sell it anyway when you don't come home."

She turned aside in tears, her shoulders shaking. I was certain that she did not mean what she said. The ranch was Davey's life, too, and for that reason she would be unlikely to sell it if anything happened to me. The words came from being heartbroken and I was sure she would get over it. I wrapped my arms around her and held her until the shaking stopped. Then I grasped her shoulders and turned her, took her face in my hands, and with my thumbs, gently wiped the tears from her cheeks. "Ree, when I found you I found life again and I don't want to relinquish that any more than you do. But I'm duty bound to do this."

She wasn't convinced, and we argued off and on long into the night, neither of us willing to give an inch. It was the first serious argument we had had in all the years of our marriage. Until then, we hadn't had much to quarrel about. We agreed on most things and when we did not, we compromised. So when her shoulders finally sagged in resignation I felt like a thief who had stolen her spirit.

The following morning we were both exhausted and cross from lack of sleep. It hurt me to see her in such a state, especially knowing that I had caused it, so I didn't linger over breakfast. She was all but inaudible and mumbled goodbye to me as I left the house to saddle a horse.

I felt nervous and restless, and the animal sensed it for it was slow settling down. On my way into Kamloops, I bypassed Jim's place on purpose, because I didn't want him to know what I was up to. I was certain he would be supportive but in the event he wasn't, I didn't need any more opposition.

The ride into town had never seemed shorter. Once there I went first to a solicitor, to put my affairs in order, then to the enlistment office in the community hall and, because of my experience, I became a sergeant with the 101st Regiment of the Rocky Mountain Rangers. I was preparing to leave when the door opened and Jim walked in.

"You're going to be the death of me yet," was all he said.

SEVEN

Over There

IT WAS A LONG, slow journey of several months from the enlistment office in Kamloops to the battlefield, and the worst of it was getting used to the Ross rifle. It had replaced the Lee Enfield and was the worst excuse for a weapon of war that I'd ever seen. It was oversized and cumbersome, and it seized up when it got hot from rapid firing. If I'd had a choice, I would have melted them all down and turned them into something useful, something on which lives didn't depend, like stove tops. Jim temporarily broke out of form and grumbled in complete frustration, "This goddamned thing'll kill us before it ever kills any Huns."

"Maybe we're using it the wrong way," I said. "Maybe we're supposed attach the bayonet and throw it like a spear."

"Let me know how you make out with that technique," he growled. Jim was edgier than I was accustomed to seeing him, but he had a lot on his mind too.

We arrived in Shorncliffe, England, a sprawling army camp a few miles southwest of Dover, where Sam Steele was the General Officer Commanding. He would have been appalled at the conditions on the ship that had brought us over. Men were jammed in bunks tiered so closely they had to get out of them to turn over, and the air was as foul as the food they fed us—a yellow slime flavoured with curry powder to mask how really awful it was. Our journey to South Africa 15 years earlier was a luxury cruise by comparison, and the only positive side to it was that the men no longer complained about their rifles. Steele would never have allowed such maltreatment of his soldiers had he any say in the matter, of that I was certain.

Typically, he came to Shorncliffe to see how the troops were doing and we lined up for inspection. Any other commander might have passed by without noticing me but not Steele. He looked at every man and could tell at a glance if part of his uniform was out of order. If he recognized a man from previous service he made a point of acknowledging it. "Strong!" he exclaimed, when he saw me, and stopped so suddenly that the officers behind nearly crashed into him. He had put on weight over the years and his neatly trimmed moustache was almost completely grey, but there wasn't an ounce less resolve and determination in those eyes. "I should have known you couldn't stay out of this."

"Right, sir," I said. "Nor could you, I see."

"It's my life. It isn't necessarily yours, though. I'm afraid this one won't be anything like chasing Brother Boer across the veld. The Boche are a different matter entirely."

"I didn't volunteer to have it easy, sir. We'll do whatever it takes."

Brave words for someone far from the front.

"I'm sure you will, Strong. I'm sure you will." He looked me dead in the eye, which might have been intimidating had I not known him for so long. "I am heartened that men of your calibre have heeded the call."

"Thank you, sir. Spencer's here, too."

"Spencer? Is he, now?"

"Yes, sir." Jim was with his own troop and Steele hadn't reached him yet. "He's just down the line."

"That's odd. I've yet to hear a single complaint about anyone pushing over British staff sergeants on their horses." He was alluding to an incident in South Africa, when Jim was in his cups and tipped over a mounted and officious British non-commissioned officer.

"He's mellowed over the years, sir."

"I'm sorry to hear that. Good luck, Strong. Stay alert."

"I will, sir. Thank you."

Later, when I told Jim what Steele had said about British staff sergeants and horses, he laughed. "I figured that's what he was referring to when he said to stay alert because the Boche were not 'pushovers.' The cagey old bugger!"

That night I was almost asleep in my tent when a droning sound worked its way into my ears and activated my brain. I sat up. At first, I thought it was a fly or a bee, forgetting that neither would be airborne in the dark. Then I heard a commotion and cries of "Zeppelin! Zeppelin!" I sprang from my cot and ran outside in my underwear. Not far off to the north I could see the dark silhouette of the airship moving across the starry sky. I remembered seeing hot air balloons in South Africa—they were a novelty then—but this aircraft was eerie and ominous, and might have been arriving from another planet. All of a sudden there was a huge white flash followed instantly by an explosion. I could hear shrapnel raining down on our bivouac area not far from where I stood. It happened so fast that there was no time to hide, but my instinct was to head for the area of the explosion and offer help. Before I could make a move, an officer barked at everyone in general, "Stay where you are until I give an order to move! Let's see where that bloody Hun is going first!"

We waited nervously but the ship disappeared. The next morning, word flew around the camp that several men in an English unit had died, along with over three dozen horses. The shrapnel that fell caused neither injury nor damage to anyone in our regiment. I hoped that we'd seen our first and last air raid in England. It would never do to be killed before we even crossed the Channel.

UNFORTUNATELY, DAVEY had gone on to Belgium before I arrived in Shorncliffe so I missed him. He had sent a few letters, as had Ree, and in the last one he said that his stellar marksmanship had earned him a job as a sniper. He was somewhere on the front, "near 'Wipers,'" but the exact location was confidential and not permitted in letters. Nevertheless, he insisted he was doing fine, sent his love and asked us not to worry about him.

What parent could ever heed that request?

In late March of 1916, we sailed for the port of Boulogne-sur-Mer, on the French coast, by a long, rough and roundabout route to avoid German U-boats operating in the Channel between Folkestone and Calais. Aside from the drabness of the port, it was a quaint town of cobblestoned streets, squares, fine old buildings and church spires. It might even have had charm if it weren't for the heavy military presence. We stopped there for two days, unloading supplies and preparing for our departure to the front. On the first evening, Jim and I went out on the town accompanied by a corporal in my troop named Freddy Wilson. We had an 11:00 P.M. curfew.

Until the war came along, Freddy had been a foreman on a ranch north of Kamloops, in "God's country" as he insisted on calling British Columbia. "Cowboying" was all he could remember wanting to do, but when most able-bodied men around him were enlisting he couldn't, in all good conscience, not follow suit. Our paths had crossed a few times before, when I was looking for horses, but I only knew him slightly. In England, however, we soon learned that he was a good man to have around. Tough, single and 10 years younger than Jim and me, he went full bore at everything he did, whether it was work or play. We kidded him about tagging along with a pair of dull married men for a night on the town but he was philosophical about it. "It don't matter," he said. "There ain't enough time to do much anyway. I thought ranchin' played hell on a man's social life but it don't hold a candle to the army!"

We visited a bathhouse first and immersed ourselves in hot, sudsy water for a half-hour, then wandered through town. The unsettling rumble of big guns at the front, some 50 miles away, was like a distant thunderstorm. It made a man want to be inside where it was comfortable, where other sounds such as conversation or music fell more pleasantly on a soldier's ear. Walking along a curved cobblestoned street slick from a recent downpour, we came upon a café chantant and found the music emanating from within irresistible. A waiter escorted us to the only empty table.

Cigarette smoke filled the overly warm room like fog, and a sprinkling of soldiers and several couples occupied the other tables. On a small stage in the corner, a man played an upright piano and sang. We ordered a bottle of wine and mussels, which came in a rich sauce with plenty of bread.

"This is more like it," observed Freddy. "The war wouldn't be so bad if we could eat like this every night." He raised his glass. "To King and Empire."

"To King and Empire," Jim and I echoed.

After dinner, we ordered more wine and, when the piano player took a break, we coaxed Jim to sing for the crowd. There was chatter as he sat down and began to play Stephen Foster's "Gentle Annie." Some music settles in the ear and stops there, but with Jim's music, the ear was merely a conduit to the heart. His singing silenced everyone and when he finished his first song they shouted for more. He sang until the piano player felt obliged to get back to work and earn his pay.

"Jesus H. Christ!" Freddy was hearing Jim for the first time. "He should be in Paris performing, instead of this rathole."

When Jim relinquished the stage, the patrons roared their disapproval, but he waved and rejoined us anyway. We celebrated his French debut with another bottle of wine. He had elevated the mood in the café to great heights, especially among those of us about to enter the fight. It was one of those moments that you wished could last forever because you knew what was coming after it.

"You know what I'm thinking, boys?" Without waiting for an answer Freddy added, "I'm thinking that music is good but some female company would be a whole lot better."

"Meaning?" I asked.

"Meaning we can find a better place than this even if we have to pay for it."

"You go ahead, Freddy," I said. "This place suits me fine."

"Me too," agreed Jim. "I've got all I need waitin' at home for me."

Freddy snorted. "But what if you don't get home? You could be dead next week for Christ's sake. Besides, no one's askin' you to do anythin' you don't want to do. Let's just see if we can find a place where we can share a drink with some women. Enjoy life while we got a chance."

Jim, his face ruddy from the wine and the heat of the café, thought for a moment, then looked at me. "Maybe Freddy's right. When I think about it, you're all I've had to look at for longer than a man ought to and it's depressing as hell. Let's do it before I get downright suicidal."

I cottoned on to the idea more readily than perhaps I should have, but too much time among all things masculine can give a man a warped perspective on life. And Freddy was right. It didn't mean I had to climb into bed with anybody, and it might prove to be a healthy reminder that another world existed beyond men, guns and horses. The several glasses of wine I'd drunk helped to make up my mind. "What the hell," I said. "Why not?"

Freddy made a discreet inquiry of the waiter who gave us directions to where we could go. Indeed, it wasn't far: around the corner and two blocks along the Rue de la Mer.

The building was quite nondescript from the street but rather pleasant inside. According to the waiter, it wasn't the best brothel in town—that one was reserved for officers—but it certainly proved decent enough. A matronly woman answered our knock and led us down a hallway into a square, slate-floored courtyard with a variety of flowering and green plants around the sides. A mullioned skylight protected it from the elements, and a small fountain adorned the centre, with a cherub streaming water from its groin. It was, altogether, quite an exotic environment compared to what we'd had to contend with over the past months. There were several tables and chairs about, some already occupied by other NCOs accompanied by seductively clad women. A red-faced sergeant-major, clearly drunk, was rubbing his hand along his companion's thigh and she was pretending to be interested, making an effort to show that for her it wasn't just a job.

The matron made a small waving motion with her hand, and three young women arose from a table on the far side of the courtyard, smiled and came over. They greeted us in French, and then ushered us to their table where a very masculine-looking older woman brought glasses, along with a bottle of red wine and a bottle of white. All business, she deftly extracted the corks. Freddy paid the tab, and she left.

Two of our companions for the evening were dark-haired and half-pretty, although one of them had a dollar-sized mole on her neck. The third had red hair and freckles, and was the plainest of the three. They might have been in their early 20s; it was difficult to tell. I'm sure that had we insisted, we could have chosen any girl in the place, but the rest were neither more nor less attractive than these three.

The most peculiar aspect of this gathering was that the girls had only a few words of English, no doubt learned from previous customers, while we spoke no French. Yet it didn't matter. They smiled a lot and were very feminine, and that alone was appealing. Then there was the wine.

Freddy became the official pourer, urging us to drink up. "Remember the sound of those guns, boys? Death and destruction. That's what's waitin' for us."

So we drank. I felt uncomfortable and gulped mine when I really didn't need it in the first place. Jim and Freddy were gulping, too. We communicated with the girls using over-enunciated words and phrases, gestures and body language. Freddy became hilariously animated and made the girls giggle with glee. He kept pouring drinks, although the girls drank very little. It was great fun and the war became a fuzzy image, as if seen through rising waves of heat in a desert.

Before long the bottles were empty and I was feeling slightly woozy. I could tell that Jim wasn't faring much better, but Freddy appeared to be gathering steam. Every now and then, a soldier would scrape his chair back and go off with his companion through one of the three exits from the courtyard, and you'd hear a door open and close. The sergeant-major left with his girl, a lascivious look on his face and a noticeable bulge in his trousers. Other men trickled in and sat unaccompanied, waiting until a girl was free. It made the outcome of our own liaison unsettlingly predictable.

As if by a prearranged signal, the girls arose and the red-head reached over and took my hand. "*Venez avec moi,*" she said, smiling, then in English, "Come weeth me," so endearingly that without thinking I obeyed, when I had told myself I wouldn't. She led me away, a woman of commerce, and yet the moment felt inexplicably innocent. Besides, wasn't I only satisfying my curiosity? Jim and Freddy and their girls followed on our heels and we all went down the same hallway but into different rooms.

The furniture was basic: a bed covered with a brightly patterned comforter, and a small counter with a sink and a towel rack. There were no windows and a strong perfume overrode an underlying smell of mustiness.

We sat on the edge of the bed, two different generations, our thighs lightly touching, and I did nothing except wonder why I had bothered to come. I felt awkward, wishing I could tell her all the reasons why this was not going to work. She stood and removed her dress. She wore nothing underneath. Her body was remarkable only for its freckles and was more alluring hidden beneath the thin garment she had shed. She sat down again and I showed her my wedding band. "I'm married," I said, the words slurring. "I really shouldn't be here. In fact, I think I'd better go."

She giggled and said something I couldn't understand. She shook her head. Did she say that it was all right? That I shouldn't worry? That there was a war raging nearby and I would get there soon enough? She slid her hand between my legs and her touch electrified me. The intimacy of the moment made me suddenly realize how lonely I was and how I longed for the touch of a woman. But I pushed her hand away and stood, swaying slightly. I took my paybook out of my tunic and, pulling out a bunch of francs, I gave them all to her. She looked cross, a woman scorned; nevertheless, she counted out several and returned the rest. How much she took I didn't know and didn't care.

My stomach was sour from the wine and I was dead tired. I went to the sink, splashed water on my face and dried off with a soft towel hanging there. I waved to her as I left the room and she said, coldly, "*Au revoir.*" I shut the door quietly behind me.

I went along the hallway and through the courtyard, and the same matronly woman who had let us in let me out with a brief smile and a nod. A stiff breeze off the sea was blowing down the Rue de la Mer and marginally revived me, although my head throbbed and I felt nauseated. I wanted to retch, but there were other people in the street and I refused to embarrass myself, not to mention the uniform. Neither Jim nor Freddy was around so I waited in a doorway for them. As terrible as I felt, there was some solace in the relief that flickered like a candle in my core: I knew I had nearly lost something, something that I would need when I faced Ree again.

WE WERE all greatly hungover the following morning but Freddy, damn his hide, was extremely chipper. Jim and I never talked about the previous evening. We didn't need to. He had a hard time looking me in the eye.

We set out for the front at noon with horse and mule convoys, transporting supplies and ammunition to the depot at the Ypres Salient. The convoys consisted of 40 or more horses laden with panniers that carried three or four large shells a side, depending on the size. Mule-drawn wagons filled with ammunition, and with what passed for food in the army, followed.

The weather was cold and dismal. The incessant rain seemed as much a part of the country as its platter-like flatness. The farther east we moved, the worse it got. Yet the rain did little to refresh the rank ditches edging the elevated roads. In places, the fetid water overflowed onto the flat land and formed ponds that, during foggy periods, looked like lakes disappearing into the gauzy distance. Where there wasn't water there was mud, a mixture of sand and clay as sucking as quicksand and just as deadly, where it was deep. Men and horses had been lost in it.

Near the front, the shell-pocked and muddy roads bisected villages and towns ravaged by the battles. Many were deserted, their inhabitants having long fled the war zone, but there were always holdouts, people who would not leave their homes for any reason, who eked out a living any way they could. Some were stubborn, others disturbed, perhaps driven over the edge by the madness around them and the stench of rotting corpses borne on an ill wind. And some were willing to put a kettle on and make a cup of weak tea for a soldier come to save them from the Hun.

Ypres was a spectacle of horror, a town of rubble and jutting, blackened, bombed-out buildings that stank of decaying bodies. I'd seen nothing like this in South Africa and it scared the hell out of me. Jim, who was rearward with his own men, didn't say much when I saw him later, but the hard set to his jaw suggested that he too was wondering what we'd got ourselves into.

Between the second battle of Ypres in the spring of 1915 and the battle of Mont Sorrel in June of 1916, the Allied and German trenches in the Ypres Salient faced each other across a No-Man's-Land that averaged about 300 yards in width. Other than the British push at St-Eloi, south of us, there were no major offensives during this period. The Allies were concentrating their efforts along the front in France and in the east at places such as Gallipoli and Salonika. Along the Ypres Salient, the strategy was generally one of containment, and the result was a stalemate. The two sides had dug in and nobody moved. Yet there were always shells exploding and guns firing somewhere, for this was a time of small artillery fire, snipers, patrols and raiding parties, and trenches. And since the salient was pretty much all that was left of Belgium not under German control, it was a matter of pride to the Allied forces not to relinquish it.

From the air, a person would have seen a nearly incomprehensible maze of trenches on both sides of the front, which had shifted so much since the war began that the Germans sometimes occupied Allied-dug trenches and vice versa. The front or firing line for the Allies was the trench closest to the Germans. When I arrived, it sliced across open fields and through small woods, and was protected by rolls of barbed wire. It zigzagged, to diffuse bomb blasts and to prevent long stretches from being taken over by the enemy. Running parallel to it, perhaps 200 yards behind, was the jagged trench of the second line, or support trench. More kinked lines, the communication trenches, connected these two main trenches just as spindles connect the top and bottom rails of a banister. From the support trench, more communication trenches ran irregularly to the reserve trenches about 400 yards back. Anyone not familiar with the system could get lost in it and many did. In some instances, soldiers accustomed to the maze acted as guides and introduced new battalions to it, and street names adorned some trenches to make it easier to navigate them.

Movement was constant, even more at night when it was safer: men rotating from the firing line to the reserve and support lines, and out to the front again; men moving supplies and ammunition to the front, and the wounded and the dead to the rear. And everything inhabiting this ungodly world, including mice and rats fat from feeding on corpses, was clad either in the grey-white mud lining it when it rained, or dust when it didn't. There was no getting rid of it. It was as much a part of trench life as the spectre of death.

Our routine consisted of about 5 days on the firing line followed by a rotation to the reserve lines for 10 days or so, then to the support line for 2 or 3 days before a return to the front. While we were in the rear lines, we were always prepared to advance in the event of an attack and were kept busy moving supplies forward, from rations and letters for the men to timber and corrugated iron to maintain the trenches. At the front, tension ran high, time slowed to a standstill and sleep was a rare commodity. Most men got some whenever and wherever they could, usually in fits and starts. If a man wasn't on sentry duty or standing to in a firing bay, he was usually working on the endless job of maintaining the trenches—reinforcing collapsed walls, replacing duckboards or digging new latrines, and anything else the officers could think of to keep him busy and his mind off dying. They were dirty and dangerous places filled with filthy, frightened men. But they were our world and sometimes it was impossible to imagine that civilization existed beyond them.

EIGHT

The Patrol

SANCTUARY WOOD WAS ABOUT a mile of deciduous forest stretching along the southeastern part of the Ypres Salient. Its northern end mushroomed out to the east and cut across both the Allied and German lines. Along this stretch of the salient the lines were, on average, about 100 to 300 yards apart. The trees, mostly maple, were not yet ravaged by gunfire and were in full leaf. Every now and then, a bird twittered. On a rather pleasant evening in July, when the sun that had baked us for much of the day was descending in the western sky, a fool might have been led to believe that all was well with the world.

I felt tense and tired as I negotiated the kinks in the trench named Bloor Street. The trench walls in this area were in comparatively serviceable shape, the parts weakened by periodic shelling reinforced with corrugated iron. Mercifully, there had been no rain for several days and the mud was drying up. Here and there, heaps of sandbags lined the parapets. I passed firing bays manned by three or four soldiers with rifles and periscopes, peering over the parapet into No-Man's-Land. A detail of men was sweating, digging a new latrine off the main trench. Numerous strands of communication wire, telegraph and telephone, ran along the trench bottoms, covered in places by duckboards. An opening in the wall ended in a well-used latrine, the smell of which was merciless, and several paces beyond, far enough from the stink, I descended three steps into 24 Sussex Drive, the dank dugout to which I had been summoned.

The place had a smell of its own, of earth, melting wax, coal oil and sweaty men, and was the home on this rotation of the two officers sitting at a makeshift table. One was eating soup and sardines, swatting at the flies that were everywhere; the other was examining some papers. On the far wall were two sets of roughly built double bunks with chicken wire for bedsprings. On another wall was a brazier for cooking and for heat, when necessary. Above it hung a tattered picture of a voluptuous, naked woman, her legs spread open. At the bottom, someone had written, "If you know of a better hole, go to it."

"Ah, Sergeant Strong," said the officer who was eating. Lieutenant-Colonel Roger Beresford was a barrister from Regina who, being well educated and reasonably well off, had bought his commission. A hawk-faced man of 35 years, he pomaded his black hair and combed it straight back, as neat and precise as his pencil-thin moustache. His eyes were dark and puffy from lack of sleep. He wore a side arm, as did most of the officers, a .45 calibre revolver that he'd had to purchase himself. He was a bit of a strange bird, and though he had some years behind him with the militia, he was new to the regiment and not yet battle tested.

With Beresford was Lieutenant Will Hoffman, my immediate superior. A successful businessman from Calgary, he had also purchased his commission. But he was an engaging, likeable man and completely unflappable, the type of person who appeared to enjoy himself regardless of his surroundings. He looked to be about the same age as Beresford and his hair, like mine, was sandy but without the greying edges. Hoffman's parents were German immigrants and though he was by no means fluent in the language, he could catch the drift of any conversation. It made him a valuable patrol officer. He was lighting his pipe as I entered and saluted.

"We're going for a midnight crawl tonight, Jack," he said, meaning that we were going on patrol. "Fritz has been too quiet lately so we'll go have a listen and see if we can find out anything. Get Gus Moretti and three good men—crawling around in No-Man's-Land in the dead of night is not for sissies—and be outside and ready at dusk. In the meantime, try to get some rest. It could be a late night."

Corporal Gus Moretti was one of the best scouts in the regiment. I didn't know him well, other than that he had an unerring sense of direction. Some swore that he could lead a patrol blindfolded.

"Yes, sir." I saluted again and left.

The weariness, at least, had gone, and I felt fully charged, as a squadron of butterflies swarmed in my stomach. Hoffman's words, about crawling around in No-Man's-Land not being for sissies, meant that I was in for something less than a good time. Patrols and raids were always perilous but were supposed to be morale builders, as much a part of trench life as lice and fleas, and every bit as welcome. They were partly designed to keep soldiers, whose main function at present was defensive, in an offensive frame of mind, lest they stagnate completely. Most of us thought they were a questionable assignment at best, but Gus accepted them as being better than the dreary task of maintaining the trenches. Few men were keen on dying, but dying during a patrol that was almost meaningless to the overall war effort was particularly unappealing.

Though I was on my second rotation through the firing line trenches and was still adapting to the ever-present tension, this would be my first patrol and I was not looking forward to it. It would have been a comfort to have Jim with me, but his rotation was currently in the support trenches. I doubted that he'd be sent on patrol anyway. It would be like one of the Rocky Mountains trying to sneak across the prairies.

I spoke to Gus, whose eyes brightened at the news, then sought out Freddy Wilson who was nowhere near as keen as Gus, but would never say no. I found two others in short order. They didn't have to go, I told them, but both had a strong sense of duty. Then, not having the luxury of a chicken-wire bunk, I found a hole in the wall of the trench, ate some bully beef, though I didn't really have the stomach for it, and tried to get some sleep. But I had too much on my mind.

I took out the postcard I'd received the week before from Davey and read it again for the umpteenth time. It was an official army card, at the top of which was printed: "NOTHING is to be written on this side except the date and signature of

case we get separated, the password to get back into this lovely hole is 'Saskatoon.' Don't forget it. Ready?"

"Ready," I answered. There were nods and mumbles of assent from the others.

"All right, Moretti, lead the way. Then the rest of us, one at a time. Let's go!"

Gus climbed onto the parapet and rolled over the top. Hoffman followed, I went next and the rest followed me, Freddy bringing up the rear.

The night was cloudy and moonless, perfect for patrolling. We moved swiftly at a crouch through the wide spaces between the trees until we reached a tangle of barbed wire about 30 yards deep. Patrols had gone out many times before and there was a zigzag route through it. Gus knew the way, even in the dark. We crawled on all fours, in close order, head to arse, the going painfully slow. It was nearly impossible to avoid being snagged or scratched by the barbs. Beyond the wire, we went down on our bellies and inched our way toward the German lines. The ground was uncommonly flat and the shallow artillery craters, which afforded a small degree of protection, had seemed far more plentiful from the trenches than they actually were. In between were long patches of rough grass, perhaps a foot high, in which I felt as vulnerable as a newborn babe.

We slithered forward, reaching out with our rifles then wriggling toward them, over and over again until the sweat rolled off my forehead and into my eyes. Every muscle in my body ached and I felt taut, like a fiddle string. I imagined a thousand guns aimed at me, ready to riddle my body with bullets in a millisecond. After about a hundred yards, Hoffman stopped us to rest. Everyone but Gus was breathing hard and trying to be silent about it. Somewhere frogs croaked and above that, three muffled explosions rent the night far to the west, followed by a burst of machine-gun fire. A raid, no doubt, or possibly a failed patrol, something I didn't like to think about.

We were about to move forward again when there was the unmistakable *whooshing* of a parachute flare ascending. In moments, it exploded open, 50 yards to our right and perhaps 60 feet in the air, and a sudden burst of light flooded the landscape. "Don't move!" Hoffman hissed, an order no one really needed. I froze, pressing myself onto the hard ground, certain that I must be denting it. The flare lasted only a few seconds, long enough for a machine gunner to get a bead on us. But nothing happened. Fritz hadn't seen us. Even in the resuming darkness we remained motionless for what felt like hours before Hoffman gave the command to start forward again. My joints seemed fused together and I could barely get them working again.

Another 50 yards and we crossed what was either a narrow, partially dried-up stream bed or a shallow irrigation ditch. It contained more mud than water but felt cool and almost refreshing. Off to our left I could see the vague shapes of trees silhouetted against the sky, the part of Sanctuary Wood that crossed both front lines. We were closing in on the German wire and could hear the murmur of voices. Whispering, Hoffman sent Freddy and another man several yards off to the left and Gus with the other man to the right to guard our flanks while he and I crept as far as we could through a partial gap in the wire. We slid forward, conscious of even the slightest noise, the rustle of a piece of grass, the scraping of a pebble, and every tiny sound boomed 10 times louder in my ears. Soon the voices were more distinct—German voices, of course. And Hoffman listened intently to them. Besides the voices, all I could hear was my heart pounding.

We stayed like that for an hour, until I wanted to stand and run, out of fear and the simple need to move my body. Then I heard a noise, ahead and well to the right, that made my skin feel like it was peeling off. For a second I didn't know what it was. The next second, it hit me. It was the sound of German soldiers rolling over a parapet. A patrol!

Hoffman heard it too. We waited, ready to shoot and run if necessary. I prayed it wouldn't be, because I didn't think we'd survive the gunfire from the trenches, and the best we could hope for would be to take some Germans with us. Luckily, the sounds of the patrol receded to our right. I wondered what Gus was thinking. He and his man must have been awfully close to it but I would wager that Gus, though not exactly relishing the experience, was cool enough to keep his partner from panicking.

We kept dead still, until we were certain the patrol was long gone, and fervently hoped we didn't run into it on the way back to our lines. Suddenly, a voice spoke out from the German trench. *"Wenn Sie bald nicht weggehen, sind wir dabei, Sie zu schießen!"* It was as if the words were directed at us, although I couldn't understand why any Boche would do such an unlikely thing.

Then Hoffman said, softly but urgently, "Shit! Time to go home!" I thought the German must have said something that scared the hell out of him.

Dark forms slipped in beside us from our right and left, the others of our patrol.

"Get us back to our lines, Moretti," Hoffman ordered. "Move it!"

Gus heard the urgency in the lieutenant's voice and didn't ask any questions. He slipped into the lead and rest of us needed no further incentive to follow. I thought we were making far more noise than we ought to because there was still a German patrol out there. They must have gone off in a different direction, yet even so, I still expected that we'd all die in a hail of bullets.

I had only a vague notion of the route to the opening in our wire, for I had lost my bearings. Gus led us straight to it. How he found it I'll never know—perhaps the silhouette of a tree against the sky guided him, or he was blessed with better night vision than most—but he made no mistake. We crawled through the gap, the barbs tearing at our uniforms.

"Saskatoon! Saskatoon!" Gus called the password in a low voice to the sentries as we stood and darted through the trees. "Don't shoot!" We hit the parapet on our behinds and slid into the trench, thudding against the corrugated iron on the far side and bumping hard against each other.

"What the hell was that all about?" I asked, trying to catch my breath, every pore in my body sweating. "What did that guy say?" The words tumbled out of me so fast that they ran into each other.

Hoffman was sweating, too. Panting, he said, "Loosely translated it was something like, 'If you don't leave soon, we are going to shoot you.'"

DURING THE debriefing, Beresford was alarmed, even more so when Hoffman said that virtually all of the conversation he had heard before that last sentence was about home, loved ones and food.

"Something's cooking," the colonel insisted, "and they didn't want to start it early. I'm certain of it. Get some rest, gentlemen. You may need it."

I asked Gus how close the German patrol had come to him and his mate.

"I could smell 'em," he replied. "Smelled like sauerkraut and fear."

I returned to my hidey-hole in the wall, pulled my blanket over my head so the rats couldn't bite my face and tried to sleep. It was 4:00 in the morning when we returned from the patrol and at 5:00 I was still wide awake, still tense. The words "something's cooking" were not exactly a soporific. I had been lucky during the short time I'd been at the front because it had been relatively quiet. But what would the approaching day bring? Already the sky was lightening in the east.

I must have dozed off for I awoke with a start, my blanket off and flies crawling around my mouth. The surrealistic events of the patrol flooded through my mind. It was fully light; the sun was just above the horizon and streaming through the trees of Sanctuary Wood. Cuckoos called from the branches overhead. I rolled from my tiny cave, stood and stretched. I felt lucky to be alive. Above the foliage, the sky was a brilliant blue, a summer morning too perfect to be anywhere in the vicinity of a war zone. Other men were stirring, preparing to stand to. I caught the smell of bacon frying as I headed for the latrine. I was just about to turn into it when the cuckoos began jabbering as if they were on to something I wasn't. I stopped to listen.

Suddenly there was a tremendous WHOOMP as a shell exploded farther down the trench line. WHOOMP, WHOOMP, as more shells exploded, nearer this time. Great gouts of soil flew into the air. Men screamed. I couldn't tell if the earth was trembling or if it was just my knees shaking. Gus and Freddy came running toward me, single file, a look of amazement on Gus's face and sheer terror on Freddy's. Another explosion tore the corrugated iron behind them into pieces. A large shard caught Freddy in the neck with such force it half severed his head. Blood splattered everywhere. Gus never even looked behind him, just kept on running, totally unaware of what happened to Freddy. All of this occurred in an instant. I turned and ran with Gus on my heels. It was only a matter of yards to 24 Sussex Drive; I reached it in seconds and tumbled down the steps, Gus falling in right behind me.

Gus expected Freddy to enter behind him and when he didn't, he asked, "Jesus, where's Freddy?" He looked ready to head out to look for him.

I grabbed his arm. "He took a real bad hit. There's no way he could have survived it." I spared him the details.

Beresford, his composure lost, was there, frantically trying to call for support. Hoffman looked as if he'd just awakened. "The goddamned lines are down!" the colonel screamed to no one in particular and slammed the handset onto the table with a loud crash. More explosions shook the earth and fine dirt filtered down between the cracks in the timbered ceiling. Another one and a small avalanche thudded down over the entrance, sending into the dugout a cloud of dust that burned my eyes and set me coughing. Beresford, Hoffman and Gus weren't faring any better. We pulled our lapels over our lower faces. Through the dust, we could see a slit of day-light at the top of the mound of earth blocking the entrance, and instinctively moved toward it, fearing that the dugout would be our grave. What was happening outside seemed a marginally better way to die.

"Grab a shovel!" It was Hoffman; Beresford appeared befuddled. Gus was ready to fight but there was no grappling with this enemy, at least not yet.

There were two spades in the corner by the bunks, kept there especially for this type of situation. I grabbed them, threw one to Gus, and we started digging. I dug with the strength of a road gang and tossed the dirt behind me as if it were as light as sea foam. In moments, we had cleared a space large enough for a man to crawl through.

Hoffman said, "It sounds as if the shells are falling behind us now. Take a look around, Strong."

I crawled out and though the noise from the artillery and howitzer explosions was deafening, Hoffman was right: most of the shells were falling behind us now, around the support lines where Jim was. I peered over the parapet in that direc-tion and saw a wall of flames and dirt. Men were staggering out of the trenches, half dead and in a daze. There were bodies everywhere. Two were draped high over a tree limb, side by side, as if someone had deliberately hung them there to dry. The clumps of blood-soaked uniform scattered about were actually body parts. I was stunned but collected myself enough to call to the others that it was safe to come out. Beresford was the first and the rest followed.

Since the colonel was useless, Hoffman was looking around, assessing the situation, trying to decide what to do. All of a sudden there was movement in the direction of the German lines and the sight filled me with horror. A swarm of grey-uniformed soldiers appeared out of the ground, advancing toward us. Some of the men in front carried flame-throwers that sent streams of fire at least 30 or 40 yards ahead of them. I had heard of these weapons but had never imagined their power. Gus looked truly scared for the first time in the short history of our relationship. There was nowhere to run, and I was so terrified that I didn't realize until later, feeling the dampness, that my bladder had let loose. Other men, who had survived the initial shelling, after seeing the wall of fire blocking their escape route behind, staggered toward the Boche lines hoping for mercy. They were either shot down or consumed by flames.

Beresford's eyes had glazed over. "I'm not staying here," he said wildly and began to climb out of the trench. I grabbed at him and so did Hoffman, who shouted, "Don't be a bloody fool, sir!" But he wrenched himself free and darted a few paces to where the trench walls had collapsed and provided an easy way out. He was above ground for only a matter of seconds, pulling his revolver from its holster, when a long tongue of flame set him on fire with such ferocity that he never even had time to scream before he died. I felt the heat of his death on my face, heard him sizzle and smelled a charcoal-like odour that was his skin cooking.

Hoffman, Gus and I had no place to go but back into the dugout. It was a terrible choice to make, but it was the only place that offered a chance that the flame-throwers might pass us by. We scrambled through the opening like turkeys voluntarily climbing into the oven, and once inside, turned the table over and hid behind it. It was a foolish manoeuvre, because it offered no protection from the flame-throwers, or bullets for that matter, but I, at least, wouldn't see my death coming. Hoffman pulled out his pistol, ready to shoot the first German who showed his face at the entrance. Gus and I were weaponless.

"You fire that if they show up here, and we're as good as dead," I hissed desperately.

"Something tells me that we're as good as dead anyway," he replied calmly, as if he were talking about something he should add to his grocery list.

I could hear movement in the trenches, voices jabbering in German. A fusillade of bullets poured through the hole and over our heads, burying themselves in the wall behind us and splintering the uprights of the bunks. Through a crack in the table, I could see German soldiers at the entrance, rifles pointing in our direction. "*Raus! Raus!*" one of them screamed. "*Mit Ihren Händen über Ihren Kopf!*"

"They want us to come out with our hands over our head," Hoffman told us.

"This is no time to argue, sir," I said, earnestly.

"*Schießen Sie Nicht!*" Hoffman yelled. ("Don't shoot!") We placed our hands where they wanted them and stood.

NINE

Boche Hospitality

A SENSE OF RELIEF filled me as they marched us at gunpoint away from the devastation of the trenches, because I had avoided being blown to bits or burned to death. But it didn't last long. Once the reality of being a prisoner of war sank in, I became anxious. While I had never spoken with anyone who had been in my situation, horror stories of how the Germans treated their prisoners abounded. Being killed might have been the better option.

Gus was angry. Being a prisoner was not on his agenda. "Fritz isn't gonna keep me long, Sarge," he vowed. "They can blindfold me and I'll find my way home. First chance I get. You can come with me if you want."

He got a rifle butt between the shoulder blades for talking. I scowled at the guard, who lifted his rifle as if to jab me. I threw my arm up to protect myself and that was as far as it went. But I got the message. We would need to tread carefully around our captors.

Well behind the German lines, we were stopped and ordered to sit on the ground. The rest was welcome at first but an hour passed, then another and another, and the sun burned down relentlessly upon us. We were given neither food nor water. A few of the men were wounded; one boy, who couldn't have been much older than Davey, was especially badly off, but the guards would not let us help him. Any attempts at talking were silenced by a guttural "*Schweigen!*" from a guard with a rifle. An eternity passed before an officer came along and spoke to one of the guards, who turned to us and barked, "*Auf Ihren Füßen. Schnell!*" He pointed his rifle at us, then swung the barrel up. "Up! Up! Up! Up!" he shouted, although it sounded more like "A pup, a pup!"

They marched us out along the Menin Road, an ugly scar on the face of a ravaged land littered with shattered wagons and gun carriages. The stink from the rotting corpses of horses and mules was appalling. Anything that might have remotely suggested that a civilization once existed there had been all but obliterated. Had it been raining, it would have been even more depressing. But the sky above was a contradictory blue, the air summer hot, and in another time and place we might have been a group heading off to the beach or for a picnic.

There were a dozen prisoners besides me: two officers, including Hoffman, and the rest private soldiers. In a second group, straggling along behind, were a half-dozen wounded soldiers. All of the guards had saw-toothed bayonets and displayed a willingness to use them should we try anything they didn't like. And yet, for me at least, it was immeasurably better than the hell I had witnessed during the attack. I had no idea what the next hour might bring but at least for the moment I was still alive. And who knew when an opportunity to escape might present itself?

In Menin, a German-occupied Belgian town a few miles behind the lines, there were soldiers everywhere and an assortment of military vehicles, both motorized and horse-drawn, owned the streets. The local citizenry, mostly old men and women with sad faces, weary of the war and the Germans, stood here and there along the street and tried to offer us food. The guards threatened them with their brutal-looking bayonets and they retreated, many showing their disapproval with hard stares.

The sight of the food only served to remind me how hungry I was and that my throat was parched from lack of water. But the lesson we had been taught soon after we left the line, that complaints or any form of talking earned a rifle butt between the shoulder blades, was well etched on our brains by then. We crossed to the far side of town and as night was falling we came to a large stable. Like the animals they probably thought we were, the guards herded us inside. One of them, who spoke passable English, ordered us to spread straw from a large pile over the floor. It would be our bed for the night. By that time, few of us cared about how comfortable it would be; all we wanted was to be off our feet.

Some civilians brought us tepid coffee and black bread made from potato flour that I wolfed down. The bread was stale and hard, and only palatable because I had not eaten for nearly 30 hours. But the coffee, which under different circumstances might have tasted like sewer water, was as refreshing as a clear mountain stream and eased the constricting dryness in my throat. Then, under heavy guard, we were allowed to sleep.

I slept like the dead for two hours, until nightmares of a headless Freddy Wilson and men on fire awakened me, drenched in sweat. Poor Freddy and Lieutenant-Colonel Beresford. But at least they had died quickly and did not linger for hours in unutterable agony, as many unfortunate souls had over the course of this war and all the wars that had preceded it. I felt sick just thinking of it, not to mention the smell of roasting flesh that persisted in my nostrils. I pushed my nose into the straw and inhaled deeply. I could smell horses and manure there, and in that smell found something connected to better times. It gave me a modicum of reassurance that there might still be some sanity left somewhere in the world. And I think it was in those moments that I came to better understand my father, or at least understand why he had drunk himself into oblivion so often.

My mother had told me what he had seen as a youngster during the American Civil War, but my own youth had barred me from truly grasping the significance of it. Now I knew, and I found a measure of forgiveness for him. The absolute horror and savagery of war had poisoned him and not even a caring wife and son could provide an adequate antidote. Now that same poison coursed through my veins and with it, a heartbreaking sorrow. Nevertheless, I could not let its grip overpower me. I would need every ounce of optimism I possessed if I was going to survive this ordeal, and I thanked my lucky stars that Gus had been captured with me.

In the middle of the night, the boy with the bad wound died. He began to ramble incoherently at first, his words falling over one another, then suddenly he stopped and very clearly said, "I'm dead, Ma. I'm dead." And fell silent.

"Jesus Christ!" a voice called out in the shadowy lamp-light. It was Hoffman, at last showing some emotion. "Can't someone help the poor kid?"

A guard rushed over and threatened him with a rifle butt to the head but ignored the boy.

I tossed and turned until daybreak, listening to the moaning and snoring of others. I worried about Jim. Had he survived the holocaust I'd seen behind me? How could anyone? But Jim was larger than life and I wanted to believe that he had. How was Davey? Far from this damned war, I hoped, thinking of his marriage to Nora and all the children they would have.

And what about Ree? Her worst nightmare could be coming true. Did anyone know that I was still alive and now a prisoner? There were so many mangled, fragmented bodies after the attack that many would not be identifiable. Would it be concluded that I was one of them? Would the Germans let the Canadian authorities know that I was still alive? I hoped so, but at the very least, Ree would hear first that I was missing in action. I could not imagine her grief, especially since she already knew that Davey had been wounded. The destruction of lives reached far beyond the front lines.

In the morning, the guards awoke those still sleeping by kicking the soles of their boots. "A pup! A pup!" they ordered. The unintentional word was fitting because they spoke to us as if we were no better than dogs, curs that one would throw rocks at in the street. Two men in civilian clothes came with a stretcher and took away the dead boy while a single guard herded off the wounded prisoners. A basket of bread chunks was brought in along with an urn of coffee.

After we ate, we formed up and were marched along bleak cobblestoned streets to the centre of town and a stately old building with an octagonal clock tower. It appeared to be the army's headquarters, for there were a lot of officers around. We were led down a narrow hall to a small room and kept there by two guards outside the door. Soon a sergeant came and took Hoffman and, a while later, his fellow officer away. Neither returned. We could not share our speculation but I could tell by the downcast faces around me that it greatly worried the men.

Not long afterward, the sergeant came and escorted me to a larger room in which a half-dozen high-ranking officers sat at a long table. The sun shone through a series of multi-paned windows behind them and the backlighting gave them an inhuman cast. My escort pushed me roughly onto a wooden chair facing the table, then went over to the door and stood there at attention with his rifle. Before the questioning began, an officer, a formidable-looking man with a scar on his cheek, came and patted my tunic until he felt my paybook. He took it out and emptied all the money from it, perhaps 50 francs in all. Then he took my watch, which had stopped because I had neglected to wind it. He gave the winder a twist and held the watch to his ear. Satisfied that it worked, he placed it, along with the money, in a drawer of the table and rejoined his fellow officers. Then the questioning began, conducted solely by the scarred officer, who spoke English as if he had learned it North America.

"How many Allied soldiers are there on the lines?"

"Too many for the German army to handle," I answered.

I saw his eyes flicker, heard movement behind me and felt a thump on the back of my neck by something hard, probably a rifle butt. It wasn't enough to knock me off the chair but it hurt like hell. The base of my head began to throb.

"Flippancy will not be tolerated," growled the officer, clearly agitated. "Now, how many Allied soldiers are there on the lines?"

"I don't know. You'll have to ask the officers. I'm not entitled to that information."

"How are they dispersed along the lines?"

And so on, question after question, some merely slight variations of previous ones, but most answerable only by a field commander. And one I thought downright silly, because only a fool would give a reply that might result in punishment. "Why are you in this war?"

"Because my country expected it of me. Just like your country expected it of you."

He scoffed. "But it's really because you hate Germans, isn't it?"

"The only thing I hate is war."

Sensing that they could not goad me into an outburst of hatred for them, they finally stopped trying. I'm certain they knew that I would not be privy to the information they sought. I can't say what they obtained from our officers, but I left feeling I had won a small victory. I was taken to another room and held there until Gus and the rest of the enlisted men had been interrogated and rejoined me. Hoffman and the other officer must have been taken somewhere else.

Afterward, we were marched back to the stable and remained

there for the rest of the day, with nothing to eat. The officers never returned. I learned much later that Hoffman was killed soon after he left Menin, while attempting to escape. He was fearless right to the end.

That night we were loaded into a boxcar on a train heading east, jammed in with other sullen-faced prisoners so tightly we could scarcely breathe. Our only source of air was two small windows, one on each side of the car. Everyone was surly, and men snapped at each other until a Canadian corporal began singing "It's a Long Way to Tipperary." He wasn't the singer that Jim was but the music pulled at my heart anyway. Slowly, the rest of us joined in until a small wave of solidarity rippled through the car.

The single saving grace of being on the train was that there were no guards and we could talk freely.

"How did the interrogation go?" I asked Gus.

"They didn't ask very many questions, mostly personal ones," he replied. "I guess they figured that as a corporal I couldn't tell them much." He grunted. "Asked me why I joined the army in the first place."

"What did you say?"

"I said because the food was good. 'You're insolent!' the guy says and I get smacked by a rifle butt between my shoulders!"

I rubbed the small bruise on my neck where the guard had struck me. "Yeah. They gave me a good one too."

Gus went on. "I was asked the question again and I look the guy right in the eye and say, 'I'm a warrior. What good is a warrior without a war?' I guess he thought that was okay 'cause he let me go."

We travelled for the next day and a half on a ration of a

single bowl of watery turnip soup. My stomach ached from hunger. And though we were free to talk, the car fell silent as we were all too tired, hungry and irritable to converse. Sleep was the only escape from our misery, but it proved nearly impossible because the constant jerking of the car made us bump against one another. The train would barely get moving before it would stop, then it would start, and there never seemed to be a prolonged period of either movement or the lack of it. It did nothing to improve our mood.

Gus and I were near one of the windows and could see farms interspersed with large stands of trees, but otherwise the countryside was featureless. Train station signs told us that we were travelling deeper into Germany. In the town of Dulmen the train stopped and within minutes the doors slid open. We detrained amid jeering civilians, waving their fists at us, and were marched to a streetcar that took us to the outskirts of the city and the end of the line. It seemed to me an odd mode of transportation for prisoners of war, but maybe Germany was hard-pressed for vehicles.

Dulmen Camp was several long, orderly rows of glass-windowed huts, generously separated by wooden boardwalks. The central boardwalk ended at an ornate obelisk with a few small trees planted in a crescent behind it. Within spitting distance of the obelisk was the hut Gus and I were assigned to, along with six other men. The place was immaculate. Clean bedding sat in neat piles on each bunk and each bunk had a tick mattress. These were the best accommodations we'd had since leaving Canada. We were pleasantly surprised but soon learned that Dulmen Camp was a "show" camp; that is, the one shown to international inspectors as proof of how well

Germany treated its prisoners. For most of us, it was merely a brief stop.

Before we could enjoy the camp's amenities, the guards marched us to a communal shower and ordered us to strip naked. The weather had turned cold and rainy, yet we stood for more than hour on a cold cement floor before someone turned on the water. Its temperature was only tepid, but by then we were all shivering uncontrollably and it almost felt scalding. We dried ourselves with towels like sandpaper and the guards sprayed us with some kind of disinfectant. Then a doctor inspected us for anything that might be contagious. They issued us with Dutch clogs but only those with badly worn shoes wore them; I stowed mine under the bunk. More important were the cards they gave us that we could send to our loved ones to apprise them of our situation. I scribbled a short note to Ree to let her know that I was in good health and hoped that she would get it.

I slept soundly that first night on a comfortable bed that did not move and jerk, and felt slightly more human the following morning at reveille. Gus and most of the others in our hut had slept well too and everyone was in a better mood. There was no breakfast, just a cup of ersatz coffee before we queued for roll call.

Every day was a workday. Some days we shovelled horse manure onto wagons that were then taken to nearby farms; other days we cleaned out the latrines that had to be kept spotless. Our daily food ration usually consisted of a child-sized portion of black bread and weak turnip soup of dubious nutritional value, supplemented at times with a thin, unpalatable slice of meat that those who cleaned the kitchen said was dog. There was also a kind of paste of unknown origin that was supposed to be porridge, so gritty that its main ingredient might have been sand. Prisoners who had been at the camp for a while said that any complaints to inspectors on one of their rare visits would result in rations being reduced even further, not just for the individual but for everyone in the hut. Hunger was an integral part of our daily existence, and the occasional distribution of Red Cross parcels was cause for rejoicing.

Our only form of amusement was a bi-weekly newspaper the Germans gave us. Named the *Continental Times*, it was primarily a propaganda sheet filled with glowing reports of German victories and virtues, designed to lower our morale even further than the bottom rung of the ladder where it resided. We called it the "Continental Liar," tore it into strips and used it as toilet paper. It was softer than the paper provided by our captors and when it contained a picture of Kaiser Bill, which it often did, it was a great pleasure to use.

Despite the difference in our ages—he was 28—Gus and I got along famously. I discovered that he had been born and raised in Winnipeg and had been a streetcar driver before he enlisted. He was engaged to be married upon his return home. Edith, he bragged, was gorgeous and that was another reason why he wanted to escape as soon as possible.

Gus wasn't much shorter than I was but his Italian ancestry was apparent in his jet black hair, olive skin and dark eyes. He was one of those people with a broad view of the world, though he had been taught at a parochial school by Jesuit brothers, many of whom were petty tyrants. He liked learning, particularly the history of the world beyond the one he was raised in.

The lessons in theology were completely lost on him, however, resulting in a lot of rapped knuckles. He was almost surprised to discover that he felt an allegiance to King and country, and this inspired him to enlist about the same time I had. His younger brother, Claudius (their father, an immigrant from Umbria, was a Roman history buff), had enlisted a little later and was last heard of heading for the front lines somewhere in France. Their father, who worked for the city's transportation company, had got both boys hired as streetcar conductors and subsequently trained as drivers. Their mother had died from tuberculosis shortly before the war.

Gus usually maintained a cheery attitude. He rarely complained and tried to see the positive side of most things, even the Boche guards. The biggest complaint I heard him mutter during our internment at Dulmen Camp was an indirect comment about the gritty paste served as food that we called "sandstorm." "You know what keeps me goin', Sarge?" he said, only half-jokingly. "The thought that when this war is over I'm gonna hunt down old Kaiser Bill and ram this crap down his fucking throat."

I thought Gus should call me Jack instead of Sarge, but to him it was a title of respect, something I had earned and therefore deserved. That I had ridden with Sam Steele during the hunt for the Cree chief Big Bear only served to strengthen his conviction.

We talked of escaping but it seemed impossible. There were a dozen or more machine-gun placements along the camp perimeter, which consisted of a high board fence topped with rolls of barbed wire and, about 20 feet inside that, a lower, barbed-wire fence. Guards also patrolled the ground, so there were few places, other than inside the huts, where a prisoner could avoid their watchful eyes. We figured that there must be an escape route somewhere, but before we could devise a plan, we heard rumours that some of us would be shipping out very soon, destination unknown.

About a week later, at roll call, the guards selected 50 men, including Gus and me, and ordered us to fall out. It was apparent that all of the men chosen were in relatively good physical condition compared to the others and that we were the ones who would be going. But where? If Dulmen was a show camp and they practically starved us, what must conditions be like in camps in remote areas? My fears were allayed, however, when an officer told us that we would be going to work on a farm. The spirits of those selected lifted visibly with this news and everyone relaxed a little. I had visions of stealing extra food that set my mouth to watering.

The guards escorted us to the city streetcar, which took us to the train station, where we were packed into a single cattle car. We rolled even deeper into Germany, crossing a river that we would later learn was the Lippe. Through the slats of the car we could see the farmland disappearing, replaced by a dirty industrial area with working coal mines and slag heaps. When the train squealed to a stop, we disembarked onto a platform blackened over the years by coal dust, like all of the buildings I could see. The station had no name. Dark grey smoke billowed skyward from a nearby factory and any optimism I might have felt at Dulmen flew off like a startled bird.

"Where the hell are we?" Gus muttered.

"I don't know," I replied. "But something tells me this isn't the French Riviera."

TEN

Slave Labourer

THE "FARM" THEY HAD told us we were going to turned out to be Arbeitskommando 54, or AK 54, as the prisoners referred to it. Literally, this meant "working command" and it was a labour camp attached to a larger stalag that was probably Dulmen. I learned later that it was in Westphalia. The camp was surrounded by a high wire fence lined with thick rolls of barbed wire and was divided into three compounds, one for the French prisoners, another for the Russians and a third for English-speaking nationalities, mostly British and Canadian. There were 80 prisoners in the latter compound, all crowded into a single, large barrack with bunks stacked three high. Everyone worked either in the mines or in a huge coke factory nearby, the one belching smoke that we had seen when we detrained. It was clear from my first sight of it, as well as of the prisoners, that this camp would not be receiving any visits from inspectors. Not only was AK 54 one of several secret slave labour camps the Germans operated to keep their war machine functioning, it was also the worst of them.

You could almost feel the despair rippling through the new arrivals, for we saw our future in the gaunt, unsmiling faces that greeted us: grey-skinned men, their pores clogged with coal dust, who had been there for months, some longer than a year. Many looked to be on their last legs. A few of the new arrivals, Gus among them, began muttering that they would not tolerate such treatment and would refuse to work. They were told by one of the old-timers, "That plan will only work if you don't mind starving to death. If you don't work here, you don't get fed, and even the revolting shit they call food here is better than nothing."

We were fumigated again, issued with clean work clothes, and told by the commandant that we would receive paper and pens with which we could write home, but they never materialized. It was just one of many lies they would tell us; the rule of thumb was to expect promises of something good to be broken and promises of something bad to be fulfilled.

Gus and I were selected for work in one of the mines. "You're lucky," a camp veteran said. "It isn't any cakewalk but believe me, it's a lot better than the coke factory. If the smell of sulphur doesn't kill you there, the heat from the blast furnaces will. We call it the 'Black Hole of Germany.'"

As we arrived for our first shift, I was surprised to see that we would be working alongside civilian miners, men and women alike. They appeared to be mostly from peasant stock, the men bearded and beefy, the women plain and chunky, with only one or two exceptions. All had sullen faces and wore clothes that were grey and dirty. Some wore clogs, others were barefoot. They spat at our feet and soundly cursed us, calling us *schweinhund*. I thought, *Even peasants need someone to look down on*, trying to be philosophical about it. I expect it was gratifying for them to have at last found someone lower on the social scale than they were.

We entered a long building where we changed into our work clothes, hanging our uniforms on hooks on one wall. On the other wall were sinks for washing up after our shift. The mine was worse than the other prisoners had described. It was a stygian hole, stiflingly hot with barely enough ventilation to prevent a buildup of explosive gases. We descended in a cage in the hoisting shaft for so long I had a fleeting fantasy that we might come out on the opposite side of the world, free men. It was fast, too, as I felt light on my feet the entire distance. I don't know how far we dropped before the cage jolted to a stop, perhaps 1,000 feet, perhaps 10,000. Panic seized me for a moment and I thought that I might suffocate. I saw fear in other eyes, too, especially Gus's—his lessons at school had taught him that this was the way to hell—but no one acted out. We had been warned that any emotional display, from fear to rebellion, would be severely punished.

We stepped from the cage into a large cavern and the guards escorted us into a long tunnel, along a narrow-gauge track. Here and there, smaller, unlit tunnels branched off from the main one. Electric lights illuminated the way; there was a slight movement in the air from the ventilation shafts but in places it was heavy and oppressive. When we reached the main seam we were split into three groups. Some, with pickaxes, chipped at the coal blasted with explosives from the seam, others shovelled it into cars and the third group pushed them to the hoisting shaft for winching to the surface. The only humane thing the guards did was to allow us to change jobs every couple of hours, although it probably had more to do with production than kindness.

Coal dust seeped into every pore and was part of every breath. When they blasted, the ground trembled so much I fully expected to be buried alive or trapped to die a slow, agonizing death. After only three days on the job, I heard a low rumble from farther along the tunnel and I feared the worst. Mercifully, it was only a small cave-in. Even so, it buried a civilian beneath a pile of coal and rock, and those of us who dug him out saw ourselves in his lifeless form.

That night in the barrack we held a meeting. The newcomers did most of the talking but it boiled down to two points: could the Germans mine the coal they needed without us? And if we refused to work, was it better to take whatever punishment they meted out than to be killed below ground? The answer to the first was "no," to the second "yes," and on that point, even most of the old-timers were angry enough to agree with us. The general feeling in the room was that a strike would be worth it if it resulted in safer working conditions. We voted by a show of hands. Who supports going on strike? A forest of hands flew into the air, so many that it was pointless to count the dissenters.

The following morning we marched to the mines with a purpose. Our strategy was to begin the strike at the pithead in hopes that it would inspire the civilians to join us. It failed spectacularly. When we refused to get on the hoist they only stared at us with hatred and got on themselves. We braced ourselves for the inevitable punishment: an immediate beating or, at worst, a bullet through the heart, which would at least be painless and fast, and preferable to being buried alive or crushed by tons of coal. Yet that wasn't how the Germans dealt with it.

Very calmly, they lined us up and ordered us to attention. Then they waited. An hour passed. Two, then three. Every half-hour a guard shouted, "Are you ready to return to work?" We answered with our silence. Then, at the far end of the line, one of the old-timers collapsed onto the hard ground with a thud and a grunt. The guards doused him with two buckets of cold water, got him onto his feet and pushed him back in line. Five minutes later he collapsed again. More cold water but this time it did not revive him. He might have been dead but the rest of us didn't move. The hours passed, 10, 20, 30. Men pissed and shat in their pants. They swayed, collapsed and were revived by the guards. Some did not come around and the guards left them where they lay. Any other movement earned a hard rap with a rifle butt, which sometimes knocked a man down.

I found a way to escape the torture by closing my eyes and moving to another place in my mind, far from this brutal spot. Ree was there, leading me through it, giving her love and offering words of encouragement. When a man collapsed, I loathed him because it jerked me back to reality and reminded me of my own feebleness and fallibility. I was so tired I wanted to weep and plead for mercy and yet somehow, with a tremendous force of will, I was able to find that other place again and stay standing. Gus, who was next to me, had found somewhere to go to as well because at one point he began calling out street names as he would have while driving a streetcar at home. He was knocked into silence and nearly to the ground by a guard.

Those of us who were able stayed on our feet for 36 hours. By then we were like trees swaying in the wind. Finally, I could not take it any longer and it was as if everyone else had decided to give in at the same time. When one of the guards again shouted, "Are you ready to return to work?" we croaked as one, "Yes."

And they sent us down into the mine to finish the shift from the day before. I had never felt so beaten, so utterly broken and worthless in all my life, not even when my father had once punched me so hard it sent me flying across the room. But the pickaxe helped me regain my spirit, as every blow I struck into the coal also went into the heart of a German soldier. Those of us who made it through to the end of the day carried out those who didn't. Gus was still on his feet, a look of hatred in his dark eyes. The flea-infested straw that was our beds was like a small slice of paradise.

No one spoke of striking again.

WE LABOURED in that wretched mine from 5:30 in the morning until 3:30 in the afternoon, 10 hours a day, 7 days a week. The Germans would have worked us more had they thought we could survive it because there wasn't enough man-power in the country for extra shifts. We were given a cup of ersatz coffee before going to work and hard biscuits and turnip soup at the end of it. At bedtime, they gave us another bowl of turnip soup and we slept until 4:30 A.M. when the guards shouted, "Raus! Raus!" ("Out! Out!"), and we started all over again. They worked us mercilessly, beyond exhaustion, so that many times I thought an explosion or a cave-in might not be such a bad thing after all.

Every day we prayed for Allied soldiers to come and liberate us, but every day was a bitter disappointment. Like most of the other prisoners, I felt abandoned. One night, after lights out, in the quiet of the late evening, a British prisoner called out, "We're lost, lads. We're plain, fucking lost. And we'll never be found." You could hear the tears in his voice and it brought tears to my eyes and despair to my heart far deeper than the mines in which I laboured. All the goodness in the world had vanished; worse, I sometimes felt as if it had never existed.

The Germans paid us the princely sum of 90¢ a week and made us sign receipts for it. That way, if the camp was discovered, they would have written proof that we were actually paid labourers and not slaves. But most of the time we were lucky if we got to keep any of it. The German soldiers who worked as foremen, or "staffers," as everyone called them, were notorious for making deductions for even the tiniest thing that displeased them. Look at them wrong, a deduction; look like you're slacking off, another deduction, and so on. We called it "strafing" and they were experts at it.

The staffers pushed the civilians equally hard and many worked underground barefoot because they could not afford shoes. They also earned a paltry sum each week, much of it lost to strafing while rampant inflation throughout Germany devalued the rest. Yet they never complained. They accepted their lot stoically and at the end of each day, they received what they really came to work for—a bread ticket. It was what kept them coming back, as a full pay envelope was not worth much when food supplies in the stores were seriously depleted. Going to work meant not going hungry.

The weeks turned agonizingly into months. I began to learn smatterings of German during my rotations at loading the cars, from one of the women who helped push them to the hoisting shaft. She was tall and thin and clearly not of peasant stock; most of the women were squat and barrel-chested. She would not talk to me at first and called me *schwein*, like the others, but the longer we worked together, the more her attitude softened and she stopped using that derogatory term. One day I mustered enough courage to ask what her name was.

It took a moment before she spoke. "Liesel," she said. "Liesel Hartmann."

That's how it began. She soon asked for my name, which she pronounced "Jock." Over time I learned tidbits about her and was pleased to discover that she knew a little English; she had learned it from a brother who had lived in the United States before the war, and the rest from annual holidays in Sweden. She came from a working-class family and had married a junior army officer when she was 19. (She was now 32 but looked to be in her mid-40s.) Her husband had been killed during the German invasion of Belgium in the early days of the war, and she hated the English for her present situation only slightly more than she hated the German government. There was no pension forthcoming and as the country's economy worsened, she was forced to take whatever work she could in order to feed her two children and her aging mother who minded them. Even so, they lived hand to mouth, with little to eat and no money for clothes. Every item of clothing they owned had been patched and patched again. Fortunately, she had kept all of her husband's garments, which her mother used for patches and in some cases altered for the children.

I wondered what her husband would say had he been able to speak. Was he glad to have laid down his life for the Fatherland? I rather doubted it. A country that didn't care for its own better than that was not worth dying for.

As I learned a bit of German, we were able to communicate more, and our moments together, though fleeting, were rewarding. She was not physically attractive—who could be down in that mine?—but she was honest and forthright, which was very appealing to me. And even a woman blackened by coal dust and aged by hard labour is better than none at all.

Christmas came and went, as did the new year. It didn't mean much to us, for the Germans needed coal and plenty of it. We dug and dug and dug some more, hundreds of tons a day. I grew thin; the muscles on my arms became hard ropes and the diet would not have sustained me were it not for the Red Cross packages of food appropriated from legitimate camps and distributed from time to time. The guards always helped themselves first, but we sometimes got such luxuries as canned salmon, beans or peas, hard bread, and for those who smoked, tobacco. Every now and then we'd receive clean underwear. Like most other prisoners, I avoided thinking of the future and lived one moment at a time. My dreams were no longer of Ree, Davey or Jim, or even freckle-faced strumpets; they were nightmares of dark abysses and Hun soldiers.

Gus was hardly faring better. His face had turned gaunt and his body wiry, and yet the Germans had not been able to completely break his spirit. They hadn't forgotten that Italy had sided with Germany until the war broke out and had then gone over to the Allies, so his Italian heritage sometimes earned him an extra rap with a rifle butt. *"Verräter!"* ("Traitor!") they'd snarl and give him a good jolt. But for Gus, every jab served only to crank his resolve to escape up another notch, and almost every conversation we had either began, included or ended with talk of escaping. We would find a way, of that we were certain. To give up on that thought would have been to give up on living.

The civilians, of course, did not have the benefit of Red Cross packages and as the war forged on, food in the stores became even scarcer. According to Liesel, the British had blockaded Germany, and everyone—except for certain segments of the population, such as the ruling classes and those with connections—was eating turnip soup to survive. While no figures were available from the government, it was apparent that thousands were dying from malnutrition. Thus the civilians wondered how it was that we prisoners had more to eat than they did. They began to complain and when no one listened, they went on strike. It was a courageous move because for many, it meant cutting off their only form of sustenance.

The Germans would not allow prisoners into the mines without any civilians there, so we got a well-deserved rest without being punished for it. But we were kept in the dark about what was happening, until a few days later when they marched us back to the work. The civilians, we discovered, had helped each other with food that, because of Germany's desperate need for coal, allowed them to stay out long enough to win a few concessions. But slowly over the next few weeks, the leaders of the strike mysteriously disappeared.

It was about this time that Liesel told me of the revolution in Russia. She was excited because there was much talk of workers around the world controlling their own fate by striking. They were sick of being exploited, sick of being slaves for profiteers who had reached their lofty positions by exploiting the working poor and using war to divide and divert them whenever a rebellion appeared inevitable. You create hatred for other nationalities, then use patriotism to pit them against each other, she asserted. And everyone had listened. But this was 1917 and hungry people rioted in towns and cities throughout Germany. Liesel and I talked of this whenever circumstances allowed, until the line between the reasons we were in the mines disappeared and I saw my plight as being not much different from hers. We had merely taken different routes to get there, that was all.

For every worker it was a dismal, cruel existence, but the prisoners had it even worse than the civilians. In camp, the guards beat us for the slightest infraction of the rules or made us stand at attention for hours at bedtime, which was at 7:00 P.M., yet still awoke us, with German precision, at 4:30 in the morning. Solitary confinement, with stale, mouldy bread and water, was a matter of course for many prisoners. I suffered through it for two days, punishment for expressing anger at a guard who had jabbed me with his rifle butt once too often. Gus also got two days, for mimicking a guard by snarling at him and calling him *schweinhund*.

That the camp was crawling with lice added to our misery

and some men had open sores from them. When they became too noticeable, the Germans would fumigate. Things would even off for a few days but the lice always won in the end because cleanliness was impossible to achieve. Though we earned enough money to buy soap—it was about the only thing that was affordable—it wasn't always available. When it was, a small cake cost nearly a week's wages, even though it was more like a bar of grease and did not lather well in hard water, nor would it remove all the coal dust that formed part of our skin.

During the winter months, the two coke stoves in our barrack provided such negligible heat that we slept in our clothes and still could not get warm. Most of us had hacking coughs that brought up phlegm the colour of obsidian. Occasionally a man collapsed and was taken to the infirmary, never to return. Some men inflicted injury upon themselves, but it couldn't be anything overt or it meant a stint in solitary. But if you pounded your wrist or ankle with a lump of dirt in a cloth, it would raise a convincing swelling after about 15 or 20 minutes. A few ate soap to make themselves vomit and some swallowed nicotine, which affected the heart. There were few limits to what a man might do to avoid spending a day in the mines or the coke factory. Still, there were some men for whom the horror of prison life was preferable to escaping and being returned to the front lines.

For those of us who coped, the hardest thing of all was keeping our spirits intact, to go on fighting to stay alive, not giving in when suicide seemed to be a viable alternative. Some knelt beside their bunks at bedtime and prayed for an end to the war. Others, like Gus and me, talked of escaping, but for the majority it was only talk. Nevertheless, a half dozen of us

felt we were fit enough to try and formed an escape committee. After much discussion we agreed that there was really only
one option: a tunnel.

Our plan was simple. The rear of the barrack was against
the barbed-wire perimeter barricade that was perhaps 10 feet
across. The fence was only heavy-gauge wire mesh strung
between posts and did not need to be taken into consid-
eration. If we went through the floor near the back wall, we
would need a tunnel only about 15 to 20 feet long to put us
beyond the fence. Access would be beneath one of the bunks
where it could not be seen. We would pry up the floorboards,
descend into the crawl space and start digging, dispersing the
excavated material evenly over the ground beneath the barrack. We would commence only if the soil was firm, because
there weren't enough boards available to shore the tunnel
completely, at least not without attracting attention. But we
didn't have far to go, which made the possibility of success
far outweigh the risks. Even so, it was a physical impossibility
for many of the men. They were too weak and the extra work
demanded energy they simply couldn't muster. On top of that,
the camp was too far inside Germany, some 50 or 60 miles,
for them to bear the rigours of the long walk out.

So a handful of us set to work in earnest, using the small
shovel kept in the barrack for loading coke into the stove. We
went down under my bunk, which was against the rear wall,
scheduling shifts of two men for two hours a night after lights
out, one digging and partially filling a burlap sack stolen
from the pithead, the other emptying it. The vertical shaft
descended through about 2 feet of gravelly, rocky overburden and then we hit good, solid clay. The digging became

extremely difficult, but we were heartened by the fact that the material would support a relatively safe tunnel with minimal shoring. As the horizontal shaft moved forward, other men, infected with our excitement, pitched in to help and allowed us more time for rest to face our shift in the mines.

Despite the torturous work, those days were some of the best I'd had since I'd arrived at AK 54. Every day that I descended into the mines was made bearable by the fact that when I returned to camp, I could work toward going home. Each night I went to bed with the thought that I was sleeping above a portal to freedom and it allowed me to arise each morning with some degree of optimism.

It took three months of excruciatingly hard digging, night after night, to drive the tunnel beyond the fence. When we at last started upward, Gus and I were given the honour of removing the overburden, while those who were leaving with us waited patiently in the tunnel. We worked our way carefully to the surface, quietly pulling down the final bit held in place by grass. Slowly, I poked my head into the beautiful, empty silence that our sentries assured us was there and climbed out. Gus gave me a boost and I was in the clear, standing on ground that did not have walls to contain me. Above were the same stars that shone down upon us inside the camp but now they were navigational symbols; I inhaled the same air but now it smelled of freedom. I knelt, reached down and pulled Gus up. Even in the dark I could see the grin on his face. Together, we helped the others out, 12 in all. Then we sneaked off into the darkness, to the road that would take us northwest to the Dutch border.

Three hours later, we were back in prison.

ELEVEN

The Long Walk

A PHALANX OF ARMED soldiers descended on us so fast there was no chance to run. It was if they knew exactly where we'd be and I wondered if one of the prisoners had turned us in for food. Crestfallen, we were marched double-time back to the prison and taken before the commandant. He paced behind his desk, scoffing at our puny efforts; he was even in relatively good humour. But then, he'd caught us handily and his reputation was intact. There were too many of us to send to solitary so our rations were reduced by half for a week and we received extra physical attention from the guards. The tunnel was destroyed, the fence was moved farther from the barrack and sentries patrolled the area at night. The Germans had won that round but it only made me more determined to win the next one.

I thought it impractical, if not impossible, to devise another plan for a group escape, so Gus and I decided that we'd be

better off if the two of us worked alone and let the other prisoners with notions of escaping come up with their own strategy.
Besides, the fewer people in on it, the better. But as tunnelling
was now out of the question, what would we do? We put our
heads together and conceived a brilliant plan that had only one
sticky side to it: we would need to acquire civilian clothes and
that meant an outside accomplice. I thought I had the solution.

I had come to know Liesel quite well over the year and a
half that I'd been at AK 54. I was genuinely sympathetic with
her lot in life and whenever I could, I brought her food from
the Red Cross packages the camp received. We agreed that
while the war had stripped her of most things she held dear,
it had done the same to me. We weren't enemies, the two of
us; war was the enemy, as were the people who profited from
it, the ones who kept both of us down in the mines. She knew
how desperate I was to find out about Davey and Jim, and to
let Ree know that I was still alive.

I remembered that she said she had kept all of her husband's clothing, so could she provide enough clothes for Gus
and me? She could have anything she wanted, anything that
was within my power to give her. I watched her eyes as I spoke
and she didn't flinch. Nor did she say anything.

That night I half-expected the guards to come and beat
me and throw me in solitary for trying to bribe a civilian, but
nothing happened. When she saw me the next day, she said
the words I wanted to hear.

"I will bring clothes for you. My husband was tall, like
you, but my mother will make adjustments for your friend."
She paused. "You could pass for a German but what of your
friend? He looks Italian."

"We'll keep off the main roads and avoid towns and villages. As long as no one gets a close look at him, he should be all right. Can you get us a map, too?"

She nodded. "You will get for me, soap."

"Done," I said.

Soap. It was an indication of the sad state of her life that a commodity that most of the civilized world took for granted could buy her assistance in such a dangerous plan. I ought to have wept for her but I felt only excitement and relief.

Two days later, she smuggled in our first piece of clothing, wrapped around her waist, and passed it to me when no one was looking. Our work clothes, like our prison uniforms, were baggy and it was a simple task to wrap it around my own waist and secure it with a piece of twine Liesel had supplied for the purpose. Piece by piece, over the span of a month, she brought in enough for both Gus and me. I took them to the barrack and spread them out flat beneath the straw on our beds. Meanwhile, we would need food on our journey so we saved as many biscuits from our daily ration as we could without starving ourselves to death.

Liesel brought a map too, hand-drawn and rough, but it at least showed the major rivers and towns, and the Dutch border. Best of all, she also brought a small compass. In good faith, I paid her in soap, over and above what she had asked for. I had no idea what her punishment would be if she were caught, and was afraid to ask. It would be serious, of that I was certain, which led me to believe that soap was only part of her reason for helping. My escape may have been her only means of revenge against the country that she felt had betrayed her.

When Gus and I each had an outfit—a thin jacket, a cap, shirt and trousers similar to what the civilian male workers were wearing—we wasted no time putting our plan into action. On a fine spring morning, we arose to the shouts of *"Raus! Raus!"* that, with any luck at all, we would never hear again. Once the guard had left the barrack, we donned our civilian clothes, tucking our caps in our waistbands, and put our prison uniforms overtop. This part of our plan was its weakest link, as our barrack mates were privy to it. We could only trust that no one would double-cross us. Besides the compass, map and biscuits, the only other item we took with us was a prison-issued razor, so that we could shave and not look like fugitives. Some of the men were teary-eyed and there were wishes of "Good luck" and "God speed."

Since we always walked to the mines in bunches, the other prisoners formed a wall around us, just in case one of the guards noticed our extra padding. In the long washing-up building, we removed our prison uniforms and put on our work clothes. I felt as conspicuous as a black spider on a white wall until we reached the dim lighting in the tunnels below. It was hot and cumbersome working in two sets of clothing, yet I could ignore my discomfort and the day sped by. With one heartbeat I ached for the shift to end, with the next I dreaded it.

Late in the day I had an opportunity to talk to Liesel. She said when she saw me, "I think you gain some weight but I know better."

"Wish me luck, Liesel. I won't ever forget you and all that you've done."

I saw a small fire in her eyes, heard the passion in her

voice. "It is all right to forget me, but you must never forget this place and what goes on here!"

She was filthy after a hard day's work and the mine had stolen much of her femininity, yet I had an almost irresistible urge to take her in my arms and hold her. I think in a way I loved her, probably because she was the only thing worthy of love in that barbarous part of the world. Our coal-stained fingers touched briefly—it was all we could risk—and in that touch was every word that needed saying.

At quitting time, my heart was in my mouth. Gus pretended to trip and twist his ankle and I knelt to help while everyone else got on the hoist. He massaged his ankle and I motioned to the staffer to go up without us. The German pressed the button and the hoist rose. None of the men wanted to spend any more time underground than they had to. We removed our prison work clothes, discarded them, rubbed our civilian attire with coal dust, and then brought the hoist down. On normal days, the ride to the surface seemed to take forever, but this time it went swiftly. I was worried that our plan was too brazen to pull off, because we had no idea what would be awaiting us on the surface when we appeared as civilians. My nerves teetered precariously on a razor-thin edge but no one greeted us. The staffers, like the civilians, were interested only in getting home and the guards were forming up the prisoners to march them back to camp. We walked to the building in which some of the civilians washed up after work—some washed up at home—and left through their exit; it was as simple as that.

According to Liesel's map, the Dutch border was about 50 miles northwest, as the crow flies. It could also be reached by going west a similar distance, but the Rhine River was a barrier that could prove to be insurmountable. Heading northwest meant crossing the Lippe River, but it was only a tributary of the Rhine and we figured that it wouldn't be nearly as broad.

Instead of setting a direct course along the westerly main road, where we risked capture, we headed south to a spruce swamp Liesel had told us about. She had said it was well-treed and would afford us protection, but warned that traversing it would not be easy. This was a small price to pay because our course initially would be nearly opposite to that which the Germans would expect us to take, and by the time they discovered their error, we would be long gone.

Reaching the swamp, we paused, and once we got our breathing under control listened for pursuers. We heard nothing above the silence of the swamp. If we were fortunate, our absence would not be discovered until the nightly bed check. I had brought the remnants of a bar of soap and we washed as best we could in the murky water. Then we removed our socks and shoes, rolled our pant legs up to keep them dry, and waded into the swamp. It was early spring; the water felt near freezing and in some places slopped around our knees. Our progress was agonizingly slow but at least we left no trail that could be followed. Our slow advance made it feel as if the swamp went on for miles. Liesel had not been able to tell us how wide it was. She did not know distances, she said, and the map she had provided was too general to show it. But she had assured us that tracking due south would eventually see us across it. Beyond, we would find a road.

We kept the setting sun off our right shoulders at first and when it disappeared behind some clouds, we used the compass. We forged on, trying our best to ignore the cold, and by dusk had reached solid ground in a densely wooded area of mostly spruce. By then we were exhausted, hungry and chilled to our core. Putting our socks and shoes on and rolling down our pants helped restore some much-needed warmth to our bodies. We had each managed to save 10 biscuits and allowed ourselves one before settling down to sleep in a hollow formed by an uprooted tree. The ground felt softer than our straw beds at the prison and we fell instantly asleep with our backs pressed together for warmth.

I awakened only twice during the night and at dawn I heard the clatter of wagon wheels and horses' hoofs. I arose to investigate and discovered we were only a hundred yards or so from a road running east to west. As near as I could tell through the trees, the vehicle was some kind of dray with a civilian at the reins. It was nothing to worry about. Gus slept right through it but I didn't sleep again. I lay there listening to the sounds of the woodland as the sun sporadically broke through the clouds and sent shafts of honey-coloured light among the trees. I heard a variety of bird calls, none identifiable; they were the music of freedom after nothing but the raucous sound of crows for so long. I would never hear the caw of a crow again without being transported back to AK 54.

After Gus awoke, we ate a biscuit each and then set out west along the empty road, heavily forested on both sides. We soon came upon another road heading northwest, the direction we had to go to freedom, and turned onto it, entering open farmland, punctuated frequently with copses of deciduous trees. We agreed that we should avoid close scrutiny but believed that our civilian attire ought to fool anyone spotting us from a distance. If we were surprised by someone, however, we would have to run unless I could bluff our way through with the German I had learned from Liesel.

When we heard or saw wagons approach, we sought a hiding place, sometimes behind a bush or hillock or in a thicket of trees. We detoured around a couple of tiny villages by cutting across fallow fields and through serene woods, and gave farmhouses a wide berth lest we set a dog or two to barking. We reached a field with a few cows in it; their relatively light udders indicated that they had most likely been milked earlier that morning, but it was plain that the supply was being replenished. The thought of warm milk was so tantalizing we climbed the fence. The first cows we approached wandered off but one was a friendly old girl and let us milk her. We had nothing to drink from, so I squirted the warm liquid into Gus's cupped palms and he did the same for me after I showed him the technique, as he had never milked a cow before. I couldn't remember the last time I'd had a drink of milk but I was certain it never tasted as sweet and delicious.

The terrain was easy to traverse so we stayed off the roads, using the compass when we needed to, and even with a dramatically zigzagging route had put several miles behind us by nightfall. By then Gus and I were feeling rather proud of ourselves. We had been on the loose for more that 24 hours, we reckoned, and had seen no sign of anyone hunting for us. It was no time to get bold, though, and we weren't about to stop being cautious in our movements. We took a long break to get some sleep and then moved on in the dark.

Just before daybreak, we reached what we thought at first was the Lippe River, which surprised us. Were we making better time than we thought? But checking the map showed us that we should have passed the large town of Recklinghausen, or at least direction signs to it, and we had seen none. We also thought that the stream wasn't wide enough to be the Lippe, because it wasn't as wide as the river we had crossed on the train. It was probably only a canal. The underbrush was thick in places along the bank and since there was no habitation in the area, we decided that it would be a waste of time trying to find a footbridge. We would have to wade it and hope it wasn't over our heads, as Gus couldn't swim.

We stripped naked and bundled our clothes in our jackets, tying the sleeves together to hold everything in. I went first to make sure the water wasn't too deep. I waded in, holding my bundle on my head with one hand and keeping my balance with the other. The bottom was slimy and weedy, and the water, as dark as a coal seam, never got higher than my chest. Once I reached dry land, I was shivering from the cold but waited before getting dressed just in case Gus had difficulty and I had to go back in for him. He did not hesitate but literally ran in and ploughed his way across the stream, unwilling to spend one second longer in it than he had to. His lower height allowed the water to rise higher on his chest but, luckily, there was no discernible current to push him over. I reached out and helped him up the shallow bank.

He was shivering as uncontrollably as I was. "Jesus, Sarge!" he cursed. "Too many of these things to cross and we'll shake into bloody pieces before we're outa this goddamned country!"

I was too cold to answer him but he was right. Our bony frames wouldn't be able to tolerate repeated dips in frigid water. I was shaking so fiercely I could hardly undo the knot in my jacket sleeves and get dressed. And we still had the Lippe River somewhere in front of us. Even if there was a bridge, bridges produce traffic and a much greater chance of being spotted. I hoped the Lippe wouldn't be our undoing.

We dressed and set out across an unused field with thickets of scrub spruce here and there. We could hear heavy wagon traffic ahead and came to a road too busy to cross immediately. We assumed it led to Recklinghausen. We hid in some bushes and waited at least a half-hour before the road cleared to our liking. We hustled across and later, in the early evening, we broke through some underbrush in a line of trees onto a dirt road following a sizeable water course. It had to be the Lippe River.

It was dark brown and appeared to be in flood, as willow bushes and tall grass poked through the edges. It wasn't wide, perhaps 60 or 70 feet, but it looked deep and there was a gentle current running. We heard a wagon coming down the road so we darted into the bush, out of sight. We made ourselves as comfortable as possible, and over a biscuit each, pondered our options.

As near as we could determine, we had only two: find a bridge or some kind of vessel, a raft or a small boat, to get us across. Well after dark, we broke from our hiding place in the trees and struck out along the road, turning left out of the woods simply because it was downstream. An almost-full moon illuminated the night enough to force us into the dark shadows cast by the trees. We had gone perhaps a mile or two, encountering no one and no sign of civilization, when we came upon a house set well back from the road. We could see light emanating from behind a curtained window, maybe from

a coal-oil lamp, as there was no electricity in the area. We may
have been on the outskirts of a village, although our map wasn't
detailed enough to show it. We stopped and listened. Other
than frogs croaking along the river, the night was silent. We
crept along the road, fearful of dogs, and opposite the gated
front yard found a short path leading through knee-high grass
and some willows down to the river. On a hunch, we followed
it and struck gold: a small dinghy complete with oars, pulled
half onto the bank, its painter secured to a bush.

We waited 5 or 10 minutes, our ears tuned to the night.
Besides the frogs, there was just the sound of the river lap-
ping against the shore. Gus untied the painter and we quietly
slipped the vessel into the water. I held the gunwale while he
climbed in, then I followed. We thought the oarlocks might
creak too much so we carefully removed the oars, pushed off,
and used them as paddles, slipping the blades into the water
slowly and smoothly so as not to create a splash. The weak current carried us only a short distance downstream and we soon
rammed the bow into the reeds along the far bank. I leapt
out with the painter and scrambled up a short, grassy incline.
Gus clambered out and I passed the painter to him, removed
my wet shoes and socks, then my pants and underwear, and
waded into the river. The water was ice cold and it instantly set
my teeth to rattling. I placed the oars exactly as we had found
them, took the painter from Gus and steered the boat out as
far as I could go without getting my upper body soaked. I gave
it a hard push into the current, leaving the painter to dangle in
the water. With any luck at all, it would be carried far enough
downriver to make the owner think that it had either become
untied or been stolen, rather than used as a ferry.

We hid in some nearby trees and slept till dawn.

The weather had remained favourable since our escape, overcast but dry, and the countryside was low, rolling farmland. Every now and then we'd take the road but there were always hedgerows to hide behind or a thicket or stand of bushes to take cover in when we didn't want to be seen. And the farther we got from prison the more I believed our appearance was enough like farm workers that we didn't have to hide as much, which might prove valuable in the event I needed to go ahead of Gus to check out the lay of the land. Near a small village I decided to experiment. While Gus hid, I did not avoid four women walking toward me on the road. I pulled my cap down low, increased my pace, and as I passed them, muttered, "*Guten tag*," as if I were in a hurry and had no time for pleasantries. They returned the greeting, far less interested in me than I was in them. I waited a short distance along the road for Gus.

The encounter buoyed our spirits immensely but did not reduce our caution. There was still a long way to go and to make matters worse, the heels of my socks were wearing out. The last thing I needed was blisters, so I tore off small pieces from my shirttails and used them as patches. It didn't take long for them to bunch up, though, and we had to keep stopping while I straightened them out. All things considered, it was better than having sore feet.

The wind increased and the sky darkened but it didn't rain. Soon after that, we made our first mistake and it nearly cost us our freedom.

TWELVE

The Second Road

WE DIDN'T THINK IT would take more than five days to get to the border and had rationed ourselves to two biscuits a day. While they were not entirely without nutritional value, they were not nearly enough to sustain us. Also, we'd not had much water and were thirsty. Nearing a farm, we saw a well pump in the front yard, and it proved too enticing to pass up. We hid among some trees and watched to see if anyone was around. After about a half-hour without any movement whatsoever, we agreed that the farmer must be away. Throwing caution out the window we half-ran and half-walked to the pump and drank our fill of cool, sweet water. Then we washed our faces and hands and dried ourselves off with our jackets.

We were set to leave when Gus suggested, "Why don't we check the place out before we go? Maybe we'll find somethin' useful. Namely food."

I looked around and there was still no one about. "Sure. But we'd better be quick about it."

We hustled to the front door of the house and found it locked, then went around to the back and came across a small shed, a stone structure with a flat, sloping, corrugated tin roof and a wooden door held closed by a rusty bolt.

Gus looked at me. "A tool shed, maybe?"

"The roof looks too low for a shed. I wonder if it's a root cellar."

I slid the bolt back and pulled the door open on creaking hinges. Inside and down two steps, four bins contained small quantities of turnips, carrots, potatoes, and onions. We ignored the turnips. They were about all we'd had for 18 months and we were sick of them. But potatoes, carrots and onions were the mother lode and we stuffed our pockets until they were bulging. So tantalizing was the prospect of these delicacies for dinner that we rubbed the dirt from two small potatoes and tore into them like ravenous animals. I might have been in the finest restaurant in the world, dining on a prime cut of beef—it was that delicious.

"Jesus," said Gus, with his mouth full. "I've never tasted anythin' so good!"

I was too busy wolfing down my own potato to bother answering.

Then a dog barked, a deep-throated sound of something large. And it was very near.

Gus was closest to the door and he bolted up the steps first, with me nearly tripping over him. The barking sounded as if it had come from the front of the house, so we ran in the opposite direction, toward a chicken wire fence perhaps

50 yards away. I looked over my shoulder and saw a ferocious dog, growling, teeth bared, rounding the corner of the house. I had no idea what breed it was except that it had short, dark brown hair and was extremely chesty and muscular. Gus and I vaulted over the fence and fell in a heap on the far side, losing some of our booty in the process. Luckily, our bones were still intact and we got up and ran as if our lives depended on it. The fence stopped the dog but its owner had a rifle and fired at us, two shots that went whistling over our heads. We were soon in some woods and out of his sight but didn't stop running until we almost collapsed from a lack of oxygen.

When we'd found our breath, Gus asked, "Do you think he knew he was shootin' at escaped prisoners?"

"I doubt it," I replied. "I don't think we would've got away if he had. He could have hit us but I think his intention was to frighten us off, not kill us. Probably thought we were just a pair of hungry tramps. Let's hope so, anyway."

Checking our pockets revealed that we managed to hang on to three carrots, a small potato and an onion, no small prize for two starving men. But fear had temporarily quelled our appetites and we moved on without eating, working our way in a circuitous route to the road. I had no sooner calmed down than my stomach began to ache from the potato. Gus had the same problem, but an ache from food hard to digest was more tolerable than the hollow ache of hunger. And there was consolation in the knowledge that our bodies were getting some much-needed nutrition.

We figured we were now about 18 or 20 miles from the border and estimated that we would reach it the following day if all went well. We plodded on, walking and resting in short spurts, our willpower alone driving us forward. Breathing was hard and I was light-headed, as if my brain was filled with helium and would soon float off somewhere without me. Under different circumstances the terrain would have been monotonous, not the sort of place one would choose for a pleasant hike. For us, though, the dread of being caught kept it interesting. It began to rain, which we thought would only aid our cause, but it also chilled us and made those last few miles more desperate than they ought to have been.

The closer we got to the border the greater was the presence of the military. The land was open but not settled, and was cross-hatched by deep ditches with trickles of water in them. We saw movement far down the arrow-straight road and what appeared to be a motorcar coming toward us. We had seen so few motorized vehicles on our journey—mostly bicycles and drays—that there was no doubt in my mind that it was military. But had we been spotted?

A ditch parallelling the road was the only place to hide. I didn't need to say anything to Gus and together we jumped into calf-deep water that was covered in green scum. We crouched, pressing ourselves against the roadside wall of the ditch, and waited. It was bloody cold. The noise of the engine grew louder as it closed on us. Would it stop? We held our breath. The vehicle trundled by and the engine noise slowly faded in the distance. Still, we waited for several more minutes. As the ditch was only about five feet deep, I slowly stood and peered over the top. I could see nothing in either direction. Our luck had held; they hadn't seen us. Visibility through the windshield with the wipers swishing across it was probably limited. I bent enough to allow Gus to stand on my knee and climb out. Then he pulled me onto the road.

There was only a bit of a breeze blowing but as we were soaked, it felt more like an Arctic gale. All we could do was move faster to get warm, and that wasn't easy to do. The rain intensified and added even more weight to our wet clothes. With each step our tired legs threatened to give out, but we knew we were nearing the border and that made it tolerable. We finally came to some woods and went deep inside them. We planned to wait until nightfall and then make the final push for Holland.

The rain stopped and the moon flickered in and out from behind scudding clouds. We ached to get moving because we were so cold, and so close to freedom. We returned to the road we had been on previously and could hear a motor running off in the distance, presumably a military vehicle of some kind at the border. We increased our pace as much as we could, running on adrenalin alone. Fortunately, we encountered no dogs. Near the border, we found cover among more trees and observed the movement of the sentries.

When the moon shone, visibility was excellent and we saw two guards, carrying oil lanterns, posted about a hundred yards apart along the straight section of the border road that we could see. They had bayoneted rifles slung over their shoulders. We watched long enough to determine that they worked in shifts of probably two hours, during which time they either stood still or marched slowly back and forth along the road. They seemed utterly bored and not very attentive, a factor decidedly in our favour. My guess was that it was probably because the Germans had no quarrel with the Dutch. But why they didn't appear to have been alerted about two escaped prisoners was anybody's guess.

After a whispered discussion, we agreed that if we waited until near the end of a shift in the middle of the night, the sentries would be even less vigilant and we might be able to sneak across between them while they were standing still, provided the clouds obscured the moon. The fact that there was no electricity in the area and therefore no lights was an unexpected bonus. Even so, we would have to be as quiet as death about it and concluded it would be best to remove our shoes before crossing the road.

It wasn't much of a plan but it was the best we could do. If worse came to worst and we were spotted, we could only pray that in the time it took the sentries to ready their rifles they wouldn't have a decent shot at us. We were reasonably certain they wouldn't chase us into Dutch territory. We ate the last of our food for the energy and strength it would provide and ignored the resulting pain in our stomachs. It didn't matter. We had walked many miles on hardly any food, even less water and not a whole lot of sleep, so we needed all the nourishment we could get. A foot placed in the wrong spot from weakness might very well be our undoing.

We waited, each of us lost in thought. I glanced over at Gus in the fading light. He looked like I felt—a physical wreck. But I was grateful to have him as a mate. His unflagging spirit had often kept me going when it would have been less trouble to wallow in despair. And would I have made it this far if I'd had to do it alone? Maybe not. It didn't matter where he was, Gus had an uncanny sense of direction. Besides, all roads led to Edith, his fiancée, and that's what kept him going, even though things hadn't been any easier for him than they had for me. During our time at AK 54, he hadn't lost faith in himself, but he had lost the religious faith that had buttressed him before the war. It had been neatly tied to an afterlife that he now believed didn't exist. Heaven and hell were here on Earth and he knew exactly where hell was—deep in the coal mines of the labour camp. No god that merited his belief would have sent him there. Heaven, on the other hand, was waiting for him in Winnipeg.

I dared to think of seeing Ree and Davey again. We would be a family once more and return to our old routines. Davey, his manhood shaped in the forges of war, would marry Nora. As a wedding gift Ree and I would look for land for them, perhaps in the Nicola Valley, or some other place close enough for frequent visits with them and our grandchildren.

I thought about Jim, too. I hoped against hope that he had made it through the conflagration because I wanted desperately to hear him accuse me of being a slacker for two years. And I wanted to hear him sing.

The evening passed at a sluggish pace. Then it was as if Providence were on our side, as if our success were part of the natural unfolding of the universe. Around the middle of the night, it had grown darker as more clouds rolled in and it began to rain again. We couldn't believe our luck. Still, we waited perhaps two or three hours before making a bid for the crossing.

The rain had stopped but the grass was still wet and the sky dark as we approached the road on our hands and knees, moving slowly, resisting the urge to run for it. Reaching a roadside bush, we stopped. Off in the distance, perhaps a mile or so, we could see lights reflecting off the low clouds and hoped it was a Dutch village. We listened but my heart was beating so wildly in my ears it was difficult to hear anything. Then I could make out the sound of boots on macadam. The sentry off to our right coughed and, in fact, must have had a cold, for he would periodically lapse into small coughing and sneezing fits. This was another unexpected stroke of luck; we slipped off our shoes and waited for the next fit when the guards were farthest from us, and stationary. Once he started coughing, we would have about three or four seconds to cross, which was plenty of time if we didn't waste any of it. We crouched there like sprinters waiting for the starting gun. When finally it came, we wasted not a second but shot across the road, bent at the waist, and slipped in behind more bushes on the far side. We hunched, listening, but heard only a sneeze from the sentry. No whistles, no shouts. We pulled on our shoes and crept away.

We crossed an open area of grass and then entered some trees, moving as swiftly as we could in the dark and concentrating on maintaining our direction. Gus led. When we felt we were deep enough in the woods, we stopped to wait for daybreak so we could see better where we were going.

Neither of us slept. We were too excited, euphoric over our success. Eons might have passed before the sun rose but when it did, we put it behind us and made our last push to freedom. In minutes, we burst out of the forest onto another road, barely able to contain our exultation. We had done it; we were free! Suddenly a blur beside us took on a human form. A German sentry.

"Halten Sie oder ich werde schießen!" ("Halt or I'll shoot!")

In our panic, we responded in English, "Don't shoot! Don't shoot." Then I said the one German word that I knew backward and forward, in my sleep. *"Kriegsgefangener!"* ("Prisoner of war!")

The sentry looked so frightened it was a miracle he didn't shoot us.

THIRTEEN

Dutch Treat

TWO GUARDS PRODDED US like cattle up a short flight of stairs and into the brick building that housed the solitary cells at AK 54. A passageway stretching from one end to the other allowed access to eight small cells. One of the guards, a sergeant, stopped me in front of the door to one cell while the other marched Gus three doors farther along. We were ordered to remove our clothes. There was no profit in being defiant, so we wasted no time complying. The sergeant then ordered us to attention and recited the rules, which were few and simple. Our daily food ration would be pushed through a small sliding door at the base of the main door. When finished, we were to put the plate and cup back where they could be retrieved. There was a bucket in the cell that served as a latrine. After our meal it was to be placed by the door where it would be replaced with an empty one. Non-compliance

would result in punishment, as would making even the slightest noise. Since solitary itself was a serious punishment, we
could only presume the sergeant meant a beating.

Finished, he spun on his heels and disappeared, leaving his
subordinate in charge. I can't say how long we stood there in that
chilly passageway, stark naked, but if the intent was to weaken
our spirits, it failed. In due course, one of the end doors swung
open and the sergeant returned, carrying two prison uniforms.
We put them on and though the material was rough and chaf-
ing, it was like wrapping my body in a warm cocoon.

The solid metal cell doors were opened and we were pushed
into our respective cubicles. The walls inside were also brick,
and a wood platform on one wall comprised the bed. I saw no
bedding but I saw the bucket sitting in the far corner. Then
the thick and heavy door was pulled shut in its metal frame
with a heart-stopping clang and I was alone.

It was pitch black at first but as my eyes grew accustomed to
the dark, I could make out the slimmest crack of light coming
from beneath the door. I might have been the last person in
the world, for if there were other prisoners in the building
other than Gus and me—as there surely had to be—I could not
hear them. No one wanted a beating.

Each morning the small, sliding door opened and a hand
pushed through a tin plate holding a chunk of stale black
bread and a cup of water. I savoured it, for that was my meal
for the day. Later in the morning, there would be a rattle of
metal in the hallway, my cell door would swing open, and a
prisoner, unable to work in the mines, replaced my bucket
with an empty one. I was always astonished at how little waste
I had to dispose of.

I tried to spend some time each day stretching and pacing the length of the cell. It measured approximately six feet by eight, so I could only get about three average paces in before having to perform an about turn. One, two, three, turn . . . four, five, six, turn . . . , and so on, counting every step until I thought I had walked about a mile. Sometimes lethargy and weariness would nearly overwhelm me and all I wanted to do was curl up in the corner in self-pity. It took every ounce of strength I had to stand and start moving, but stand I would and somehow get past the aching joints that cried out for lubrication.

I lived inside my head because there was no other place where I could find solace. The trick was to try not to think of where I was and the situation I was in. That kind of thinking could drive a man crazy. So I sat on the platform when I was awake and thought of my life and all the people in it. I was able to recall even the smallest incident from my childhood. Memories of my father and his cruel fists, and my mother and the saint-like patience that ultimately deserted her, brought tears to my eyes. I thought of Charity and Becky, and the all-too-brief span of time I shared with them, and I thought of Joe Fortes. How to reconcile the monsters here with those sweet, generous souls? They had to be a different species.

I listened to Jim sing. "*I'll take you home again Kathleen, across the ocean wild and wide . . .* ," his tenor voice, rich and soaring, filled the concert hall of my mind and spilled out into the cell. It was so present and real that I felt he must be alive, so loud that when I came to my senses I feared the guards would come and beat me.

I spent a lot of time with Ree and Davey. I worried that they did not know I was still alive. How would it change their lives? Ree could be selling the ranch at that very moment. I imagined Jim and Maggie buying it from her and I was comforted, knowing that it would be in good hands. And I imagined Ree and me buying it back from Jim and Maggie, the hilarity of it, and our laughter rang in my ears.

After four days of almost total darkness, a board covering a small barred window above the cell door was removed. I was given an extra ration of bread and ate breakfast in the luxury of the twilight the window afforded. But that night the board was replaced and I was in darkness again, back on my one piece of bread and water. Four days later the board was once removed again, and four days after that. Each time I was rewarded with an extra ration of bread. After a month had passed Gus and I were released from those dark holes.

A single guard marched us to the commandant's office. He must have had a soft heart for he let us talk to each other. It took a moment to find my voice, and Gus's voice sounded surreal after I had heard it only in my head for so long. He looked weak but far from defeated.

"How're you doin', Sarge?" he croaked.

"I've seen better times but I ache so I must be okay. How about you?" My voice was low and raspy.

"Peachy," he croaked again.

The commandant, a round-faced man with jowls, who was clearly better fed than his charges, had only passable English. Strutting like a rooster, as was his habit, he gave us a stern, 10-minute lecture on the errors of our ways and finished gloatingly, "No one has ever successfully escaped from

Arbeitskommando 54 and no one ever will! Not while I am commandant!"

His chest protruded almost as far as his belly and he appeared so bloated over our capture that I wondered if he had even informed his superiors of our escape, although they would have known that with our capture. Perhaps at this stage in the war, with far more important things to worry about, the German higher command didn't care all that much. We waited for him to ask how we had obtained the civilian clothing but he never did. Gus and I had vowed that we would die before revealing our source. Done, he clicked his heels and ordered the guard to escort us directly to the mine.

Words fail me to adequately describe the assault upon my resolve to stay strong as I descended beneath the earth, the cables of the hoist creaking out my anguish. My nerves were raw, as if someone were rubbing the ends with a file. I had to escape again or this place would surely be the death of me. I was hanging onto my sanity only by brittle fingernails. Gus and I stepped from the hoist and made our way to the coal seam. Liesel was there and when she saw us, her eyes widened as if she'd seen a pair of ghosts and her shoulders sagged. We passed her without saying anything—there was a staffer nearby—but her demeanor and watery eyes said all we needed to know. I desperately wanted to boost her spirits but all I could do was wink, as if our return was all part of a greater plan.

Later, when I was able to talk to her, Liesel was incredulous, her voice heavy with emotion: "*Gott im Himmel!* I thought you had made it! I prayed you had made it!"

"I thought we had, too," I said with bravado so that she wouldn't see the effect my recapture had had on me. She had too much of a stake in my freedom; I couldn't let even the smallest amount of the despair I felt affect her. I told her how close we had come, that we'd been done in by our own carelessness. We had assumed there was only one road to cross out of Germany but there had been two, the second also manned by sentries. Yet as I told the story to Liesel, I found a kernel of optimism, that I would escape from the horror of this place again. "We can't let it get the best of us. We have to consider it a rehearsal. There has to be another way out of here and we'll find it. Will you help again?"

"*Ja!*" she said. Some life returned to her eyes and some of the sag went out of her shoulders.

In the barrack that night our comrades were keen to hear the details of our escape and what had led to our capture. Most found the irony stunning, amazed that we had made it so far, only to be nabbed in the last few hundred yards. Yet they were impressed that we had actually reached the border and offered whatever support they could give for a second attempt. The encouragement further lifted our spirits.

It took fewer than two days of being back in the mines for Gus and me to concoct another scheme, and the only person we needed to let in on it was Liesel. Though no one had ratted the last time, we still felt that the fewer people who knew about what we were doing, the better. In the bathroom of the building in which we changed our clothes and washed after each shift there was a small window with a single vertical bar down the middle, mortared into a brick sill and lintel. There was no glass. Without the bar, there would be just enough room for a slender man to slip through, and Gus and I more than qualified for that description.

We needed a short piece of stiff wire that could be easily concealed, which we could use to dig the bar out of its mortise. This proved to be more difficult than we thought. Though the camp was surrounded with miles of stiff wire, it was not readily accessible to us. Liesel came to our rescue and brought us an awl from which she had broken the wooden handle. It was perfect, and over the next four months, during our turns in the bathroom, we slowly picked away at the mortar, standing on the toilet to reach it, until we were able to loosen the bar.

Liesel smuggled in more clothes, which again were hidden beneath our mattresses. No one else knew what we were up to until the day of our escape. When Gus and I pulled out the civilian clothes and donned them, our barrack mates applauded lightly. Several patted our shoulders as we left for the mine. When our shift was over, we joined the others on the hoist and went with them into the wash house. Then, as if we did such a thing routinely, we went into the bathroom together. Hurriedly, we stripped off our prison garb. Gus climbed onto the toilet and worked the bar out of the window. He went first and I followed. Given the way the rear of the wash house faced, there wasn't any danger of anyone seeing us as we slithered through the narrow opening and fell headfirst into some bushes. When the shifts had changed and the area had been vacated, we walked into the open and headed for the swamp. We didn't need a map; we knew the way.

This time it was late summer and it was much safer to raid farm fields than root cellars, as long as there were no dogs or farmers with shotguns. We ate better than we had expected on our journey, and besides vegetables we managed to add a few apples to our diet. Decent nutrition combined with knowing the way put us at the border in four and a half days. Much to our relief, we even managed to find a bridge over the Lippe River. The weather was fair and warm all the way, which was not what we hoped for at our destination.

We hid in the same woods and waited, praying for the weather to change, for some clouds and rain to roll in from the North Sea, but it remained the same. Since it was high summer, the nights weren't as dark, which would work against us. We waited for two days, consuming the last of our rations, until we either had to retrace our steps to find more food or try crossing the border regardless of the weather. After some discussion, we decided that we did not want to take even the smallest step back in the direction of AK 54, that we would place our fate with the border.

We still reckoned that the best time for crossing the first road was at a shift change in the early hours of the morning, and it proved to be easier than we thought. Shoeless, we sneaked across one at a time, me first. On the far side we slipped our shoes on and crawled across the grassy area and into the trees. We moved slowly and quietly, glimpses of the stars overhead providing our direction. We had no timepieces, of course, so I can't say how long it took us to traverse the woods to the next road, but it probably seemed longer than it was. We knew when we were getting close because the ambient light ahead changed. We stopped and listened, as still as stumps.

There was movement on a paved surface some distance off to our left. Footsteps came toward us, passed, then turned and came past us again. The process was repeated and each time, the light changed slightly. After the third pass, I peeked and made out the figure of an armed sentry, carrying a lantern, slowly marching off. I looked the other way and saw another swaying lantern in the distance. It didn't come near us so we were probably in the middle of a patrol area. This road was not as heavily guarded as the first, which I thought strange, but perhaps the Germans believed that the first road formed a tight enough net. We removed our shoes again and waited for the sentry's fourth pass, and just before he reached his turn-around point we dashed across the road into the woods on the other side. We waited there until the sentry had come and gone again, then moved off. As there were no clouds, we had not seen the lights that we had thought, during our previous attempt, were the lights of a Dutch village reflecting off them. Nevertheless, we held our direction and after some time saw bright lights through the trees. To our utter disappointment it wasn't a Dutch village at all.

It was actually the real border crossing, a wide road fully lit, with evenly spaced, manned, sentry huts on the near side. The trees had been cleared back from the road about 25 yards on the German side and 50 on the Dutch side, although scrub brush had not been cut. As near as we could tell, there was no Dutch presence, perhaps because there was no crossroad. We watched for about an hour and the guards did not appear to be overzealous in their work. Holland was, after all, a neutral country and for the first part of the war had quietly acted as a conduit for goods entering Germany. It was easy war duty for the sentries, who sometimes congregated to talk, laugh and smoke. Their rifles were slung on their shoulders. We reckoned we could make it across the road before the guards were able to unsling their weapons to shoot at us, and if we could make it into the brush without being shot, we should be home free. Whatever the case, a bullet in the head was a better alternative to a slow death in AK 54.

We waited until the guards had gathered once more for a confab and stood, stretching our legs to get the kinks out. Dawn was breaking. Gus put out his hand to grasp mine, saying softly, "Here's to good luck, Sarge."

"And the smell of Dutch air. Are you ready?" My heart was hammering in my chest.

He nodded curtly. "Let's do it!"

We broke from the trees and onto the road, running as hard as our limited energy and spindly legs allowed. We did not look toward the guards but had our eyes fixed on the brush ahead. Our prediction that they wouldn't have time to get off a shot was right, although we heard lots of shouting. We tore through the bush, bent at the waist, the branches grabbing at our clothes and stinging our faces. Then we were in the trees, with scant underbrush, although the ground was still rough and uneven. Even so, we continued as fast as we could, Gus leading the way. We had no plans for stopping until we were certain we were deep in Dutch territory. I don't know how long we ran but it must have been for a considerable distance when suddenly, Gus went crashing to the ground, crying out in pain. I tried to avoid stumbling over him but tripped anyway and thudded into a tree, taking the brunt of the collision with my left shoulder.

"Shit! Shit!" Gus cried in pain. "I think I've busted my knee!"

I was dazed for a moment. I felt my shoulder and while it was sore and I'd probably soon have a sizeable bruise there, I still had full movement of my arm. I looked in the direction we'd come from and neither saw nor heard anyone in pursuit. I crawled over to my friend.

"Which leg?" I asked.

"My right!" he groaned from the deepest part of his chest.

He was in too much pain for me to pull up his pant leg, but in the twilight of the forest, I could see that below the knee his leg was twisted at an odd angle that couldn't be natural. He moaned as I touched it.

"It doesn't look good, Gus." I made a quick decision. "I'm going to scout ahead and see how far we are from a road where we can get some help. As near as I can tell, there's no one coming after us, so we must be in Holland. You should be all right here."

"Okay," he gasped.

I hated to leave him but there was nothing else I could do. So that I could find my way back, I dragged my toes in the forest floor to create a recognizable trail. Before long I came upon another road. It was empty—a good sign, I thought. The forest ended abruptly here and across the road was open farmland. A few hundred yards to my left I could see what looked to be a small settlement. I retraced my path to Gus, who was coping much better with the pain now that the initial shock of it was over.

"There's a road just ahead, Gus, and some kind of settlement nearby. I'm positive it's a Dutch village. At least there aren't any German soldiers around."

"Hallelujah," he responded.

"You've got two choices: I can help carry you to the road or you can wait here while I get help. Maybe I can find someone with a litter. That'd be easier on you."

He didn't have to give it a second thought. "Go for help. The leg's tolerable as long as I don't move it. I'll be okay."

I patted his shoulder. "Don't worry. I won't leave you here long."

Once I was on the road, I headed for the settlement and spied two men walking toward me. They were not at all concerned about my presence. Approaching them I asked in German, "*Haben Sie ein Gegenstück?*" ("Have you a match?")

They looked at each other, confused. While the German and Dutch languages shared many similarities, they hadn't quite understood what I had said. They must be Dutch! I pointed at myself and said, "Canada! Canada! *Kriegsgefangener! Kriegsgefangener!*" I hoped that the Dutch words for "Canada" and "prisoner of war" were not too much different from the English and German words.

Apparently they weren't.

FOURTEEN

Repatriation

DUTCH NEUTRALITY IN THE war made Gus and me hot potatoes. Worse, there was much confusion at first because army
records showed that we had been killed in action. They must
have assumed that our bodies had been blown into pieces,
beyond all recognition, and scattered along the front line, as
no one had seen the Germans take us prisoners. But the Dutch
were humanitarian enough to move Gus to a hospital and tend
to his injury, while they sent me by train to an internment
camp near the border with Belgium, originally established for
Belgian refugees who fled their country at the onset of the war.

Over the next several days, they treated the septic sores I
had from lice bites and gave me clean clothes. My shoulder was
so sore from colliding with the tree that I could barely move
my arm. I was a physical and mental wreck, even though the
stress of the prison camp and mines and escape attempts were

behind me. I felt as if I had collapsed inward. I kept to myself in the refugee camp and showered as often as I could in the huge stalls that provided only cold water. Once the authorities had everything sorted out, they shipped me to a hospital in Ramsgate, England. I could not find out what had happened to Gus before I left but after many inquiries at the hospital, I received news that stove my heart in.

Jim had died during the attack on Sanctuary Wood. My good friend was gone, his beautiful voice silenced forever. Although badly hurt, he had survived the bombardment but instead of retreating, he and another soldier had manned a machine gun and cut down several attacking Germans before being killed themselves. Jim's actions didn't surprise me. He wasn't the kind of man to go meekly to his death. He and his mate had been posthumously awarded Victoria Crosses.

I barely had a chance to absorb the fact of Jim's death when I found out that Davey had never got his Blighty. His wounded leg had become gangrenous and he died during the amputation in a field hospital in Belgium. He was interred in a cemetery there. The news knocked me down into a chair, as if an ornery horse had kicked me squarely in the gut.

What had I wrought? While I was enduring the hell of the prison camp, Ree must have been enduring a hell of her own. Everything that she had feared had come to pass, even, as far as she knew, my death. The hospital administration sent her a cable saying I had survived, but the telegraph company in Kamloops wired back that it was undeliverable. That could mean only one thing. She had sold the ranch and moved somewhere else, leaving no forwarding address. I figured it was best that way. I had ruined her life and she would be better off without me in it.

The world I had known no longer existed, blown to smith-ereens by the war. I perhaps should have felt some consolation that I had survived both the front lines and a slave labour camp, and that I was one of the few people to have escaped from one, but I did not. I had devastated the lives of those who meant the most to me, and had hidden in a hole when the Germans came instead of fighting, as Jim had. I was mortified.

The camp and the mines haunted my dreams, and so did Ree, Davey and Jim. The burning men returned, and the smell too. Tears came unbidden and I was lethargic. It sometimes required a Herculean effort just to get out of bed and face the day. I had experienced something similar when I lost Charity and Rebecca, but this felt a hundredfold worse. I was losing my hair and I had been malnourished for so long that the hospital's medical staff had to take great care to get me back on a normal diet; the pain in my stomach and bowels was at times excruciating and my heart fluttered madly in my chest. And paradoxically, now that ample food was available, I had no appetite for it and the weight I regained was minimal. I remained a walking skeleton.

Yet it was my crying that concerned the hospital staff the most. I didn't sob—the tears merely seeped from my eyes, and my nose ran—but crying was what women did; in men, it was an obvious sign of femininity and therefore weakness. I tried holding off the tears until I was alone but was not always suc-cessful. One day a burly orderly came on to the ward and said, "Please come with me, Sergeant Strong." I asked why but he shook his head. "Just come with me, please."

I followed him down two floors to an office in the basement where he introduced me to a Dr. Waddell, a short, balding, cheery-faced man who held the rank of major. He sat behind a large oak desk, shuffling some papers around on it.

"Have a seat," and he pointed to a metal chair opposite him. I sat down.

Waddell opened a folder and rifled through the papers it contained. His demeanour suggested that he might be looking for some good news to tell me. He cleared his throat and smiled. "I see by your files, Sergeant Strong, that you are, um, frequently seen crying."

His statement surprised me. Men didn't usually discuss such things with each other, not even if they were good friends. Was he a psychiatrist? He hadn't said so, and I hadn't asked to see one. I felt uncomfortable answering. "I didn't think it was frequent, sir. A little, I suppose. Not too much."

"And how much do you think is 'not too much,' might I ask?"

I shrugged. I did not want to be talking about this, especially to someone whose smile hid a superciliousness I was growing to dislike. Yet I felt compelled to justify my tears and began explaining what I had gone through, what I had lost. I didn't get far before he interrupted me, still smiling.

"I know your story, Sergeant. It's all here," he said, referring to my file. "It is certainly tragic and believe me when I say I am deeply sympathetic. But we have had men here who have been through much worse. Much worse. Men who didn't feel a need to cry about it, I might add."

Where was this going? Had I been brought here to be reprimanded for crying? "I guess I'm different, sir," I said, defensively.

His eyes widened and his smile turned into a grin. "Are you

now." He arose. "You must come with me. There's something you need to see. It may change your mind."

I followed him into a room next to his office. In the centre of it was a table-height wooden slab with broad leather straps across it and a large machine beside it. A number of wires with metal brushes attached to their ends came out of the machine. A longer, thicker wire ran across the floor and connected the machine to an electrical outlet in the wall. We stood beside the table.

Waddell laid his hand on the machine, almost fondly. "I devised this myself," he said proudly. "It is normally used to stimulate the wasted muscles of men who have been seriously wounded." He picked up two of the brushes. "These are electrodes. They are attached to the affected area and a faradic current is sent through them." He smiled even more broadly, as if he were a teacher and I, his favourite pupil, was faithfully absorbing the lesson of a lifetime. "You probably don't know what a faradic current is but, briefly, it's an alternating electrical current that can produce a mechanical reaction, if enough power is applied. In other words if these electrodes are placed in certain areas on your leg, the muscles will jump. My patients tell me that it is sometimes quite painful but it is usually very effective. The gain outweighs the pain, so to speak." He laughed at his small rhyme.

"But here's the part that will be of interest to you, Sergeant Strong—what an interesting name, by the way! The sort that almost demands living up to. But I digress. I have recently discovered that my machine can also be very effective in other kinds of therapy. For example, if I strapped you down on this table and attached the brushes to different parts of your head, it might be just the thing you need to stop the tears."

I looked at him, befuddled at first by what he was saying; then it became all too clear. I imagined myself strapped to the table, writhing in insufferable pain as currents of electricity flashed through my brain like lightning bolts. With as much conviction as I could muster, I said, "I don't need it, sir. I'll be okay."

He chortled, a Hun with a smile on his face, and clapped me on the shoulder. "Good man! I knew you could be reasoned with."

THE TALK throughout the hospital was of the pending cessation of hostilities. The staff was happy, as it meant the end at last to the long line of torn bodies and souls coming their way from overseas. For the patients, however, many of whom were amputees and mental wrecks like me, the war would probably never be over. On November 11, 1918, when the guns finally fell silent, there was a huge sigh of relief, especially from those whose bodies had mended well enough to warrant their return to the front lines.

I was among the first contingents of wounded and sick repatriated to Canada. As I sailed from Southampton, I wondered fleetingly if Ree had returned to her parents' home in Exeter. But no. I really didn't think she had. She had said many times that Exeter was her past, not her future. My guess was that she had probably gone to Victoria, for she had loved the city during our frequent visits. Yet even if I had known that she had returned to Exeter I could not have gone there, nor could I have cabled or even telephoned her parents. Inasmuch as these options, as well as others, were open to me—the army even owed me leave—I deeply believed I should not contaminate Ree's life any more than I had.

The Atlantic Ocean was in its usual foul winter mood but I scarcely noticed it and spent much of the journey in a haze. From Halifax I went first to Ottawa where I received an honourable discharge, a $35 clothing allowance, a $375 War Service Gratuity, a travel voucher to go anywhere in the country, and free medical care for a year. I was also entitled to full pay for the time I had spent as a prisoner of war but since I had been listed as dead, miles of red tape needed sorting out before I would see a penny of it. Some people said the government was so far in debt that I should not expect payment any time soon, if ever.

But the gratuity was cash in my pocket and the first thing I spent it on was alcohol, which, despite Prohibition, was readily available for medicinal purposes. I used my free medical care privileges and visited two local doctors who, other vets had told me, had no qualms about prescribing a bottle of whisky for a soldier who had served on the front lines. In this way, I acquired enough to stay drunk for almost the entire journey west.

I STEPPED down from the train in Kamloops, depressed and hungover, my nerve endings frayed. It was snowing lightly and a cold wind swept through the town, swirling the flakes around so that they seemed never to touch the ground. The valley that once felt open and beautiful was now narrow and constrictive, the low clouds clinging to the hillsides oppressive. The physical appearance of the town hadn't changed much since my departure nearly three years ago, but whereas I used to recognize people on the streets, I now recognized no one and even if I had, I had changed too much for them to recognize me. I rented a horse from complete strangers at the livery stable.

On the way to the Bar JM, I wondered why I was going there, why I had even got off the train in the first place, when I felt more like crawling into a hole somewhere. And yet I couldn't help myself, which overrode my concern about how Maggie would react to my return. Jim very likely would not have enlisted had it not been for me. I remembered his words, now prophetic, during our encounter at the recruitment office: "You're going to be the death of me yet."

And I had been. The least I could do was apologize to Maggie.

By the time I reached the ranch I was frozen stiff, wishing I had bought a warmer coat in Kamloops and maybe a bottle of whisky. Maggie had probably not heard me ride up in the snow and wind, so I tied the horse in a small shelter for visitors, climbed onto the porch and knocked on the door. It swung open and Maggie stood there. She wore denim trousers and a plaid flannel shirt, and looked more like a rancher than a rancher's wife. I thought she had aged 10 years since I'd last seen her. She did not recognize me at first, then she turned as white as the snow I'd just ridden through.

"Jack?" she cried. "Oh my dear God, Jack! You *are* alive! We've been hearing rumours that you were but didn't dare believe them!" She wrapped her arms around me. "Oh, it's so good to see you," and she pulled me into the warmth of the house.

It was just as I remembered. The long kitchen counter and white apron sink, the once-new but now well-used wood-burning cook stove, the cast-iron pots and pans suspended from the ceiling. The living area had hardly changed over the years and contained the same furniture. The wolfskin still adorned one wall and the upright piano that Jim had bought just before the war stood against another. A fire crackled in the fieldstone fireplace. It was all so familiar and yet strange at the same time. It was the first home I'd been in since I left The Little Karoo, and it made my head spin.

While she brewed tea, Maggie apologized for the mess the house was in, but running the ranch without Jim kept her much too busy for mundane household chores. The two youngest boys, Jimmy and Tommy, were still a handful when they were at home but they were at school. Peter, now 15, was helping her run the ranch and he was also at school. It was terrifically hard work for the two of them, yet they were doing reasonably well and, with the help of the widow's pension she received each month, were able to hire an extra hand when they needed to. She did not know how much longer she would hang on to the land, because the boys had expressed interest in pursuing more lucrative careers than ranching. I said I was sorry for not warning her that I was coming and told her, without going into detail, where I'd spent the last two years, and that the cables to Ree about my survival had been undeliverable.

"Yes, but they can't keep their mouths shut at the telegraph office, even though they're supposed to. Word leaked out that you were alive. I wanted to believe it and write Ree but what if it wasn't true? It would have been cruel of me to give her false hope."

"Where is she?"

"She went to England to be with her parents until she decided what to do with her life."

So I was wrong. She had not gone to Victoria after all. She had been in Exeter while I was convalescing, there as I departed from Southampton.

"She must have sold the ranch then."

"Yes. I bought it. I couldn't bear to see the land owned by someone else. Just say the word and it can be yours again for the same price I paid, plus taxes. Anyway, she certainly got the cable informing her that you were dead, just as I got the one about Jim." She paused, the memory being almost too much to bear. "That was such an awful time. The only thing that got us through was that we had each other, and three kids to worry about. Then two days later, she got another one about Davey. That almost did her in completely. It nearly did me in; the loss was just too horrific to even think about. And yet, I'm certain that if Davey hadn't died she might have stayed on at the ranch. He was so good with horses. But with him gone too . . ." She left the sentence hanging. "I'm so sorry, Jack."

"So am I," I said, "and I owe you an apology, Maggie. I thought I was doing the right thing but all I managed to do was destroy a lot of lives."

"Nonsense, Jack! If you're referring to Jim enlisting, he would have done it without you. You shouldn't feel any need to apologize. He had talked about it many times and I simply told him it wouldn't be fair to Ree to involve *you*. As it turns out, you were both on the same track. And who can fault you for doing what a multitude of other men did? Where would those poor people in the conquered countries be if no one had answered the call? You and Jim went to ensure their liberty and I believe it was the honourable thing to do. You should be proud!"

It was either a magnanimous gesture or a way of explaining and coping with her loss, I didn't know which. "That's what I believed in the beginning. Now I wonder how so many of us could have been such bloody fools."

"Dear God, Jack, you mustn't reduce what was done, what

you and Jim did, to mere foolishness. It's utterly unfair, not only to yourself but to every man who went overseas and put his life on the line."

I did not want to argue with her so I said nothing, and she went on in a different vein. "What about you and Ree? You must return to England and find her. Or send a telegram, at the very least."

Returning to England was not only beyond my means, it was unthinkable, and even a telegram was out of the question. "I can't. How could I face her? Everything she feared has come true and it was entirely my doing. I've already ruined her life once and that's enough. I'd rather she went on believing I was dead."

Her eyes widened with surprise. "But you just can't ignore her, Jack, like some old saddle you've no more use for. I know that I can't ever imagine what you've been through, but Ree is your wife, for goodness sake! She was your life!"

"It's not a case of ignoring her, Maggie. I just believe it's best this way. Look at me. I'm not the same man she married."

"I can see how much you've changed. God knows the war has changed all of us. But you're still Jack Strong, aren't you?"

Still Jack Strong? I never was Jack Strong. I was Caleb Caine, the same name as my drunken father. Maggie knew that but did not mention it, so I said only, "To tell you the truth, I don't know who Jack Strong is anymore."

"Well, you still have your life, and that's more than Jim has," she said softly.

"What life is that, Maggie?"

The bitter sadness in my voice clearly bothered her. She opened her mouth to say something and thought better of it. Finally, she asked, "Where will you go?"

The question evoked memories from over 30 years before, when my mother had asked the same thing. My answer was not much different. "Away from here. Maybe Vancouver. I'll get Ree's address from you and I promise to contact her when I feel better about things. That's the best I can do right now."

Maggie half smiled. "I understand. But don't leave it too long, Jack. If you don't mind me saying so, I think you need Ree as much as she needs you. Perhaps more. And please don't forget about me. I'm a friend. If you need money to get to England, I'm sure I could arrange some for you."

I nodded. I had to get off the topic so I asked her if any of the boys had taken up the piano.

"Peter has. He has some talent for it, and he can sing, too. He plays the songs his father used to sing."

"I'm glad about that. And Nora? How did she take Davey's death?"

"She took it hard, even though nearly a year had passed since she'd seen him. But she had youth on her side and she's managing now. Even has a new beau. A nice young man, new to the area. I try not to compare him to Davey."

Maggie begged me to stay over but I declined. I needed to be alone. Before I left, she showed me the letter that she had received advising her of Jim's death and the medal he had won. The letter came from the Honourable A.E. Kemp, the Minister for Militia and Defence, and read in part:

> I desire to express to you my very sincere sympathy in the recent decease of your husband, 798641 Sergeant James Edward Spencer, who in sacrificing his life at the front in action with the enemy

has rendered the highest service of a worthy citizen. The heavy loss which you and the Nation have sustained would indeed be depressing were it not redeemed by the knowledge that the brave comrade for whom we mourn performed his duties fearlessly and well as became a good soldier, and gave his life for the great cause of Human Liberty and the Defence of the Empire.

Jim's medal was nestled in plush velvet in a small box. I thought of Ree. She had undoubtedly received a similar letter, twice. It was what they said about all the soldiers who died. And who could blame any wife or mother if they believed the claptrap it contained? It was something to hold on to, something to lend meaning to an incomprehensible circumstance. But, I wondered, was the medal a better deal than the letter? Had it reduced Maggie's grief by even the smallest measure? It would have been too mean-spirited to ask. All I said was, "I miss Jim terribly."

She hugged me and clung for a long time. She had been the strong one during our reunion, yet I think she was trying to collect herself, for I heard her sniffle. "So do the boys and I, Jack. Indescribably. You take care of yourself and try to put some meat on those bones. And remember, I couldn't think of a better outcome to this sad affair than to have you and Ree as my neighbours again."

Maggie stood on the porch as I climbed onto my horse and rode out of the yard. I waved and she waved back. Few artists could have captured the loneliness I saw in that scene.

FIFTEEN

The King of English Bay

VANCOUVER NOW HAD A population of nearly a quarter of a million people, far different from the short row of wood-frame buildings that had lined the waterfront and housed perhaps 200 when I arrived in 1884. The downtown core was thick with tall brick and stone buildings; trolleys screeched and clanged along the streets; the residential districts stretched far beyond what I could see. The forest and the salal-lined path that ran through it, which I had once followed to the brothel where I mistakenly believed I had become a man, was now a railroad yard. I craved anonymity and the busy, rainy January streets were just the place to find it.

The city was flooded with men home from the war, looking for and expecting work in this remote part of the Empire that they had, for the most part, volunteered to defend. But jobs were as scarce as compassion in the higher echelons of government and veterans went begging after they had used their gratuity. If that didn't go toward food and shelter, it went toward steeping them in alcohol to forget the hell they'd been through and the sorrowful fact that they themselves had been all but forgotten. This was possible because Prohibition was even more of a sham in Vancouver than it was in Ottawa. No need for a sympathetic doctor here: alcohol was as close as the nearest bootlegger. In fact, I hadn't gone far from the station when a Sikh, operating from the entrance to an alley-way, sold me two pints of whisky. "Visky, sir?" he asked as I passed by and I stopped immediately, nodding. He had little English but we communicated perfectly. He led me a short distance down the alley to a recessed doorway, unwrapped his turban to reveal a small cache hidden there and removed two bottles for the money I handed him.

When I was on the street again, a skeletal beggar wearing a shabby suit and a haunted, hungry look asked if I had any spare change. I should have cared more and asked him if he was a veteran but I didn't. I said, "It depends. Can you tell me where I can find a cheap hotel?" He directed me to the Devon on Hastings Street and I gave him a dime.

The Devon was just what I was looking for: not much out front to advertise its presence. Inside, there was a small lobby with an alcove and counter where a desk clerk sat, a tight-lipped, rat-faced man with steely eyes who asked only how long I'd be staying. Monthly rates were the cheapest so I paid a month's rent in return for the key to a third-floor room.

Voices emanated from the rooms I passed on the way to mine, through open transoms and the large gap between door bottoms and the linoleum floor: drunk conversations, arguments and, out of one room, the sound of a man and a woman's lust. The place reeked of stale cigarette smoke. My room contained sparse, well-used furnishings—a scratched chest of drawers, an upholstered chair, a rickety bed and a small, rust-stained sink with a single, cold-water faucet. A light fixture dangled from the ceiling and the bathroom was at the end of the hall. Doors banged incessantly in the hallway but I could not have cared less. I stripped down to my underwear, climbed onto the bed with the two bottles of rotgut whisky for bed-partners and drank until I couldn't put two coherent thoughts together.

I awoke the following morning feeling extremely sick with a monstrous headache, vowing never to visit the Sikh again. I staggered to the sink to wash my face, and when I peered into the mirror, the image I saw startled me. I saw an older version of my father, and I hated it. I recalled that during my drunken stupor the previous night, I had considered moving elsewhere and reverting to my birth name. As Ree and Maggie were the only ones left who knew of my name change, I could easily become the world's cleverest vanishing act. Wild Jack Strong be damned. I had proved unworthy of the name, so why not let him disappear from the face of the Earth forever, followed by the resurrection of Cal Caine? In my twisted thoughts, it rang true.

I did not want to be that man in the mirror. Yet my depression weighed on me so heavily it was almost suffocating.

FEBRUARY ROLLED in, cold and dreary, the days passing in limbo, one barely distinguishable from another. I stayed away from the whisky, lay around a lot, slept and, when I had the energy, walked or whiled away the time in a greasy spoon, sometimes talking to other veterans. Like me, they all had stories to tell but kept them to themselves. One morning, as I was heading out for some toast and coffee, I passed a newspaper kiosk that I normally ignored. I don't know why, but I happened to glance at the front page of the *Province*, perhaps because its headline was big and bold. It was so stunning that I bought a copy of the paper, nearly throwing the coin at the vendor, and stood in the street, reading the story that had grabbed my attention. I could not believe my eyes.

Sam Steele was dead. Something that I had always viewed as nigh impossible had happened. He had seemed indestructible, so much larger than life that not even death could conquer him. At Loon Lake during the hunt for Big Bear, and in the South African war, I had seen him attract more than his share of gunfire yet the bullets never found him. It was as if an invisible shield, which death dared not penetrate, protected him. Sadly, it now appeared as if it applied only to bullets. He had died from the flu, the very virus that had taken tens of thousands of Canadian lives and millions of others worldwide.

The news item called it the "Spanish Flu" for no reason other than that Spain, being neutral during the war, was the only western country without censorship for its newspapers, so it provided relatively reliable reportage. The illness had become so much a part of life then that sometimes, while walking down the street, I would hear young girls skipping rope to the rhyme, "I had a little bird, its name was Enza, I opened the window and in-flew-enza." Adults were terrified of the disease, yet there were many, for whatever reasons, it never touched, and I was one of them. But poor old Sam had caught it.

I couldn't imagine him lying on a bed, suffocating to death from pneumonia, which was how the flu typically took its victims. The article referred to him as "one of the conquerors of the western wilderness," who should have died "in a blaze of glory and mingled his valiant dust with the lost riders of the plains." Instead, he had died a passive death in Putney, England, while awaiting his turn to come home. The article went on to say that he had retired from service in July of 1918, not long after he had received a knighthood and many medals. He had turned 70 just three weeks before his death.

Sir Samuel Benfield Steele. I felt proud to have known him. I had followed him through every major historical event of the last 35 years and we had survived them all. But this last one had got him and not me, and I thought that the world might have been a better place had it been the other way around. That he was gone and I remained was baffling.

That spring, I discovered that my former father-in-law, Alexander McRae, had died of a heart attack while I was overseas. I assumed that he'd been buried next to Eleanor, Charity and Becky, but for the longest time I was unable to find the strength to visit their graves. When I finally got around to it, apprehension ate at my gut as I boarded the trolley that would take me to the cemetery. It was a peaceful place, as cemeteries tend to be, but my anxiety intensified as I walked among the sombre vaults and gravestones. At first I didn't recognize the ones I'd come to see, for they were now enclosed by a low, wrought-iron fence, and the latest marker was grander than the rest. But there they were, side by side: Charity, Becky and Eleanor, in the shadow of Alex's polished marble obelisk.

I stood there, outside the fence, my thoughts a jumbled mess, not knowing what to do. Then it struck me that there had always been flowers on Charity's and Becky's graves while Eleanor was alive but now there were none. That was something I could do. I returned to the entrance of the cemetery where there was a kiosk and bought four fresh-cut daffodils. I placed one on each grave and left with an overwhelming sadness cloaking my heart. So many of the people who had been close to me had died tragically: my mother, my father, Charity, Becky, all those killed at Frog Lake, Jim, Davey, even Sam Steele. It was as if it was their punishment for being part of my life. Not that I thought I was a murderer; rather it was more like I had some sort of deadly touch, a disease that killed others who came in contact with me while I remained alive. I felt cursed.

Despite such self-loathing thoughts, the depression that had swept down me like an avalanche in England did not seem nearly as suffocating now. Reasonably good days crept sporadically in among the bad, but I was still a long way from thinking that Ree needed me back in her life. However, on a warm Sunday in June, with the sun hotter than usual, I felt in good enough form to pay a visit to my old friend Joe Fortes.

Not everyone knew Joe personally but most people had at least heard of him, in spite of Vancouver's phenomenal growth and size. By chance, I had seen him walking toward me on the street one morning, burly and confident, an unmistakable figure, even among the crowds. I turned down an alley so that I wouldn't have to meet him, although I'm not certain he would have recognized me even if our shoulders had touched in passing. I was still as thin as a lodgepole pine and what was left of my hair had turned completely grey. Yet I knew that it was entirely possible that reconnecting with Joe might be the best thing I could do for myself.

People packed the sandy beach on English Bay, sprawled on blankets, taking in the sun. Others strolled along the long wooden pier jutting into the bay. Everyone appeared bliss-fully carefree and I envied them. I sat on a driftwood log and spotted Joe out on a large diving raft anchored just offshore. It had a springboard fixed to it and he would jump off, pull his knees to his chest, as much as a big man can, and make a huge splash that caused the kids in the water to squeal with delight. Then he'd climb onto the raft again and wait his turn for the board, which groaned under his weight as it launched him into the air. He coaxed and cajoled the kids swimming around him, and chastised them if they weren't kicking their feet properly. I could hear his voice over the water, "Kick your feet, child, kick your feet!" Or, pointing at a skinny, shivering boy hugging himself on the raft, "Come on, boy! You jump in before I have to throw you in!" And to prove he meant what he said, every now and then he would grab a kid still on the raft and heave him or her into the water, having altogether too much fun for someone pushing 60.

It was late afternoon before he came ashore, a barrel of a man dripping water from his striped grey swimsuit and down his bare brown shoulders. He grabbed a towel from the lifeguard's highchair and wiped himself dry, then hung it up neatly. Waving at the kids, he walked along the water's edge and beneath the pier. People on the beach smiled and called hello to him. I followed, and saw him climb a flight of stairs to a cottage, open the door and go in.

I went to the bottom of the stairs and stood there, wanting to simply turn around and walk away. But I didn't. I ascended the stairs and quickly knocked on the door before my courage ran out. It opened and I said, "Hello, Joe."

He stood there in his wet bathing suit, confused about who this scarecrow was at his door. "Jack? Is it you?" he asked tentatively.

"Yes. It's me."

"Come in! Come in!" We shook hands and his grip was almost crushing. "The last I heard you'd gone off to the war and I said to myself, 'That's just like Jack!' I was hopin' you'd come back in one piece, but it looks like you might have broke in other ways. Come and sit down. I'll put the kettle on and get changed." He guided me to an old sofa. "Sit down, my friend! Sit down!"

He disappeared into the kitchen and I heard him fill a kettle with water. He came back through the living room and went into a small bedroom, shut the door and reappeared a few moments later dressed in a light shirt, slacks and sandals. He returned to the kitchen and I heard tableware rattling and water splashing into a pot, then he carried in a tray with two cups and a teapot on it. He sat on the sofa, placing the tray between us. "How're you keeping, Jack? Or maybe I shouldn't ask."

I put my thoughts in order and started at the beginning. Like the gentleman he was, he listened intently but never interrupted. When I finished, the tea that he'd forgotten to pour was cold.

Joe shook his head. "That's a bad spell you've had, Jack, and I can see you're hurtin'. You remember what I told you a long time ago, when you were just a boy?"

"I do now. Something about it's always best for a man to step out in times of trouble."

"Nothin' wrong with your memory, and that's a fact I can state. You did it then and you surely need to do it now. You got to step out of your troubles and move on. You can't draw in and hide, which is what you been doin'. You seen a lot in your life, too many bad things, and I can't imagine what it's been like, but it's done and you ought not to put yourself through it anymore. You say it's all your fault, but that don't make no sense at all. You're giving yourself way too much credit for the way the world turns. You just got caught up in it, that's all. And you need to be careful, my friend. You go splitting yourself too far apart inside and you might not get back together again."

I definitely had that sense, as if there were two of me in a tug of war for my soul.

"How are you doing, Joe?" I asked, moving on to something besides my troubles. "I saw you on the raft today. It looked like you were having fun."

"Oh, indeed I was. I always do. I have a good life, Jack. I always have."

The city had built him this cottage, right on the beach, and paid him a policeman's wage to be a lifeguard and manage the rowdies who sometimes frequented the area. It was what he'd done on a voluntary basis, but the citizens had finally recognized his worth and demanded that he receive compensation for it. After all, hadn't he taught many of them to swim when they were children? And their kids, too, now sent freely to the beach unchaperoned because he was there and would ensure their safety. "You mind what Joe says," the parents said and the children did.

"I saw those people nodding and saying hello to you on the beach. They admire and respect you." I managed a small grin. "I believe you're the King of English Bay."

He laughed. "I'm no king, Jack, but everybody calls it 'Joe's Beach' and I do get the respect of most people who come here. And every summer I have a hundred children that are like my own. I get to teach them how to swim and I play with them every day and it keeps me young. I don't know what else a coloured man could ask for without gettin' some of the white folks all stirred up."

"You never asked for anything, Joe, that you didn't deserve. And what you've got, you earned. I'm glad things have worked out so well for you."

"Best you get them workin' out for you now."

I declined Joe's invitation to stay for dinner. The length and intensity of the visit had drained me. I left with a promise that I would reconsider my stance on contacting Ree and that I would come see him again soon, especially if I needed a place to sleep. During the walk back to the hotel, the world seemed less black. I had enjoyed Joe's company and it made me realize something that hadn't occurred to me: I was lonely.

I lay awake a long time that night, thinking about Ree.

My bank account was dwindling and I still hadn't heard anything from the government about the money it owed me, though the address I had listed with them was the hotel's. Part of me desperately wanted that money but a small part thought that not getting it might be more of what I needed. It would force me to find work somewhere, even if I had to go cap in hand for it, and work was probably the best antidote for grief and self-pity. If I was going to contact Ree, I needed to pull myself together. Then a couple of days after my visit with Joe, I passed by the news kiosk, on my way to the usual greasy spoon for toast and coffee, and the day's headline again caught my attention. Sam Steele was finally coming home. It had taken this long because there was no room for the dead on the jammed transport ships bringing back the troops. (I doubt that Steele would have minded—he had always made sure that his men were looked after first.) Apparently, he had received a large funeral service in England but the government had another planned for Sunday, June 22, a few days hence, in Winnipeg, where he had wanted his remains interred.

I had to get to that funeral, whatever the cost.

I had enough cash for a return ticket, plus a little extra, and my room was paid for until the end of the month so the trip was financially possible. I would be in desperate straits once I returned but I would deal with that then. I let the hotel clerk know that I'd be going to Winnipeg for a few days.

SIXTEEN

Irony

I STOOD OUTSIDE UNION Station in Winnipeg in the warm
noon sun. I had not had anything to eat since I left Vancouver
and was famished. Directly in front of me, Broadway Avenue
stretched away to the west, its twin streetcar tracks flanked
by grassy boulevards lined with lovely shade trees. A narrow
stream of people poured out of the avenue and joined a larger
stream coming from the south along Main Street. The majority of them were men, with a few women and children mixed
in, and there was purpose in their steps. I doubted it had anything to do with Steele's funeral. This was no funeral march;
these were people on a mission. A young man in a tweed cap
brushed by me and I caught up with him.

"What's going on?" I asked.

He stared at me as if I had just landed from another planet.
"Where've you been, Mac?"

"I just got in from Vancouver. I've been out of touch."

"I'll say."

"Any place a man can get a bite to eat?"

He laughed. "You might try Regina," he said, his words fat with sarcasm. "You won't find much open here. The whole city's on strike and there's a demonstration at City Hall. We're protestin' the arrest of all the strike leaders."

His flippancy grated on me. I dropped behind and simply followed the crowd. At Portage Avenue, a tributary of people swelled our stream as we continued along Main Street, past tall, stone buildings, mostly banks and retail stores, toward a sharp dogleg to the right. The street was now a logjam of people. Jitneys and Ford automobiles were angle-parked along the curb, while others sat parallel to it. Still others had stopped in the crowd, unable to move. We got as far as the corner of the block on which City Hall was located and could go no farther. I could see the shade trees fronting the brick-and-stone building, ornate with its twin turrets, clock tower and matching staircases rising to meet at the entrance. Across the street was the Union Bank building and beside it, Stanfield's Underwear store. Behind me was Moore's Funeral Home and the crowd was thinner there. I found a spot against the wall and wondered fleetingly if Steele's body was inside.

There was a hum of people talking but otherwise the crowd was quiet and orderly. I heard a voice that I instantly recognized call, "Sarge!" and saw a thin man with a pronounced limp pushing his way toward me. My mind could scarcely believe what my eyes beheld. It was Gus Moretti.

"Gus!" I shouted, extending my hand.

I admit to having mixed emotions about our chance

encounter. I would rather have been alone but Gus and I had shared a lot during our two years of captivity, and I knew he was not a man to sit in judgment of friends. I had thought about him many times, curious about how he had fared after our separation in Holland. It was not difficult to see that his broken leg had not healed well.

He grasped my hand and shook it mightily. "Goddamn, but it's great to see you!" he exclaimed, clearly happy about running into me. "How're you doin'? You come for this?" He motioned toward the crowd. "Or the funeral?"

"If you mean Sam Steele's, yes, I did. But I didn't expect anything like this. Haven't been keeping up with the news."

Gus explained that 30,000 workers had walked off their jobs five weeks before and the city was in an ugly mood. The war had boosted the Canadian economy but had sent inflation soaring and seriously affected the buying power of workers across the country. They wanted a fair slice of the pie and rightly so. The revolution in Russia, the one that Liesel had told me about, had given the working class worldwide a sense of solidarity and there was talk of forming One Big Union to oppose the capitalists. I remembered hearing similar chatter in Vancouver but I had paid it scant attention.

In Winnipeg, the metalworkers had been the first to approach their employers and ask for a raise that would allow them to meet the higher cost of living. When the owners refused, the workers went on strike and the rest of the building trades followed in sympathy, under the umbrella of the Winnipeg Trades and Labour Council. The owners accused the strike organizers of being Bolsheviks, claiming that enemy aliens had influenced them and that their actions threatened to tear irreparably the political and social fabric of the country. The government called them conspirators and was preparing to deport any who were foreign-born. Businessmen formed the Citizens' Committee of One Thousand to oppose the strikers and since the local police force sympathized with the latter, the city had hired 2,000 special officers, mostly unemployed ex-servicemen willing to do just about anything for money. In the event that proved unsatisfactory, they had also brought in the Royal North-West Mounted Police.

"You'd think we asked for the fucking moon, for Christ's sake," Gus complained indignantly. "All we want are decent wages and the right to bargain for them."

"Good luck," I said. "I don't need to have read the newspapers to know that you might as well try to get blood out of a stone. I'd wager that the people you're up against would sooner part with their sons and daughters than with their money."

"Don't I know it! Sometimes I think they're worse than the bloody Huns. They'd have us work in the same conditions for the same slave wages that we had in AK 54 if we let them get away with it."

My clandestine discussions with Liesel flooded in, of unions and workers tired of being exploited by profiteers, but I had built a dam that diverted them to the back of my mind. While I sympathized with Gus and his fellow protesters, I had enough problems of my own without adding another. I wanted nothing to do with it. I changed the subject.

"Do you know anything about Steele's funeral? That's really all I came for."

I could see the wheels of his mind turning, as I think he expected a more interested response from me. "Tell you what.

Stick with me until this thing's over and I'll see that you get some grub and fill you in on the funeral. Might even be able to find us a drink. Far as I know, the bootleggers haven't joined the strike."

A streetcar occupied by two army officers approached from the south and nosed slowly into the crowd. People moved out of its way, protesting loudly, till someone ran behind the vehicle and pulled the trolley off the overhead wire.

A voice suddenly split the air, coming from the steps of City Hall, amplified by a bullhorn. "His Majesty the King charges and commands all persons being assembled immediately to disperse and peaceably to depart to their habitations or their lawful business, on pain of being guilty of an offence for which, on conviction, they may be sentenced to an imprisonment for life. GOD SAVE THE KING!"

It was the Riot Act. A roar arose from the crowd. Just then, the clatter of hoofs echoed among the buildings. Surging toward us up Main Street was a wall of about 50 red-coated Mounties on horseback and behind them another wall of riders, special constables, dressed in khaki uniforms. All of them carried clubs. They broke into a trot and the crowd parted before them, squeezing onto the sidewalk, jamming against the buildings. Men yelled and women screamed in anger and fright. Gus and I had our backs to a car parked at the curb and now had front-row seats. Farther on, the crowd refused to move and the Mounties and specials urged their horses into it, swinging their clubs. We could hear the dull thud of wood smacking raised forearms and exposed shoulders, even heads. Men shouted in pain and and people roared in anger. What had been a peaceful scene was now bedlam. The horsemen charged through the crowd, which flowed in behind them like a creek around a stone, a mob now. Many went to the side of the streetcar and tried to topple it. They heaved but got it only part way over before the weight proved too much for them. A fender came off in the attempt and they had to be satisfied with that. I looked up the street; the Mounties and specials were returning, only this time at a full gallop.

Unwilling to be bludgeoned again, the crowd parted. Several men ran to a construction site across from City Hall, gathered stones and bricks, and pelted the Mounties as they rode by. The horses of the specials panicked at the barrage of missiles and bolted forward. One man was thrown from his animal and swallowed by the crowd. After a block or so, the Mounties regrouped and charged back again. The specials stayed behind.

A stranger standing next me tried to force a stone on me. "Use this!" he urged, his eyes wide and wild.

I took it.

The Mounties stormed up the street under another barrage of stones and bricks. I was frozen, not from fear but from the shock of what was happening. I could not throw the stone I held in my hand, not at a Mountie, regardless of what they were doing. It would have been like throwing it at Steele himself. I let it fall to the ground. Two Mounties were knocked from their horses; one was dragged into the crowd on the far side while the other fell right in front of Gus and me. I dropped my valise and, instinctively, we leapt forward and pulled him from the road.

The people behind us created enough of a path for us to drag him into the funeral parlour. He was unconscious but still alive, bleeding profusely from the side of his head. A man, perhaps the mortician, brought a gurney from another room and we laid the wounded constable on it. It was tempting to stay in the quiet safety of the parlour but we were compelled to go back outside. In the excitement, I had forgotten all about my valise but it was right where I'd dropped it, the crowd engaged in more important things.

The Mounties had gone up the street and were returning again. They galloped past us, regrouped and turned for a third charge. This time they held their clubs and reins in one hand and revolvers in the other. As they spurred their horses toward us, a thunder of bullets rent the air and I saw a man run onto the street to grab a broken brick. He was about to throw it when a bullet struck him in the chest and he flopped to the ground as if someone had ripped out his leg bones.

Some of the people had retreated along William Street, which flanked City Hall's south side, and the Mounties went after them. Others had climbed aboard the streetcar and set it on fire; grey smoke poured from its windows. Down Main Street, an army of special constables, on foot, armed with baseball bats raised above their heads, marched into the crowd, beating individuals ferociously. Men fled to safety, into buildings and down alleyways. The specials chased after them.

"Let's get the hell out of here!" Gus yelled over the din and pulled me down a lane next to the funeral parlour. He limped along as best he could and I kept glancing over my shoulder. I spied a metal bar about two feet long and scooped it up. If those bastards caught us, they weren't going to get off lightly.

Gus led us north, up side streets; dozens of other men were doing the same thing. The farther we got from City Hall the safer we thought we were and the slower our pace became. We came upon some railway tracks and followed them west. I felt we were safe enough then and threw the bar into some deep grass beside the railbed. I was puffing madly and Gus was wincing in pain from negotiating the uneven ties. We were both sweating profusely. We left the tracks and negotiated more side streets, onto a narrow thoroughfare lined with dilapidated houses, unkempt, fenced-in front yards and small, neglected apartment blocks. Despite its seediness, it was a peaceful haven after Main Street.

We turned into one of the apartment blocks, went up a short flight of worn wood steps and through double doors in need of paint. We were in a wainscotted hallway with a plank floor, dimly lit by a filthy skylight. Ahead were two varnished doors, side by side. The one on the left bore the number "2"; the one on the right, nothing.

"Hang on a sec," Gus said, and went through the numberless door into a bathroom. I could hear him relieving himself as I leaned against the wall, waiting.

When he came out, he grinned. "Didn't think I was gonna make it. Help yourself," he added pointing to the door. "Wait here when you're done. I'll be right back."

The toilet was rust-streaked and filthy, and old newspapers were piled on the tank top for toilet paper. Afterward, I waited about five minutes before Gus returned with what I suspected was a bottle under his coat. He pulled out a skeleton key, opened the door marked "2,"and led me down a short hallway into the kitchen of a tiny two-room suite that might have been a later addition to the rear of the building. An oil stove sat against the far wall, and to the left of it, a multi-paned window faced the blank, grey side of another building. Against the wall to my left, beneath another window, looking out into a thumbnail-sized yard overgrown with weeds and nearly filled by an apple tree, was a table with four chairs; papers were piled and strewn across the tabletop. A small counter and sink with a cupboard above them were situated on the wall behind me. There was hardly enough room to turn around. To my right an archway led to a sparsely furnished bedroom with a cot below a single window. It was low enough that I could see children playing in a bare dirt yard.

Gus took the bottle out and put it on the table. It was gin, a last-ditch drink; if you wanted one you took what was available and cheap. He got two mugs from the cupboard, cracked open the bottle and splashed generous amounts of the clear liquid into them. He handed me a mug and I raised it.

"To King and Empire," I said acerbically.

"Yeah," Gus acknowledged, "where would we be without them?"

The gin burned down my throat and once it was in my stomach, it sent waves of warmth through my body. It was like an enemy come to visit in the guise of a friend.

I glanced around the place and since it was definitely the home of a bachelor, I asked, "Didn't you tell me that you were engaged to be married?"

"I did and I was." He paused and cast his eyes downward, groping for the right words. Gus usually had no shortage of them but, as was the case with most men, they didn't come easily when it concerned affairs of the heart. I didn't interrupt his thoughts, just let him find the ones he could use. Finally, he slapped his bad leg. "She decided that she didn't like men who weren't 'whole' and couldn't support her in a fashion she figured was her birthright."

"Jesus, Gus, that's terrible. I'm sorry to hear it."

In reality, I was angry. I knew Gus probably as well as any man, had seen him at his best and his worst, and he was a caring individual with a well-developed sense of decency. How anyone could treat him so cruelly was unfathomable. But it was plain that talking about his ex-fiancée was a touchy subject, so I changed tack. "What happened in Holland? Weren't they able to fix your leg properly?"

"The damned thing got infected and just about ruined my knee before the docs were able to get around to fixin' it. Then they couldn't set it right and even talked about amputation for a while. I begged them not to do that. I was lucky. I was able to fight off the infection but not before the damage was done. I couldn't get my old job drivin' streetcar because of it—I can't stand or sit in one place too long without it gettin' painful. Since I got home I've been findin' work wherever I can, mostly menial shit." He showed me his hands. They were red and chafed. "That's from washin' too many dishes in rat poison cafes. But it pays the rent and sometimes feeds me, as long as I'm not too particular about where I live and what I eat. The bastards still haven't sent me any money for my time as a prisoner. How about you?"

"Not a cent, so far."

He went on, bitterly, "That goddamned war, anyway! I lost my girl and I lost my kid brother, Claudius, at the Somme. Then the Boche might as well have put a bullet in my father's head because it did him in as well. Had a heart attack. Thought he'd lost me, too, when he got a letter sayin' I was killed in action."

There was a streak of cynicism in Gus that hadn't been there before. Though his deep, dark eyes were still direct and honest, he looked different. He now sported a dark moustache that, with his changed attitude, gave an almost mean cast to his face and the mostly cheery disposition that I had enjoyed during two years of imprisonment had turned sour. It was easy to understand why. The only difference between his losses and mine was that I still felt that I had been the cause.

He asked, "What about you, Sarge? How's things with your wife—Ree? Was that her name? And your boy, Davey?"

"Yes, Ree and Davey," I said, and like Gus, went searching for words that were difficult to say. The gin helped. "I haven't seen Ree. Like your father, she was told I was dead and as far as I know she still thinks that. I'm inclined to keep it that way." I continued, stumbling over the next words because they were so painful, "Uhh, I'm afraid Davey, uhh, didn't make it." I had to clear my throat before I could go on. "Neither did my, uhh, good friend, Jim."

"Shit. If that don't take the cake." Gus paused for a moment, thinking. "It's none of my business, Sarge, but why would you want Ree to think you're dead?"

He was right; it was none of his business but I answered the question anyway because I felt I owed it to him. "She was dead set against me joining the army. Against Davey joining, too, but I encouraged him. So I'm responsible for destroying practically everything she held dear. I'd be surprised if she wanted any more to do with me, even if she knew I was alive. I think it's best this way."

Gus didn't say anything, just shook his head slowly. We were silent for a moment, steeped in our losses. Then he stood and moved around a bit, his leg clearly bothering him. He went to the cupboard over the sink and pulled out a can of pork and beans. He removed the label and opened the can with a lever-type opener. He then placed it on a two-burner hot plate that sat by the sink and turned the element on high.

"Supper," he said. "Sorry, but it's all I got to offer at the moment."

"It'll do just fine. I've got some cash so maybe later we can go get something better."

We sat at his modest kitchen table, ate the beans out of cracked bowls and drank more gin. While I liked its effect, I didn't like the taste and I drank it slowly. That wasn't a bad thing. We talked of the war for a while, then of the day's events. Every time someone from the apartment block used the bathroom, we could hear the door open and close, urine splashing on water, noisy bowel movements, the toilet flush and water running to fill the tank.

"Nice, eh, Sarge? Every time I hear that and look around this fucking place it makes me feel real good about riskin' my life for my country and being a goddammned cripple." He slapped his leg. "And knowin' that this thing'll only get worse as I grow older is a real bonus."

He took a sip of gin. "We won the war for the big boys and lost a pisspot full in the bargain. When we should be enjoyin' prosperity, vets are workin' for next to nothin' compared to those greedy bastards down on Wellington Crescent."

He was referring, when I asked, to an enclave of wealthy businessmen and monied families on the south side of the Assiniboine River, and he was angry.

"That's why we went on strike. They keep gettin' richer and

richer and we keep gettin' poorer. How fair is that? Shit, we've gotta eat, too! We're doing all the fucking work. And we're the ones who went overseas and put our lives on the line while they stayed home and got stinkin' rich. Then the bastards lie about us, every one of us who went and fought for democracy. They call us revolutionaries and accuse us of bein' more communist than the Russians. What a load of crap! They got everybody else in the city scared of us, like we're two-headed monsters about to destroy the country. But I'll tell you this, Sarge. There wouldn't have been any trouble today if they'd just left us well enough alone. There'd've been a few speeches and everybody would've gone home. They started it, not us."

Once Gus got going it was hard to stop him but he eventually had to come up for air and when he did, we walked to a nearby store, before it closed, where I bought a few groceries and a pouch of tobacco for my friend, as he had run out.

Later in the evening, Gus said he was hungry again so he cooked some of the bacon and eggs I had bought and talked more while we ate. He spoke of the frustrations of being part of the strike committee and the roadblocks constantly placed in the way by the Committee of One Thousand. "They print somethin' in their newspapers and it's called the truth; we print somethin' in our newsletters and it's called propaganda and lies. They quote from the bible and it's righteous; we quote from the bible and it's seditious. Let me show you what I mean."

He rummaged beneath some papers on the table, found a bible and opened it to a bookmarked page. "This is Isaiah, Chapter Two. It's one of the things the strike leaders were arrested for. 'And they shall build houses and inhabit them, and they shall plant vineyards and eat the fruit of them. They shall not build and another inhabit, they shall not plant and another eat; for as the days of a tree are the days of my people, and mine elect shall long enjoy the work of their hands.' Pretty threatenin' stuff, eh?"

"When you know you're wrong, the truth can be more threatening than a pointed gun," I offered.

"But I'm not sure they know they're wrong. They probably think they're entitled to the bags of money they've got in the bank."

Gus fell silent and we sat for the longest time without a word, sipping gin, each knowing the direction the other was coming from. Finally, Gus spoke, "I'm beat, Sarge. I gotta turn in."

I went to use the toilet and when I returned Gus was unfolding a blanket on the four kitchen chairs that he had put side by side. He said, "You take the cot, Sarge. I'll sleep here."

But I wouldn't hear of it, not with his leg. "The hell you will. Since you insist on calling me Sarge, I'm pulling rank." It took some doing but I convinced him that he should sleep in his own bed.

I scarcely slept at all in the beginning of the night. Every time I moved, the chairs slid apart on the linoleum floor and the edges bit into me. My feet hung over the end and there was no getting comfortable. I finally had enough of the chairs and bedded down on the floor beside the stove. It wasn't any worse than the German labour camp and I could leave anytime I wanted to.

SEVENTEEN

The Rescue

SAM STEELE'S FUNERAL CORTÈGE was at 1:00 P.M. and Gus and I walked into town to see it. As it turned out, the funeral home into which we had dragged the Mountie was indeed where Steele's body was being kept. All the time the Mounties had been charging up and down Main Street, one of their best ever was lying in a coffin mere yards away. I wondered what old Sam would have thought of the fiasco. He was an officer who always obeyed higher authority, but he was also a man of integrity and I was certain that he would have done things differently, that he would have let the strikers have their way as long as they went about it quietly and did no harm, just as they had been doing. He would have thought that hard-working men deserved at least that much respect.

It was crowded around the funeral parlour, as it had been the day before, but the tenor of the crowd was vastly different.

Everybody knew of Sam Steele, and it would be difficult to find someone who didn't hold him in high regard. The crowd fell silent when the hearse containing his body came out of the lane beside the parlour. Tied by the reins behind it was a saddled, riderless black horse; Steele's service boots, freshly polished and gleaming, were reversed in the stirrups. Behind the horse came a troop of Mounties, bearing the force's colours. A multitude of cars carrying dignitaries constituted the rest of the long procession. Along the sidewalks, some of the same men who had thrown bricks and stones at the policemen less than 24 hours earlier now removed their hats in deference. All of Main Street was lined with people, families come to say goodbye and curious onlookers, as we followed the cortège to St. John's Cathedral where the service was held. We couldn't get near the place, and had to wait until long after the crowds went home to pay our respects at his grave in the cemetery beside the cathedral. I could think of nothing profound to say but I knew that Sam would have appreciated my being there.

In the aftermath of "Bloody Saturday," which was what the newspapers were calling the attack on the strikers, one man was dead—the man I had seen shot by the Mounties—and about a hundred were injured, both civilians and policemen. Another civilian would die from gangrene. Three days after Steele's funeral, the strike ended. The metalworkers, who had precipitated it, saw their work week reduced from 55 hours to 50 but they didn't receive a penny more in wages.

"It's just like the war was for a lot of us." Gus sounded as if he'd just eaten something that left a bad taste in his mouth. "You can't win for fucking losin'."

The telephone operators, who were a public service and

had walked out in sympathy, had to reapply for their jobs. The only way they could get them back was if they pledged never to strike again. The same thing happened to firemen and postal workers.

I spent another night with Gus and as I prepared to leave, he asked me to stay and get involved with union organizing. "Come on, Sarge," he pleaded. "You can't have gone through what we went through without wantin' to do something about what's goin' on in this country. We can't let those bastards beat us down. If we don't stand up for our rights, we might as well be back in that goddamned Boche coal mine. We gotta stick together!"

"I can't argue with that, Gus, but Winnipeg isn't the place for me right now. I've got too many things that need sorting out."

He nodded, clearly not convinced. "Sure. Just don't forget what happened here."

His words jolted my heart because they were almost exactly the same as the ones Liesel had said to me.

"I won't," I assured him. "You can count on it."

I WAS glad that I'd run into Gus. His fighting attitude was inspiring, and I boarded the train with a small flame of optimism burning in my gut. But as we sped across the prairies and deep into the mountains, the fire guttered low and soon burned out. The events in Winnipeg evaporated from my mind and the war was my only history; it was my parent, and I was its mutant offspring, unrelated to the rest of humanity. I felt useless and hopeless, and the weight of my depression began crushing me again.

In Vancouver, I bought a pint of whisky from the Sikh before making a beeline for the hotel. I half recognized that I was hungry but ignored the gnawing in my belly. I needed a drink and solitude more than anything. The same bored clerk sat behind the desk, as if he hadn't moved since I left. Before I could say anything to him, he held out an envelope along with my room key.

"This came for you," he said blandly.

"For me?" I asked, dumbly. It was the first piece of mail I'd received at the hotel. I glanced at the return address and saw that it was from the government.

I went upstairs. In my room I threw the valise and envelope on the bed, removed my jacket and put it there too. I retrieved the bottle and poured myself a stiff one, then added a tad more for good measure. I sat on the bed, took a long swallow and placed the glass on the nightstand. I picked up the envelope, turning it over a couple of times. Was it money or an apology? Did it matter? I tore it open. On official government station-ery, it was a letter that I had to read twice before it sank in. I would be remunerated for my two years in prison, although at reduced pay. All that was required of me was to confirm my address and a cheque would be mailed immediately.

I really didn't know what to think. In one sense it was a slap in the face, as if I hadn't contributed to the war effort enough to warrant a soldier's full pay. Even so, having stood on the threshold of the poorhouse just moments ago, I was now flush again. It was fortuitous, because I think I had subconsciously decided during the train ride from Winnipeg that Jack Strong was finished and that I would become Caleb Caine again. What happened to him would concern no one. When the money arrived I would pull my disappearing act and move to Victoria, where it all began. It seemed right.

I was aroused from my reverie by a knock on the door. It was another first. In the months that I had lived in that seedy room, no one had ever knocked on the door, not even the desk clerk. Maybe he had forgotten to tell me something. I went to the door and opened it. The clerk stood there, holding another envelope. He said, "This is for you too, Mr. Strong. It came yesterday and was accidentally placed in the box next to yours. My apologies."

He didn't look apologetic at all. I took the envelope from him, said thank you and sent him on his way by shutting the door in his face.

The return address was the Astor Hotel, here in Vancouver, although there was no stamp on it. My name was handwritten across the front of it and in my depressed state, I failed to recognize the writing at first. I thought it might be Maggie's and wondered if she was in town. If she was, I really didn't want to see her. Then it hit me. I stared at the envelope, afraid to open it, fearful of what it would say. I sat on the bed, placed the envelope next to me and had another drink. My heart thundered like a passing racehorse and my mind couldn't rest on a single thought. Finally, I picked up the envelope and ripped off the end.

Inside was a note, dated the day before, that read simply: "My Darling Jack, Thank God you are alive! You must come to me upon your return, I beg of you. I am at the Astor Hotel in Beatty Street, Room 305. I love you always. Ree."

My head nearly spun out of control with images from the last 20 years. I was befuddled and didn't know what to do. It had been easier to deny Ree when there were a continent and an ocean between us instead of mere blocks. I don't recall how long I stood there, holding the letter, my hand trembling, tears forming in my eyes. Then I put the letter down, went to the sink and washed my face and hands, rinsed my mouth and ran my damp hands through my hair. I did not look in the mirror for fear that what I saw there would make me run the other way. Donning my jacket, I went out the door without bothering to lock it. I rushed downstairs, past the curious desk clerk who had never seen me move so fast, and went as rapidly as I could, without falling flat on my face, to Beatty Street.

In the Astor's lobby, I ignored the elevator, found the stairs and took them two at a time. I misjudged a step once and stumbled, scuffing the heels of my hands as I pitched forward. On the third floor I paused for a few seconds to ease my hard breathing, then walked down the hallway and found room 305. Filled suddenly with apprehension, I felt like running away and hesitated before letting my knuckles fall on the door, a soft rap, followed by a louder, more urgent one. I could hear something creak, and muffled, hurried footsteps.

The door swung open. Ree stood there as startled as I was, our appearances having changed so much over the years, especially mine. Her once-chestnut hair, now streaked with grey, streamed onto her shoulders and she was thin and frail, but no less beautiful.

"Jack!" she cried. "Oh Jack!" Tears welled in her eyes and spilled over.

I could not speak as I gathered her into my arms.

EIGHTEEN

The Not-So-Roaring '20s

THERE WAS A KNOCK on the front door and it opened. "It's just me, Uncle Jack," said Peter Spencer as he saw me coming out of the bedroom where Ree was still getting dressed.

"Morning, Pete. Come on in and sit down. A bit early, aren't you?"

He held out a parcel. "Ma thought you might like some of her cinnamon bread with your breakfast."

With his dark hair and handsome features, Pete looked so much like his dad that I sometimes thought Jim had been resurrected. Named for his maternal grandfather, he was a strapping, intelligent lad of 18, who was good at most things he put his hand to. He could sing, too. Not as well as his dad—few people could—but he had a fine voice and was not as shy as Jim had been about using it. He was determined to attend university and become a lawyer but for now, he was my official broncobuster when I needed one. Ree and I were back in the business of harness-training horses and sometimes we'd get a couple of wild ones, so Pete would come over and show them that a saddle and rider on their backs wasn't really anything to go frog-hopping around the corral about. I was glad to have him since it's a younger man's game and my bones were getting too brittle for it.

Ree came out of the bedroom, greeted Pete and thanked him for the bread. I got a fire going in the stove and put on a pot of coffee while Ree cooked some oatmeal. Pete had already eaten but joined us at the breakfast table for a cup of coffee and a generous slice of cinnamon bread. Afterward, I brushed my teeth, scraped a razor over my lower face and went with Pete out to the corral in the warm June sun to get down to the business of breaking horses.

This was a world I had always loved and I was back in it, thanks to Maggie and Ree. Indeed, had Maggie not intervened while I was mired deep in a depression in Vancouver, I might have ended up dead in some back alley, just as my father had. She had got fed up with not hearing from me and decided to find out where I was. She went into Kamloops and from a public telephone began calling the hotels in Vancouver. She had started with the A's and found mine after only three tries. She then telegraphed Ree with the news that I was alive, telling her where I was living and how desperately I needed her whether I knew it or not.

Not surprisingly, Ree understood the situation far better than I had. She had been devastated by the news she had received about Davey and me, and at first blamed my patriotic pig-headedness for destroying her life. (She would not even accept the widow's pension offered her by the government, which ultimately was a blessing in disguise because we would have had to pay it back upon the discovery that I hadn't been killed in action after all.) But in England she had had many long talks with her parents, who staunchly believed that if a man did not stand and be counted in the face of an aggressor, then who would? Did a people simply lie down and let the tanks roll over them? Britain would always be grateful that the citizens of her colonies heeded her call for help to defeat the belligerent Germans. Over time, Ree came around to her parents' way of thinking, yet she had been more right than we both knew. When she read the telegram from Maggie, the words nearly caused her to faint. She wasted not a moment booking passage on a ship to Halifax.

Our reunion in Vancouver was tearful and that first night in bed we simply held each other until we fell asleep. We revelled in each other's company for several days, paying a visit to English Bay where we waved to Joe who was sitting on the raft shouting commands at the kids in the water around him. He did a massive cannonball in our honour and swam to shore to greet us. It was the first time I'd seen Joe's eyes wet when the cause wasn't seawater. The following day we took the train to Kamloops and went to see Maggie, who burst into tears when she came out of the house and saw us driving a rented buggy into the yard. The three of us hugged. "Dear God," she said, "I hope this means what I think it means!"

We bought The Little Karoo back from her. We didn't have the full price, but I worked some of it off by helping her and the boys operate the Bar JM. She was still running a small herd of about 300 head of cattle. Those that didn't stream out of the hills at the onset of winter had to be rounded up and they all had to be fed when the snow got too deep or crusty. Their calves needed branding in the spring and the two- and three-year-olds and the dry cows had to be cut out and driven across the Thompson River to the Lease, a property of 20,000 acres where the hills were rich with grass and the cattle could fatten up for the summer markets in Kamloops.

Riding onto The Little Karoo was emotional for both Ree and me. Weeds had grown thick around the house but other than that it looked none the worse for wear. The basic furniture was still there—Maggie, who had removed all the bedding and kitchenware, returned what she still had—and the place really needed only a good dusting and airing. Once primed, the water pump worked as well as it had the day Ree left. The only thing missing was Davey, and I doubted we'd ever get used to that. But now, two years had passed since our reunion, and life was pretty good.

EARLY IN July, Ree packed me a good "feed bag" of beef sandwiches, hardboiled eggs, carrots and apples; I saddled up Jennie Gee, a smart cutting horse, and rode over to the Bar JM to meet the Spencer boys. We were heading up to the Lease to pick out their fattest cows and drive them to market in Kamloops. Since cattle fatten up at different rates, we would repeat the trip in August and in September. The boys were ready when I arrived and Maggie was in the yard to see us off.

Riding with the boys was always a treat. They called me Uncle Jack, but I felt more like a father to them than an uncle. I was no replacement for Jim, but I know Maggie was happy for them that I was around. We laughed a lot and if the two youngest weren't joking around, they wanted to hear stories about my days of fighting Indians, driving a herd of cattle over the Dalton Trail, or the Boer War. (They avoided asking about the last war, probably at their mother's behest.)

Though we didn't really need four men on these trips—three was ample—it would have taken a cruel man to make either Jimmy or Tommy stay at home. Jimmy was 16 years old and Tommy was 14; both boys were high-spirited and, like Pete, were not afraid of hard work. And they enjoyed these trips, not only because they wanted to ride with me, but because it gave them the opportunity to visit Kamloops, to wander through stores that sold just about everything a person needed, and to marvel at what the locals took for granted: electricity and telephones. Like their older brother and parents, both Jimmy and Tommy had dark hair, and whereas Pete was the spitting image of his father, Jimmy had his mother's features and Tommy seemed to have the best of both. They were all going to be big men when they reached full maturity and Maggie was run ragged just trying to feed them.

It was hot as we rode along the old Brigade Trail and even hotter as we descended through the heavy sagebrush and into Kamloops. We bypassed the town—its amenities would be enjoyed only after our work was done—and crossed the old wooden bridge over the Thompson River where we stopped for lunch. Afterward, it was a short ride of about four miles to Lac Du Bois where the cattle were grazing.

The Lease was owned by one of the wealthier ranchers in the area, who had purchased the rights to it from the government because he needed more grazing land. He helped out the smaller ranchers in the area, like Maggie, by letting them fatten their cattle on it for a small fee that, according to Maggie, when you're selling your beef by the pound, was money well spent. Above the sagebrush, the country was a carpet of hilly grasslands, dotted with many small alkali lakes suitable for cattle and a few spring-fed lakes fit for humans. A cowboy, paid by the Lease's owner, camped at Lac Du Bois and kept his eye on the cattle, from the spring when they were brought in until the fall when last of them was gone.

At the lake we let the caretaker know that we were on the property and began rounding up our cattle. We had brought in 100 head in the spring and they had, as cattle usually do, split into smaller groups. Even so, they weren't difficult to find and in about an hour we had them gathered into a single herd. We then cut out the fattest ones—38 altogether—and trailed them to the stockyards in Kamloops. They brought 81¢ a pound, which was a good sum of money to deposit into Maggie's bank account, a task that I always loved doing for her.

As it was late, we liveried our horses and got rooms in a hotel for the night. After breakfast the following morning, I let the boys loose on the town while I tended to business. I trusted Pete to keep his younger brothers out of mischief but always breathed a sigh of relief when we met up and rode home. I didn't want to have to do any explaining to their mother.

IN SUCH a manner, my time was filled; in such ways I was becoming whole again. I still had the occasional dark day, but they were rare, and instead of a deep hole that at times seemed impossible to claw my way out of, they were mere dips in the road that were easily handled. Ree was always there when I needed her, and having the Spencer boys around frequently was a blessing.

Ree was helping train the horses now and they seemed to respond to her gentle manner. We sold animals to buyers as far away as Texas. The world beyond the ranch passed by mostly unheeded, except during trips to Kamloops and Vancouver when I caught up on the news. On one such trip to the coast in February of 1922, I learned that although I had arrived on time to meet a prospective buyer, I was too late for something vastly more important.

Joe Fortes had died. He had come down with pneumonia and was taken to Vancouver General Hospital where doctors were unable to save him. His funeral had been held the day before my arrival in the city and I only found out by seeing the headlines in the *Province*. According to the article, the funeral had been the biggest the city had ever witnessed. The church was packed to overflowing for the service and thousands lined the street as the funeral cortège made its way to Mountain View Cemetery. Joe would have been humbled by it all.

The news was a hard blow to the heart. Joe, like Sam Steele, was one of those people who seem indestructible, who give the impression that they might never die but if they do, it will somehow be in a blaze of glory. For Joe, that would have meant something like giving his life to save a drowning child. After I finished my business, I went to the cemetery to bid him farewell. I felt a bottomless sorrow as I stood over his grave, remembering. Among many things, I saw a young man with few resources, on his way to the prairies to fight Indians, finding $20 in his lunch bag along with a note that read: "Jack—just in case you run yourself short. Your friend Joe."

That was Joe. He could always be counted on to be there if you ran yourself short, and it didn't necessarily have to be money.

THAT WAS just one of several changes that came to our lives as the years slipped by. On rare occasions, a motorcar trundled by the ranch, and Ree, Maggie and I pitched in and bought a truck that the two ranches could share. Electricity and telephone poles came soon after, and then a radio for news and entertainment. Peter went off to the University of British Columbia to obtain a degree in commerce, after which he hoped to article with a law firm in Vancouver.

IN DECEMBER of 1924, I received a letter from the Board of Historic Sites and Monuments in New Westminster. Through other government sources, they had been able to track me down to inform me that as one of the two remaining survivors of the massacre at Frog Lake—the other was Bill Cameron—I was invited to the unveiling of a monument, on the grounds where it had occurred some four decades before. This would take place next June.

I looked forward to being reunited with Cameron. I had lost touch with him over the years and knowing Bill, he'd probably have many tales to tell. Ree stayed at home while I took the train to Kitscoty, a whistle stop in Alberta, where I met my old friend, holed up at Busby's Hotel. I had arrived a day early, hoping Bill might be there, and he was; he had been there for a couple of days, working on a book about the massacre. He was 63 years old but I recognized him straight away. He'd put on weight and was balding but the long nose, small mouth and wide ears were still evident.

It took him a moment to recognize me, however. I was several years his junior but had lost more to the passage of time than he had. We shook hands warmly.

"Hello, Bill!"

"Wild Jack Strong! Good to see you! *TÐnisi nikwa kÐitha?*"

I couldn't remember the last time anyone had called me Wild Jack, and it brought back a rush of memories, many of them unpleasant. And it had been years since I'd heard Cree but I remembered the simple greeting for "How are you?" I responded, "*NamwÐc nÐnitaw*" ("I am fine").

Bill would rather have walked while we renewed our acquaintance but the weather was foul, so Busby made us coffee, and Bill and I retired to my room to share stories.

I was surprised to hear that he had lived in Vancouver for many years. Or at least he had been based there. Despite having a family that included two children who, as he put it, "are now as old as I was at the time of the massacre," he could never settle down. "I wasn't cut from the strong cloth that makes a good husband and father. I was more interested in leaving than I was in staying, and my family and I simply drifted apart." He shrugged. "My friends have nicknamed me the 'Wandering Jew.' Not in the biblical sense, of course, but because I'm a nomad."

He'd spent some time as the editor of *Field & Stream* magazine, and wrote articles for it and other magazines that often took him away from home. In time, he ended up returning to the place that he loved most, the old Northwest—he had even visited Frog Lake—and was now mainly involved in some large real estate deals around Battleford, Saskatchewan.

When Bill asked about me, I gave him only sketchy details about the Boer War and my time in a German slave labour camp, and spoke mainly of Ree and the ranch. His ears perked up when I said that I trained horses, because he had taught me how to ride.

The next morning dawned warm and sunny, and one of the locals, hired to take us to Frog Lake, was keen to get an early start. Another car would wait for the train carrying the attending dignitaries, which was scheduled to arrive before noon. Bill and I climbed into a 1923 Model T Ford and the driver headed north. We had about 40 miles to cover and the roads were mostly rough, muddy tracks. We spent more time being bounced around than we did talking.

The site of the village was overgrown and scarcely discernible from the rest of the landscape. All that remained of the buildings was the stone basement of the Roman Catholic church where I had found four bodies, all friends of mine, burned so badly I couldn't identify them. I remembered vomiting then, and felt nauseated just thinking of it. In a small clearing there were eight grave markers and a large fieldstone cairn draped with a Union Jack.

Bill and I were greeted by the ceremony's organizers and we waited, along with a small crowd, for the officials to arrive. By mid-afternoon they still hadn't shown up so those in charge asked if we wouldn't mind giving a guided tour. Bill was eager for the task, so I let him do most of the talking. He pointed out where the buildings had once stood and where the bodies of our slaughtered friends had lain, and seemed in his element, as if he had done this sort of thing a hundred times before. He named the Indian participants—Wandering Spirit, Big Bear and a few others—and all of the white members of the community who were killed. He spoke of his capture by the Indians and my escape. He could remember even the smallest detail, but then he had made copious notes after the incident and was writing a book on the subject. He said it would be published next year and encouraged everyone to buy a copy. Its title would be *The War Trail of Big Bear*, which I didn't like at all because it was misleading, but I kept my thoughts to myself. It was his book.

By suppertime the VIPs still hadn't shown up and the crowd went home. Bill and I and our driver were put up at the home of one of the organizers.

The main party arrived early the next morning, car trouble having kept them in Kitscoty the previous day. A surprising number of people returned for the delayed ceremony, and Bill and I were asked to unveil the monument. After several speeches, we pulled the lanyards securing the flag and it fell to the ground. It was Bill's and my first glimpse of the bronze plaque fixed to the monument. It listed all the people whom "Rebel Indians Under Big Bear Massacred": "Fathers Fafard and Marchand, Tom Quinn, John Delaney, John Gowanlock, Bill Gilchrist, George Dill, Charles Gouin and John Williscroft." Below their names it read, "They took prisoners, Mrs. Theresa Delaney, Mrs. Theresa Gowanlock."

I saw Bill stiffen slightly and it was clear, perhaps only to me, what was wrong. The ceremony ended and he and I answered more questions until everyone left. Then we climbed into the Ford for the bumpy ride back to Kitscoty. It wasn't until then that Bill vented his feelings.

"Jesus Christ, Jack! They invited us all the way here because they knew of our role in the massacre, even paid our expenses, but never put our bloody names on the plaque! I guess I can understand why they might omit yours—you escaped—but I was taken prisoner too, along with the ladies!"

He was inconsolable and remained in a foul mood until we went our separate ways at Kitscoty, he to his nomadic lifestyle and me to the haven of Ree and The Little Karoo. I neither saw nor heard from him again, nor did I read his book. But I've always believed that omitting his name from the plaque was an inconsiderate, terrible oversight. As for my name, I didn't give a damn. I was thankful to have survived.

WE WERE kept busy during the closing years of the decade. The market for horses was still thriving and the Bar JM was now keeping about 400 head of cattle. By 1929, Jimmy and Tommy were pretty well running the show, although I still went with them on the drives to and from the Lease. We had long since paid Maggie in full but I never missed an opportunity to ride with boys. Pete had finished his degree at UBC and was articling with a large Vancouver law firm. I usually had lunch or supper with him during my trips to the coast, provided his bosses weren't overworking him at the time. Then in the fall of that year, the bottom seemed to drop out of the world.

NINETEEN

Depression

"GOOD GOD!" EXCLAIMED MAGGIE, after Jimmy, Tommy and I had returned from a trip to the Lease. "Forty cents a pound is outrageous! How's a rancher supposed to survive on that?"

That was 1932. By 1934, Maggie and the boys were selling their cattle for one cent a pound. Some ranchers in the region, who had kept on buying up property during the good years of the '20s, could no longer carry their 8½ per cent mortgages and were selling out or losing their land and homes to the banks. The Spencers were managing because to augment their income from cattle, they had begun to train horses. There was still a thriving market for them, and there were wild herds back in the hills that Jimmy and Tommy and I went after in winter when it was easier to chase them down. Once broken to harness or saddle, they went for good money, often to buyers south of the border.

While we hummed smoothly along, the muddy track in which the country's economy was mired was apparent right on our doorstep. Men on foot, carrying bedrolls, would stop by looking for work. Occasionally, we could offer them a day's work but rarely more than that. Mostly, we would simply feed them, put them up in the barn if they needed a place to stay for the night and send them on their way with a bag of food. In Kamloops, men were begging for handouts and waiting patiently in long "soup lines" for food.

When the Spencer boys and I made our first trip to the Lease during the late spring of 1934 and crossed the bridge over the Thompson, we were stunned at the size of the hobo "jungle" in among the trees. It seemed to grow exponentially from year to year, and now there must have been several hundred men in rough-built shacks or tents, some just sleeping on the ground. All were jobless and hungry for a decent meal. Every day, dozens of transient men jumped down from or climbed on freight trains, outside the town limits so the railroad police wouldn't catch them. Many of the townspeople were sympathetic and gave them food, but quite a few considered them good-for-nothings and possibly dangerous. One grocery store owner complained to me about the "bums" who came into his place looking for "something for nothing."

"Why in hell don't they go to the relief camps?" he grumbled. "That's what they're there for! Instead of hounding decent folks like me."

With that attitude, I figured he didn't need me in his store either, so I never patronized it again.

A necklace of relief camps was strung out across the country, meant to provide work for the unemployed—building roads and airports, among other things. The men in them would be clothed, fed and housed, and paid 20¢ a day for their labour. The camps were the brainchild of Major-General Andrew McNaughton who was disturbed by the awful waste of manpower in the country. How would such men be able to fight in the next war? Why would they even want to, when the government was treating them so shabbily? Worse, they were susceptible to communist propaganda, and to McNaughton and Prime Minister Richard B. Bennett, that could lead to only one thing: a revolution!

The camps seemed like a great idea and many unemployed men took advantage of them in the beginning. But they soon discovered that most were worse than the jungles. The camps were run by the military with its characteristic discipline. The housing usually consisted of tarpaper shacks that were freezing in winter and stifling in summer. The food was awful and most of the work was unfulfilling. Men dug holes that other men filled back in. Roads were built by pick and shovel while heavy equipment sat idle. Anyone contravening the rules of peace, order and good government could be imprisoned for 14 days in solitary confinement, solely at the camp commander's discretion. Being displaced from their home constituencies, the men were disenfranchised. Though the camps were generally in remote areas, no leisure time activities were provided, and there was nary a female to be seen. The men could come and go as they pleased, but they were blacklisted if they left and were unable to get relief anywhere but at another camp. And in reality, there was nowhere else for them to go, so the camps were considered by most to be no better than prisons, at best slave camps. All that for 20¢ a day, or $4 a month, when the working poor were earning $50.

The government, of course, would have everyone believe that the camps were Shangri Las and that the men in them were picking its pocket. But I began to learn about their true nature from the transients who came by our ranch, men who had suffered in them and left, because they felt begging was less degrading. It bothered me greatly. I remembered Steele's parting words to the regiment upon my return from South Africa: "Boys, never forget that you are Canadians and that Canada, as a country, has no superior in the wide world. Be proud of being Canadian!"

Well, I had been, and I had been loyal, too, heeding the call each time I thought my country needed me. But this wasn't the country I had fought for and I was finding less and less to be proud of, the relief camps being the worst example. How far removed were those camps from Germany forcing its war widows to work in the coal mines? Such thoughts led to Liesel and I wondered if she had survived the horrible treatment she had received at the hands of her callous government.

I thought about Gus, too, and the work he had been doing in Winnipeg during the general strike. Without a doubt, he would be involved in any organized protests in Winnipeg, like the many that were happening nationwide.

And what was I doing? Making a reasonably good living, far from the desperate struggle of a large number of good men in this country. It didn't sit well with me.

Ree knew something was weighing heavily on my mind. One morning over breakfast, she said, "For a man who works as hard as you do, you don't seem to be sleeping very well. Those dark rims you used to have under your eyes are returning."

I sighed. "It's the men we see coming by here looking for work or handouts, not to mention the ones in town. Some of them are willing to trade a day's work for a bowl of soup. A bowl of soup, for God's sake! It's enough to break your heart. Then there's that hobo jungle across the river I've told you about. If it gets any bigger it'll need a mayor and council, and streetcars to get around in it. Men shouldn't have to live like that, and they shouldn't have to live in those damned relief camps, either. Those things eat at me."

Ree reached over and covered my hand with hers. "I understand your feelings but you can't be held responsible for what's happening."

"But in a way I am, at least partially, because I'm not doing anything about it."

"You give them food, work and a roof over their head when you can. What more can you do?"

"I don't know, but I know all too well what it feels like to be considered less than human, no better than the slop we throw to the chickens. It's bad enough to treat a prisoner of war that way; it shouldn't be happening to good men in our own country."

"Then you'll have to think of a better way to help, won't you?"

IN LATE February I had to go to Vancouver on horse business, so I made a lunch date with Pete Spencer. Pete was 30 now and a practising labour lawyer. He had a small office on Dunsmuir Street and much of his work was on behalf of unions, negotiating contracts and representing individuals in employee-employer disputes. We stood in line at the White Lunch, a nearby cafeteria, bought soup, sandwiches and coffee, and found a table against the wall. Pete asked about Ree and the ranch, the Bar JM and his mum and brothers, whom he hadn't seen since Christmas. Then the conversation turned to the economic hole into which the country had fallen.

I told Pete about how the hobo jungle at Kamloops had grown, and the number of men who came by the ranch looking for work or food. "Going into town isn't enjoyable anymore. The look of despair on some of those men's faces is heart wrenching. But I don't suppose it's any better around here."

Pete, who also had great sympathy for the plight of the men, said, "Not by any means, and it was 10 times worse when the men in the relief camps walked away from them in December and came here. You've probably heard that they sent a delegation to Victoria. The premier kicked them around like a political football, and they came away with nothing. Most of the men have gone back to the camps. They had to. It was the only place they could go. I don't know if I've ever seen men more frustrated."

"It's a bloody shame," I exclaimed. "What's needed is for every man in those camps, right across the country, to march en masse on Ottawa and lay their demands on Bennett's desk. Give that tight-fisted SOB something to think about!"

"He's got a heart of iron, old R.B. He doesn't mind hoarding his millions of dollars while other men starve. And he's scared stiff of communists and revolution. They might take his wealth away from him."

"Then you'd think he'd come up with something better to help a penniless man than self-imprisonment for 20¢ a day."

"He's not going to do anything to rectify the problem unless someone makes him. And getting thousands of men to Ottawa is probably neither affordable nor logistically feasible."

"There must be a way."

Pete was quiet for a moment. "I've been doing some pro bono work for the Relief Camp Workers' Union. It aims to help the men in the camps get organized so that there'll be a chance of changing their lives for the better. I've sat in on a couple of their meetings and they're scrupulously democratic—everything's put to a vote. They've done pretty well so far, and they want to do what you suggested but no one's come up with any good ideas as to how to go about it. Anyway, one of their best men is Slim Evans. He's with the Workers' Unity League—it's an umbrella organization for many of the provincial unions, including the RCWU. Maybe you'd like to meet him. At least you'll see the calibre of leadership the union has."

We walked over to Evans's "office" on Cordova Street, which wasn't so much an office as it was a small meeting hall, with a desk and a couple of chairs. A handful of other men were there, all talking informally. Evans came over to greet us and Pete introduced me as his uncle, adding that I owned a horse ranch south of Kamloops.

Arthur Evans, or "Slim," as his friends called him, lived up to his name. He was tall, too, with reddish hair parted down the middle, blue eyes that saw more than they let on and a jaw as square as a child's building block. He walked with a limp and wore carpenter's overalls over a green shirt. Now in his early 40s, he'd been involved in union organizing for most of his adult life and had been in and out of jail a few times for it. During a miners' strike in Colorado, he'd received two bullets in his leg for his trouble, hence the limp. He had been a staunch supporter of the One Big Union, the movement that Liesel had talked about, which eventually fizzled out. He'd even been blacklisted by the United Mine Workers of America for using local funds to feed striking mine workers in Alberta when he was supposed to send the money to head office. Now he worked with the WUL and, according to Pete, was a rebel down to the tips of his leather boots.

We shook hands and the three of us traded small talk for a bit until the conversation settled on the union and its efforts. I repeated what I had said to Pete, about marching on Ottawa, and Evans listened. His response was polite and soft-spoken. "You're right. And as Pete knows, we've given it some serious thought. So far we've come up with nothing that'll work, or even how to handle the incredible amount of organizing it would involve. That would be a feat in and of itself."

"Without a doubt, but Pete tells me that organizing is what you do best. There's got to be a way."

Evans's mouth broke ever so slightly into something that passed for a smile. "If you think of anything, let me know. We may not be open to bullying by the government, but we're always open to suggestions."

"If I can help, I will."

He was smart enough to know that as a horse rancher, I probably wasn't starving. If he saw in me the possibility of a generous donor to the cause, he gave no hint of it, nor did he ask for anything. I wondered, briefly, if he thought I might be an informer because I sensed that he was a bit cautious and guarded in what he said. And maybe the question he asked next was a way of feeling me out in that regard.

"What's your stake in it, Jack?"

I didn't have to think about it. "A good night's sleep and keeping a promise I made to someone in a German slave labour camp where I spent two years during the war. I learned then what it's like to live on a bowl of soup a day and be treated like something lower than dirt."

Evans's nod was almost imperceptible but I sensed a slight shift in his attitude toward me, that I had gone from possible informer to possible donor. He said, "Tell you what. Our first goal is to get the camp workers on board with the union. We're getting there, but there's still a lot of work to do. We've divided the camps into five divisions, and delegates from those divisions, along with me, are meeting in Kamloops on March 10 to discuss issues of concern and to plan a strike some time in April. Why don't you come along and see for yourself what we're doing? I'll be there so you won't need a card to get in."

"I'd like that. I'll be there, barring any unforeseen events."

He told me where the meeting was and that it would start at 10:00 A.M. sharp and probably last two days. We said our goodbyes and I walked with Pete back to his office. "Attending that meeting probably won't do anything to enhance your reputation with some of the locals in Kamloops," he said. "Slim and a few of the others in the union are card-carrying communists, and even though the majority of the members aren't, the government and the newspapers paint them with the same red brush. Maybe I should have told you beforehand."

I shrugged. "Communist or not, they're just hungry men who want the dignity of decent, paying work. And even if they are, who could blame them? Sometimes a man has to go to extremes to get people to sit up and listen to him."

After I left Pete, I went to my bank in town and had a draft for $100 made out to the RCWU. I left it in the hands of Pete's secretary, saying that he'd know what to do with it.

TWENTY

Tin Cans and Snake Parades

I DROVE INTO KAMLOOPS early on March 10, with Ree's blessing and a reminder to stay safe. The Relief Camp Workers' Union meeting was in an empty store on Victoria Street and the place was packed by the time I arrived. Evans was already sitting at the head table, but he saw me and waved to the man at the door that it was okay to let me in. When the proceedings got under way, they were orderly and run according to strict parliamentary procedure. Much of the early discussion centred on some of the problems of getting the camps organized and problems within the camps themselves. In Revelstoke, the government-paid storekeeper had stolen $200 and as a result, the men's rations had been reduced; in Princeton, camp directors were opening the workers' mail, trying to sniff out and thwart any attempts to get organized, and so on. That went on for the rest of the day.

The following morning, after the meeting was brought to order, Evans stood up to speak. He wasn't the soft-spoken man I'd met in Vancouver. His words were fiery and meant to incite passion in the men.

"I owe allegiance to this country but not to the parasites who own it. I want to see it become a beautiful place for everybody to live in, not just for the people who close up the mills and factories and have elevators stuffed to overflowing with food!"

He continued in that vein for several minutes, rousing the men, and finished by calling for a general strike in the camps on April 4. "That's right after payday, so the men will have some money in Vancouver. And even if some of the workers aren't members, my guess is that they'll follow the lead of those who are."

There wasn't a dissenter in the place.

The meeting then dealt with the logistics of the strike and ended with the official adoption of the demands that had been taken to Victoria in December: that unskilled camp workers be paid a minimum of 50¢ an hour and skilled workers union rates; that they be covered by workers' compensation and that first aid facilities in the camps be improved; that the military system of blacklisting workers from further relief should they leave the camps be abolished; that workers be represented in the camps by democratically elected delegates; that a program of unemployment insurance be established; that camp workers be given the right to vote regardless of their location; that all anti-vagrancy laws be abolished.

The meeting was adjourned and the delegates, happy to have established a goal, rallied in the street outside. I had a brief moment with Evans before I drove home.

"What do you think?" he asked.

"I like what I heard. There wasn't anything you've asked for that isn't deserved and that isn't long overdue."

"Did we inspire any ideas?"

I grinned. "Not yet, but I'm still thinking about it."

THE RANCH kept me busy over the next while. It was time for branding, cutting and moving Maggie's sellable stock over to the Lease. Nine dollars for a cow was still better than nothing.

The camp workers' strike went off as planned. On April 4, over a thousand men streamed into Vancouver, arriving there from as far away as Revelstoke by their usual mode of transportation: on top of boxcars.

And that's what triggered the idea.

I ran it by Ree. She shook her head in disbelief. "Having crossed the country in the relative comfort of a sleeper car, I can't imagine anyone making the trip like that. But they surely are desperate men. Maybe you should talk to Pete."

But I held off. The idea seemed preposterous and needed more thought. While it was definitely affordable, the logistics of pulling off such a feat could prove to be Evans's worst nightmare. But I did call Pete, because I wanted a first-hand account of what was happening in Vancouver.

"It's incredible," he told me. "There are things going on here that might not generate change but ought to at least make the history books."

He went on to say that the day before, at every major intersection, not only downtown but all the way to New Westminster, striking relief camp workers had stood with tin cans, collecting money so that they could eat and keep the strike going. They worked in four-hour shifts and there were always men standing by to replace those with the cans should they be arrested. Some were, but in no time the jails were so full that it became too expensive to keep them there and authorities were forced to let them go. Over $5,000 had gone into union coffers by the end of the day. At a cost of about $500 a day to feed the strikers, that meant they could continue for another 10 days.

"And there always seems to be a parade of some sort going on to garner public support. They've even got our mayor yammering at the feds to do something about the situation!"

I rang off, telling Pete that I would be down in May.

Later in April, the strike went to a level that Evans and his colleagues had never wanted and had even feared. All of the strikers lined up four abreast on Hastings Street. They linked arms and weaved their way from side to side along the street, in a tactical "snake parade" that would make an attack by the police difficult. They moved west, then turned south onto Granville and snaked their way toward the Hotel Vancouver at Georgia and Burrard. Storekeepers along the route hastily closed and locked their doors. On the corner of Georgia and Granville, dozens of men broke off from the parade and entered the Hudson's Bay store, which hadn't locked its doors. They snake-paraded through the aisles until the police came, and the men responded by smashing glass counters and overturning them. Then they smashed the police, crippling one for life and breaking the skulls of three others. Two strikers were arrested and the rest retreated outside to join the main parade at Victory Square.

The mayor had a temporary office across the street; 12 strikers formed a delegation and visited him, demanding that the city give them food and shelter. He would have none of it and sent them packing. Outside his office, the police arrested them for vagrancy and a van took all but one, who happened to have money in his pockets, to jail. Then the mayor came into the street and read the same words to the crowd that I had heard six years before in Winnipeg: the Riot Act.

The strikers withdrew to plan for another day, while the mayor went to the radio station and told the public that the strikers' goal was to "change our system of government into one of communist authority and soviet power."

Few people were fooled by the rhetoric.

A few weeks later, on May 18, while two divisions of strikers marched in the streets as a diversion, a third division occupied the Vancouver Public Library. Again, their goal was to obtain food and shelter. Once the library was under control, the marchers headed for the building and gathered in front of it. A banner was hoisted that read, "When do we eat?" The White Lunch, the cafeteria where Pete and I usually ate, sent milk cans of coffee to the occupiers, and onlookers sent in cigarettes and candy. The mayor, who was at the Vancouver Yacht Club, conceded to the strikers' demands and gave them $1,800 for food and shelter. It wasn't much, but it would see them through the weekend.

REE WAS worried when I left for Vancouver near the end of May. "More people are bound to get hurt there soon," she warned. "It's only a matter of time. Promise me you won't be among them."

I pulled her into my arms. "I wouldn't admit to being too old for anything—except rough stuff. So don't worry. I'll stay as far away from it as I can."

After completing my business, I met Pete at the White Lunch. He was worried, too; I could hear it in his voice when he spoke. "I don't know what Evans is going to do. The union's all but broke and the public aren't so quick to back the men anymore. If he doesn't come up with something, there's bound to be violence, maybe even a bloodbath."

"I have an idea," I said. "It may be outrageous, but it's got to be better than nothing. How did those men get to Vancouver? On top of boxcars! They do it all the time and they're good at it. Why can't they go to Ottawa that way? After all, a lot of them came from the east in the first place. And they could pick up others along the way. There could be thousands of men involved by the time they reached Ottawa. And I doubt that the CPR would stop the trains—it's in their best interests to keep them running—and there probably isn't a railway cop in the country who'd be willing to take on that many men!"

A look of excitement transformed Pete's face. "That might work, and it would be much easier to organize now that most of the workers are here. It could be just a matter of convincing them that they could do it. At the very least, the union membership should have the opportunity to say yea or nay to it. There's a meeting tonight at the Avenue Theatre, so why don't we go? You can present your idea, because as far as I know, no one's come up with anything better."

The theatre was packed, with close to a thousand strikers. They were mostly ragged young men in their early 20s, but I saw a few older men, some probably veterans of the war like me. As I looked at the crowd from the back of the theatre, a wave of compassion washed over me. The majority of these men had come to the west coast well before the camps were set up, for no other reason than to avoid the frozen, harsh winters that gripped the rest of the land. Here, it rained often, but at least frostbite was far down the list of problems a man had to worry about. Yet the change in climate had not altered some things: they still had to cast their dignity to the wind, either by staying in the camps, holding their hands out for scraps of food or standing in long queues at soup kitchens. When they went door to door, some people fed them while others politely refused them. And some slammed the door in their faces.

The first thing Evans did was put forward a motion to continue the strike. It passed with a two-thirds majority. He outlined the problems facing the strikers and called for more militant action. A man stood and said, "That won't work. People will just get hurt. We need to negotiate directly with the feds and the only way we can do that is to go to Ottawa. All of us."

Someone shouted, "And how do you propose we do that?"

When the man shrugged, I stood up. Every face turned to me, an old man among youngsters.

"The floor recognizes Comrade Jack Strong, a union supporter." Evans paused for a heartbeat. "And a man with a good idea, I hope."

I laid it out, just as I had for Pete, and it was greeted at first by total silence. Then the place erupted in noisy support until Evans had to call for order.

The On-to-Ottawa Trek was born and it would leave in four days.

Later, Evans sought me out. "That idea was a long time coming, but it was worth the wait, I think. I've never seen the men so enthusiastic. By the way, we'll need leaders on the trek and I'm wondering if you're interested? Since it'll need all the discipline of a military operation, you'd be perfect for the job. You also have nothing to gain from it other than a clear conscience."

Oh, the memories that went stampeding through my mind at that moment, in particular Liesel, that angel of mercy in the guise of a miner in filthy clothes and coal dust who thought that I would forget her. I hadn't, not for a moment, and I hadn't forgotten the mines either. I would join the trek for her and I would join it for Gus. I would join it for all of the men here and their shattered lives. It seemed to me a battle worth fighting and a debt long overdue. "I told you I would help if I could."

"Then make sure you carry some money with you at all times. That way you can't be arrested for vagrancy."

I phoned Ree afterward, guessing that she would be opposed to my involvement in the trek, just as she had been opposed to my going off to war. She was, but only mildly. "I personally think it's time for someone else to fight the wars, Jack, but I know you have to do this. So don't worry about the ranch. Jimmy and Tommy will be around and so will Maggie if I need her. You just take care of yourself and come home in good health."

"It's been a long time since I told you I love you, hasn't it?"

"It was yesterday, before you left."

"See what I mean? I love you."

"I love you, too, Jack. And really, I couldn't be more proud."

I joined the trekkers on Sunday, June 2, at the picnic ground near the murky waters of Lost Lagoon in Stanley Park. A warm sun and a blue sky elevated spirits that were already high. We feasted on a picnic dinner that some of the townsfolk had provided out of the sympathy and kindness in their hearts. Slim Evans made a speech. Everyone was in good humour and a blind man could have told that the men felt something stirring in their breasts that they hadn't felt for a long time— power: the power of a united front that would right a world turned on its head. After dinner, we fell into the three divisions that Evans and other union leaders had formed, just like soldiers. I led the third. On a signal, we stepped out, nearly a thousand strong, 12 abreast, arms linked, and marched from the park in the dusk and along Coal Harbour, singing:

Hold the fort for we are coming,
Union Hearts be strong,
Side by side, we battle onward,
Victory will come!

That many men, connected both physically and spiritually, and singing lustily, created a heady elixir and I expect that few thought we would not ultimately prevail.

We passed the huge, round oil-storage tanks that fronted the harbour and raised our voices even louder as we neared the towering Marine Building, now a symbol of wealth and a system that had failed to include everyone. I was nearly hoarse by the time we reached the Canadian Pacific Railway yards below Gore Street and stood beside the long line of boxcars. We climbed the steel ladders to the roofs, 24 men to a car, with such precision it was as if we had rehearsed it a dozen times. We positioned ourselves shoulder to shoulder, seated, along the narrow catwalks than ran the length of each car. The whistle blew and the train jerked as it inched from the yard. Beside the tracks and on the rooftops of drab buildings, thousands of onlookers cheered and waved goodbye. We waved back and began to sing "Hold the Fort" again. It made my scalp prickle. We were on our way to change minds, if not the country, and the men were more optimistic than they'd been in years.

It was fully dark by the time the train departed from the Vancouver waterfront. I had left this place many times, the first more than 50 years before, when I was still a kid as green as fresh-cut timber. This rail line had not even existed then, nor had Vancouver, for that matter. And the country had lain stretched out before me like a love-starved woman, as eager to embrace me as I had been to embrace her. The memories were so vivid, it might have happened only yesterday.

The boxcars rattled and swayed, the couplings groaned, and the wheels screeched so that conversation below a yell was nigh impossible. As the train rolled along the industrial edge of Burrard Inlet and the North Shore mountains became towering black shapes against the stars, an increase in speed bent the smoke from the engine's stack and sent it billowing rearward, engulfing the men on the lead cars. It was funny none of us had thought of such an obvious thing, and those without handkerchiefs had to pull their jackets over their faces for protection. But ultimately it didn't really matter. We were on our way and that engine stack could blow pure hell and it wouldn't stop us.

TWENTY-ONE

Eastbound Train

I WAS GRATEFUL THAT we went through the Fraser Canyon under cover of night. As it was, there was enough light to see the white, foaming rapids far below, to have some sense of the height above the river and the danger every time the train lurched around a bend. We clung to each other and to the catwalk for fear of being thrown into the maelstrom. For men like me, who had never ridden on top of a boxcar, it was a terrifying experience. But I had resolved that I would see this thing through, regardless of the consequences. There are some principles worth dying for.

We had expected food to be awaiting us in Kamloops but there was none, other than a box of sandwiches that Ree and Maggie brought. Evans had promised a meal, and thus bore the brunt of the grumbling and complaining. He said it was a failure of communication and vowed that it would not happen again.

"This was unfortunate," he said. "The people haven't yet realized the possibility of our movement but they will very quickly, and then our worst difficulties will be over. Now, who's for continuing the trek and who's for leaving?"

Evans mesmerized people with his tongue; he was the kind of man other men listened to, and the kind of man they did not want to let down. No one quit. Instead, many went door to door through the town, begging for food and money. A man wouldn't get fat on what was offered but it was better than going hungry. Content for the time being, we sought rest beneath the trees in a riverside park. I didn't sleep that night. I could not stop the sensation of motion from the train.

Golden was a slice of heaven in a beautiful mountain valley. I could smell the food before we even got down from the train and it set my belly rumbling. In a park close by, there were bathtubs and wash boilers brimming with lamb stew, simmering over open fires. Dumplings the size of watermelons floated on top and freshly baked loaves of bread covered the tops of several trestle tables. A couple of dozen women from the town and outlying communities were overseeing the cooking, led by an elderly lady with grey hair and glasses, and a smile larger than the size of her mouth.

"Come and get it, boys," she called. "Fill your bellies. It's all for you!"

I remembered that Sam Steele would always ensure that his men were fed first, before he ate, so I hung back and let the others go ahead of me. They got the stew and dumplings, got the bread and filled their bellies, certain that they were in the presence of saints and satisfied that Slim Evans was a man true to his word.

Then Evans was gone, needed in Vancouver for matters apparently more important than the trek. I sensed an uneasiness among the men as a dour Scot named George Black tried to fill the gaping hole the organizer had left. Yet I had experienced similar feelings before myself and recognized that they were a normal reaction to the loss of a general. As leaders, generals created the state of mind necessary for forward movement. Evans's departure interfered with that motion, in the same way a sudden headwind slows the speed of a boat. But I knew Black to be a capable man and that given the necessary co-operation, he would do the job. I told that to the men in my division, and told them, too, that it was as much up to them as it was to Black to make this thing work. They understood. And with their hunger and uneasiness appeased, I led them back to the train and we were carried away among the great mountains.

Old men should not be doing this, I thought. I was no stranger to extreme discomfort but riding on top of a boxcar was as bad as anything I'd ever experienced before. I was as stiff as the catwalk we sat on but did not want to show the younger men that I might not be fit for the task, did not want them to know I was hurting. Whenever I had to climb down I tried to do it fluidly, which required great effort on my part. When I stood, it was like taking the bend out of an iron pipe.

After Golden came the Spiral Tunnels, two smoky hellholes that almost did me in. They weren't as long as the five-mile Connaught Tunnel through the Selkirks, but the steep gradient slowed the train to a crawl and the tunnels winding back on themselves made them giant smoke traps. The men who had jars of drinking water soaked their handkerchiefs and covered their faces so that they would not choke on the smoke. Those without water pissed on their handkerchiefs. I was one of them. Even so, a young man in one of the other divisions nearly succumbed. Red Cross workers accompanying us managed to revive him.

The train swept through the foothills, with Calgary visible down the line. I remembered that view from many years before, when a nondescript town awaited me rather than a city; nevertheless the sight of the prairies thrilled me, as it always had. We debarked from the train in the west end, formed into lines and marched to the city's centre. People stood on rooftops and cheered.

We stayed in Calgary over a weekend, because a man can only spend so many days in a row on top of a boxcar before he needs a good break. The atmosphere in the city was party-like. Bands played and we paraded and picnicked courtesy of some of the more generous Calgarians.

We were on the train by 7:00 sharp on Monday morning, boarding with the same military precision we had at the beginning. A massive crowd came to see us off—we were pulling the citizens of the country over to our side—and a group of women brought 2,000 sandwiches and a side of beef to tide us over until our next stop. Other women offered to accompany us on our journey to provide female companionship. Most of the men could only speculate on what that meant, but this was no place for women and we refused the offer. No one declined the offer of another 300 men though, relief camp strikers from the Edmonton area who wanted to join the trek. Another man had walked nearly 50 miles to be part of it. They formed a separate division, and the CPR added seven boxcars and three gondola cars—freight cars with low sides and no top—to the train. The impression given by the railway company was that it was trying to be co-operative, but I believed I knew that the underlying reason was no different from why we had received co-operation in Vancouver: the authorities merely wanted us out of town.

The train jerked ahead, its whistle evoking cheers from the throngs of well-wishers who had come to see us off, and rolled out of the city toward the east where huge storm clouds were gathering on the horizon. We sped into the night through a cold, driving rain that would have been bad enough even without the forward motion of the train. It was like being hit by steel pellets that burst into liquid on impact. My mackinaw was soaked right through, as were my pants and cap. The only consolation was that the rest of the men were in a similar condition, although those riding in the extra gondola cars were more out of the wind and slightly better off. I could only pull my jacket tighter, draw in toward my companions for the minimal warmth they provided and try not to think that below me, protected from the miserable weather, were cattle and horses.

In Medicine Hat, the mayor offered us $200 not to stop in his town. We declined the offer. We would march through these streets just as we had the others, garnering support for the trek. We had become a travelling show that people were eager to see, and you could not put a dollar value on something like that.

Boiled coffee awaited us in the athletic park when we arrived, vats of it, and I thought that I might need several gallons just to restore some warmth to my bones. We built bonfires and gathered around them to dry out. Despite the miserable ride, it was behind us now and everyone was in high spirits, full of talk. We had survived the mountains and some nasty prairie weather, and there was a heady feeling of pride and accomplishment that was infectious. Lesser men, we knew, would have packed it in by now. Indeed, a few had.

The fire crackled and sparked with flames as tall as a man. I had turned from them to let the heat sear my backside when I glanced over at the trees lining the edge of the park and saw an apparition appear out of the twilight, limping toward the fire. It was Evans. Amid the greetings from everyone, he came and stood beside me for the warmth cast by the flames.

"How are you holding up, Jack?"

I was the oldest man on the trek and since riding on top of boxcars was not a common pastime for most sexagenarians, he was concerned.

"I'm holding up. No better or worse than the rest of the men."

It was a lie, of course, and Evans probably knew it, but all he said was, "Your presence makes a difference, Jack. I'm especially glad you came."

"Wouldn't have missed it for the world," I said, and hoped I sounded convincing.

MORE SPEECHES beneath granite skies at Swift Current, words necessary to inspire the men and keep them determined to see this thing through. I did not need the stoking but I understood that many of them could not continue without it. It made me think of other times and other places, of men like

Big Bear, Sam Steele and General Buller, who knew how to get that extra mile out of a man, knew how to make him care about things greater than himself.

A member of the local unemployed association spoke first, from the deck of a flatbed truck, and condemned the Bennett government for its lack of compassion. Then Evans took the bullhorn and talked at length about the importance of solidarity. He complimented the men for maintaining the discipline with which they had begun the trek 10 days before in Stanley Park. If they were going to finish the job they'd come to do, they would need discipline as much as they needed food. "I have said this before," he told them and paused for a moment, looking at a handful of reporters standing off to the side with pencils poised over notebooks, "but I will say it again for the benefit of the press. The men riding these trains are not communists, nor is this trek controlled by communists. I would not deny that I am a communist and that communists support the trek but so would anyone with any sense of compassion and justice. The common people seem to understand this better than the bureaucrats in Ottawa, for they are the trek's greatest supporters. Ottawa continues to ignore a simple demand that can be summed up in three words, 'work and wages.' It's all we've ever asked for; it's all we've ever wanted. Work and wages!"

Cheers arose from the men in a deafening roar. Evans's words had cemented their convictions and common bond even more firmly. Nothing but an army could stop them now!

Issued meal tickets, compliments of the province and town, we ate in shifts in Swift Current's few restaurants. Once again, the main course was stew but it was impossible to grow tired of it when it was free and meals were so hard to come by. Afterward, we formed up and marched to the train singing the song that had become our anthem: "*Hold the fort for we are coming . . .*"

As we swarmed over the train like ants, cattle mooed and horses neighed from within, as if affronted by our return. *Why not*, I thought, as I climbed the ladder myself. First-class passengers had always looked down their noses at those riding in economy. That's just how the world worked.

In Moose Jaw, crowds stood on overpasses spanning the railway tracks, shielding their eyes from the setting sun, cheering our arrival. People wanted to see us and to tell others that they had seen us. Moreover, we wanted to be seen, for it validated our action. It was as if we had achieved celebrity status by dint of our misery. Whatever the case, the plan was to stay in Moose Jaw long enough to determine if there was substance to the rumours that the government would stop us in Regina. If so, we would need to decide what to do about it.

We marched to a nearby park and bedded down for the night on the grass, the single meal we'd had earlier in the day a distant memory. I figured my stomach must have shrunk to the size of a thimble because I wasn't often hungry, and when I ate, it didn't take long for me to feel full. It was both the upside and downside of being without three meals a day. I felt as thin as the slats in the cattle car, but then I'd pretty much felt that way since the war.

During the night, it began to rain. Some men were able to find shelter underneath the bleachers but there wasn't room for everybody. I, along with the other division leaders, made sure everyone had a turn out of the rain while the rest huddled beneath soaked blankets and tried to keep warm. By morning, everyone was drenched, cold and miserable. Nevertheless, morale remained high as I led my division to the restaurants on Main Street. There was a kind of sweetness in the fact that Mounties, in aprons, minus their tunics and guns, served us the obligatory stew. I thought about cornering one of them with my stories of how I had fought with Sam Steele on these very prairies, and in South Africa, but it was so long ago, and these men were so young, they probably wouldn't care.

We spent the next several hours trying to keep out of the pouring rain, then returned to the park in the afternoon where the size of the crowd that had gathered to hear the trek leaders speak had doubled.

It was true. The government did indeed have plans to stop us in Regina and they would do it by not allowing us on the trains. Boos and catcalls greeted the announcement. One of the speakers shouted angrily, "We'll bloody well carry on with the trek if we have to do it in our stockinged feet!"

The men roared their approval.

Evans, who had taken the bus to Regina and returned with the unwelcome confirmation of the news, urged the men to stay united, that this was a class struggle and only solidarity and discipline would see us through. "There could be trouble ahead in Regina. But I can tell you this much: if we're going to break those pot-bellied political heelers and financial parasites, we're going to need all the discipline we can muster. Unless we maintain order, the public won't sympathize with us and the cause will be jeopardized. If this does not sit well with any of you, I would ask that you leave right now."

No one left.

THE EARLY morning wind was cold, driving the persistent rain into my back as I turned from it. But even with the rain, the prairie here was so flat I could see the buildings of Regina off in the distance. The train lurched as it began to slow down, and came to a halt at a crossing some distance from the station. We descended from the car, formed and marched four abreast to the livestock building on the exhibition grounds. The smell of hay filled our nostrils as we entered and some of the men mooed in jest while others neighed. This was our temporary home and as it was for animals, there was considerable irony in it. It was at least out of the rain and warm.

The powers that be had created a barricade, just as we assumed they would. Stories circulated that the CPR had allowed us on the trains out on the coast only because the company feared we would precipitate a strike among its own workers, and that the trek had been allowed to go as far as Regina for one reason: it was the training depot for the RCMP, which meant the force was represented there in large numbers. As far as the officials were concerned, we would be moving neither east nor west out of the city.

Prime Minister Bennett had invited a delegation to Ottawa, expenses paid, to discuss the situation. No one liked the idea and thought our leaders would receive only lip service from the government. But to refuse the invitation would be to negate all the work that had gone before, in building good relations with the public.

With the delegation, led by Evans, gone, I helped keep the men busy and out of trouble. We ate at restaurants, compliments of the provincial government, and attended rallies as well as meetings. We watched softball games at the stadium on the fair grounds and enjoyed picnics put on by the citizens of Regina, biding our time, waiting for word of how the delegation was faring with Bennett.

While we waited, another 300 men arrived from a camp up north to join the trek. Word came from Winnipeg that thousands there were waiting to join. Though we had not kept in touch, I had a hunch that Gus Moretti was somehow involved in organizing it.

TWENTY-TWO

A Matter of Duty

"WHAT A FARCE!" EXCLAIMED Evans upon his return from Ottawa. "Bennett is an arrogant man. He can't seem to get it through his thick skull that we want nothing more than jobs and fair wages. To him we're revolutionaries and communists out to bring the country to its knees, and he seems to have no intention of ending his camp program. At one point, he even said to me, 'I remember when you embezzled the funds from your union and were sent to the penitentiary.' What did that have to do with why we were there? I called him a liar and told him the men knew I used that money to feed themselves and their families, rather than line the pockets of a bunch of overfed union agents. I tell you, that man isn't fit to be prime minister of a Hottentot village!"

"Damned straight," interjected another delegate. "He was afraid of us, too. There was at least one cop hiding behind the window drapes in his office—I saw his boots!"

The result was that the trekkers could travel no farther by train, and the police had set up roadblocks to restrict movement east by any other means. A few men tried and were arrested for their trouble. It seemed obvious that Bennett was afraid of what would happen if the trekkers reached Winnipeg and joined the multitude there. He believed that he would have a full-blown revolution on his hands, and as far as I was concerned, he deserved nothing less for his monstrous indifference.

Plans, devised by both the federal and the provincial governments, were under way to expand an existing camp near Lumsden, northwest of Regina, and to escort the men there like prisoners. Very few of the trekkers, who numbered well over a thousand now, were in favour of that option.

"The best we can do at this point," Evans insisted, "is to get Bennett and his henchmen to allow us to disperse on our own, and maybe negotiate a means of getting us all back to the coast or to our homes."

For that, the trekkers would need support from the local citizenry, so a rally was planned for the approaching holiday weekend, at 8:00 P.M. on Dominion Day. Meanwhile, we would try to get as much of our case as possible into the newspapers and onto the radio.

ON THE evening of the rally, the majority of the men stayed behind to watch a baseball game rather than attend, which was a good thing in my opinion. Tempers could flare and people could get hurt. But I formed up those who wanted to go—about 300 in total—and we marched over to Market Square, an empty, unpaved city block that had served as a farmers' market in better times. It was a warm, pleasant evening. Young couples and families strolled by, and it struck me as odd how life could appear so civilized for many of the people in the towns we had passed through. Yet it was merely an illusion. A truly civilized country would not force its most needy to the top of boxcars to bring attention to their plight. A truly civilized country would not have backed them into a corner in the first place. Yet that was the thing about governments, wasn't it? They would use you shamelessly when they needed you to fight their wars and cast you aside like jetsam when they didn't.

By the time we arrived in the square, a large crowd of about 1,500 had already gathered, among them families with baby carriages. A flatbed truck equipped with microphones and loudspeakers served as the speakers' platform. Precisely at 8:00, Evans and the other speakers climbed onto the truck to begin. The scene seemed as normal as such scenes can be.

But there were things we did not know, that we wouldn't discover until later.

Over on the southeast corner of the square, the city's chief constable stood with warrants for the arrest of Evans and the other trek organizers. The chief was waiting for a team of plainclothes RCMP officers whose job it was to rush the platform and get into place so that Evans and the others on the truck couldn't escape. The team itself was waiting for three moving vans, each filled with a troop of RCMP constables, to take their places on the north, west and east sides of the square. A block south of the square, a fourth troop of RCMP barricaded the only other possible escape route. In the city garage, on the south side of the square, a flying column of 29 uniformed city policemen had formed into ranks of four. They wore "bobby" helmets, in the fashion of British policemen, and carried sawed-off Woolworth baseball bats that weighed nearly a pound, euphemistically referred to as "batons."

I watched and listened as George Black made introductions and explained the purpose of the meeting. Evans was sitting on a chair, looking around, and I could tell that he sensed something was up when the three vans pulled in. Suddenly a shrill police whistle pierced the air. The doors of the city garage flew open and there were cries of "Police! Police!" just as the flying column emerged, moving swiftly, its members holding their batons vertically at their waists. Evans, guessing that he was about to be arrested, jumped to the ground and straight into the arms of some plainclothes officers. The crowd panicked at the sudden show of force and moved hastily away from the truck. Many people bolted from the square before the rear doors of the vans burst open and the Mounties poured out to form a line around the square's three remaining sides. Other Mounties rode in on horseback, wielding batons.

There was pandemonium. Vignettes of horror unfolded around me, all at once. A woman screamed, "Holy Mother of God!" as some people, in their rush to escape, trampled her. Baby carriages were knocked over, the infants in them sent flying. Near the flatbed, a woman crumpled to the ground from the blow of a policeman's baton. Another policeman, hit in the head with a brick, dropped like a ton of them, bleeding profusely. Yet another had the baton ripped from his hand and was being beaten with it. Closer to me, three policemen began clubbing a trekker, pounding, pounding, drawing blood. Instinctively, I went to pull them off. I heard hoofbeats behind me, turned, saw the distinctive uniform and a baton descending and was not agile enough to avoid it. I threw up my arms for protection and cushioned the blow to my head but went crashing to the ground anyway. I struggled to my hands and knees, stunned as much from the knowledge of who had delivered the blow as from the blow itself. Then I collapsed in a heap.

I AWAKENED in the hospital with a bad headache and a few stitches in my scalp as souvenirs. Yet it wasn't the physical injuries that bothered me as much as it was the knowledge of who had struck me down. I could not reconcile those men with the likes of Sam Steele or, for that matter, the men who had served us stew in Swift Current. Worse, they represented the country I had fought for in two wars, the country that Davey and Jim had died for, and I felt betrayed.

Some time afterward, I found out that the rally had turned into a full-scale riot that lasted over two hours and had spread out over several blocks near Market Square. Over a hundred people were injured. Many trekkers were battered and bruised by batons and wounded by police bullets, as were a few innocent bystanders. At least half of the injured were law enforcement officers, both city policemen and Mounties, hit by bricks or beaten with their own clubs wrested from them by trekkers. A city detective was killed, and each side was accusing the other of murder. Shop windows were smashed and dozens of trekkers were arrested for rioting. Evans and Black had been apprehended under Section 98 of the Criminal Code, which banned any association whose intent was to provoke change by violence.

With the help of a matronly nurse, I managed to reach Ree by phone. I had only wired her during the trek, and to actually speak with her made me feel connected to more solid ground. She had heard of the melee on the radio and was frantic with worry. I made light of my physical injuries and kept the other to myself. I simply told her that the trek was finished because it had run into a brick wall known as government and that there was nothing more we could do that wouldn't shed more blood. I would be home in a few days.

Relief filled Ree's voice. "Thank God, Jack! I won't be happy until you're here safe and sound!"

I returned to the exhibition grounds just as the police were loosening the cordon they'd maintained to prevent the trekkers who hadn't attended the rally from joining the riot. The men were angry and frustrated, and the only good news was that that most of those arrested had been released and the charges against Evans and Black dropped due to lack of evidence.

Saskatchewan's premier realized that sending the men to the camp near Lumsden, rather than dispersing them to their homes or back to other relief camps, might prove to be a costly mistake and lead to an even bigger riot. Tired of the prime minister's recalcitrance, he said that his government would accept responsibility for disbanding the trekkers. The offer provided Bennett with the perfect opportunity to abdicate his government's accountability for ending the trek, and he did not hesitate to accept. So the men were provided with railway tickets and a food allowance. They marched in an orderly fashion to the station and the trains that would whisk them away from Regina, away from their disappointment, some eastbound, most westbound, but all "riding the cushions" instead of the top of a boxcar.

I paid for my own ticket and went home to Ree and The Little Karoo.

A COMMISSION was set up to investigate the riot and, after several months of interviewing witnesses, of which I was one, it concluded that the trekkers alone were responsible. I can't say that I was surprised—decisions are easy to reach when only one side of the story holds sway. The commission dismissed all of the trekkers' testimony, as well as that of Reginans who had witnessed the event. But I can say unequivocally that the riot began with a police attack and a sham arrest, not with a few harmless words from George Black. And there had been ample opportunity to arrest him and Evans prior to the rally, so why wait to do it in a place where a riot was a distinct possibility? Moreover, the authorities knew that all Evans wanted was to negotiate a way to get the men out of Regina in peace and with some measure of dignity. I think Bennett wanted to crush him, and crush the trekkers too.

A federal election saw Bennett ousted from office and replaced by William Lyon Mackenzie King, who kept his promises of shutting down the relief camps and ridding the Criminal Code of Section 98, the law that Bennett had so loosely interpreted. The men remained out of work and on relief, though, and it took a war to end that. When the call to arms came, they enlisted by the thousands to fight on behalf of the country that had treated them so cruelly. After all, it was work, even though it was the most dangerous job in the world.

Bennett retreated to England to become a peer of the realm. Evans, despite his defeat, would not lie down. He returned to British Columbia to fight the good fight and do what he did best—organize unions. I never saw him during my infrequent trips to Vancouver, but Pete said he always maintained that the idea for the trek was his.

I didn't mind. The man had put himself squarely on the firing line to help the relief camp workers, which is more than I can say for our politicians. They should have pinned a medal on him as far as I was concerned. Sadly, he was struck down and killed by a car in Vancouver in 1941, probably still thinking he could change the world. But in the grand scheme of things there isn't much that ordinary people can do to alter the minds of powerful men forged in the fire of self-righteous entitlement. There will always be the haves and the have-nots, and the one will never willingly share with the other.

Evans was right on one count, however, when he told the men at the Kamloops meeting that a wealthy, modern state ought to take better care of those it might one day call on to defend it, and that if a man has a responsibility to his country, then his country ought to have an equal responsibility to him.

Those words contained no small truth; it was simply a matter of duty.

EPILOGUE

The Little Karoo, Late Summer, 1943

THAT TRAIN JOURNEY STILL plays regularly on the stage of my mind. Some days it doesn't stall in Regina but keeps surging forward, on to Winnipeg where another 1,000 men join, then on to Thunder Bay, Sudbury and Toronto, collecting strikers all along the way. From Toronto we move on to Ottawa, 5,000 strong, and occupy the front lawns of Parliament. In a single voice we insist on our right to share in the wealth of this country. And Bennett, that old thief, commits the most incongruous act of his life by loosening his government's purse strings and giving the men back the dignity he had stolen.

Such were my fantasies on days like today, as I sat in a reflective mood on our front porch looking out over the lake, nursing a small whisky and glad that the day's toil with the horses was behind me. Not that it was overly difficult; I just lacked the stamina that I once had. Through the screen door I could hear Ree in the kitchen making dinner, humming along with a Glenn Miller tune on the radio. We were having a quiet dinner on our own to celebrate our 41st wedding anniversary, after which we'd join the Spencers for a few drinks. Maggie was making the trip from town for the occasion.

A breeze wrinkled the lake's surface and the trembling aspens made their lovely rustling sound. The sky was streaked with mackerel-scale clouds and the air was warm and humid, which probably meant a thunderstorm later on.

Had I ever lived up to the image of Wild Jack Strong? What man outside a dime novel could? Certainly not me. Then again, I had not become my father either, despite trying hard twice. We like to think that we know where we're going, but more often than not we arrive at a completely different destination. Chance is the common thread woven into the fabric of everyone's life. But if a man has stories to tell, then it must count for something, and I have told my stories: some that still haunt me and some that set my spirit soaring. I can see them all, like shimmering ghosts; I can hear them, too, like a whisper across a silent room . . . the men slaughtered during that violent spring of 1885, women screaming, Indians whooping . . . a good man who could not accept that his way of life was disappearing . . . a wife and a child snatched brutally from this world . . . cattle trailed through an unimaginable wilderness . . . bullets whistling across the South African veld . . . a good woman found in the most unlikely of places . . . a good friend and a son lost to the ravages of war . . . an angel deep in a coal mine . . . and the trek. They are all there, neatly slotted into compartments in my mind.

A distant rumble of thunder in the west reached my ears and the wind was ruffling the lake more intensely. A horse whinnied. Chickens, sensing the coming storm, pecked their way to the henhouse. I took another sip of whisky. I couldn't count the times I'd sat here, enjoying this view that had never turned stale over the years, even though it was substantially the same as it was when we first moved here. I drank it in deeply because it soon wouldn't be ours.

There was another great war raging across the world, more blood being spilled, men dying like dogs because of a few megalomaniacs. Pete had put his law practice aside and was a captain with the 1st Canadian Infantry Division somewhere in Sicily. All we could do was wait and hope for the best. A couple of nights before, there was more talk on the news of conscription, if more volunteers weren't forthcoming. Ree had given me her best "cross" look and said, "Don't you dare even *think* about it!"

I laughed. I was 74 years old and the war would do just fine without me. Besides, after Regina, my loyalty had been centred more on Ree and The Little Karoo. Truth to tell, I was getting too old for the rigours of ranch life, let alone war. It's something few men care to admit, but it needs addressing. I was faring all right—there was nothing wrong with me that being 20 years younger wouldn't cure—but I couldn't say the same for Ree. That old enemy of the aged, arthritis, had lodged itself in her joints and she wasn't as mobile as she thought she needed to be to help keep the ranch going. So by summer's end, The Little Karoo would no longer be in our hands.

We were moving to Kamloops to be nearer medical treatment, and to be nearer Maggie who had made the move a couple of months before. Jimmy and Tommy were taking over our operation, since it would be theirs anyway when Ree and I passed away. It was in our wills. Jimmy was married and starting a family of his own, and they would occupy our home, which would give them some breathing room. Pete would share in the ownership too, but the younger boys would work it and were planning to increase their cattle herd to around a thousand to meet the steadily rising demand for beef. The brothers were two of the best cowboys I'd ever seen and the chances of the war swallowing them up, at least at this point, appeared slim.

The wind had gathered even more speed and the air had cooled, as if it had slid down from a high mountain pass. I finished my drink and went inside. On the radio, a girl with a beautiful voice was singing "In the Still of the Night." Ree was setting the kitchen table, and I placed my glass on the counter and went to her. From behind, I enclosed her slender frame in my arms. She turned and pulled me tight and laid her head on my shoulder, the melding of two into one. I whispered in her ear, "Tell me the truth. Have you ever wished for a different life?"

"Yes," she said, letting her head fall back to look into my eyes. "A long time ago on the African veld. Who said wishes don't come true?"

We swayed to the music, then moved slowly around the floor. If a man didn't have a good woman to give definition to his life, then he didn't have much of a life at all, for I held in my arms what was perhaps my best story. And as long as we were able, we would dance in the unfinished stories of our lives.

Author's Note and Further Reading

AS IN THE PREVIOUS two volumes of the Wild Jack Strong trilogy, fiction occupies the driver's seat in this, the final volume. Nevertheless, I have tried to remain true to the historical record by referring to the following books: *Kamloops Cattlemen*, by T. Alex Bulman, (reprint) Sono Nis Press, Victoria, BC, 1993, for ranching in the Kamloops, BC, area; *The First World War*, by John Keegan, Random House of Canada, Toronto, 2000, for World War I; *Sixteen Months in Germany*, by John Evans, in *Canada at War*, Penguin Books, Toronto, 1997, for Jack's slave-camp experience; *The Great Depression*, by Pierre Berton, McClelland & Stewart, Toronto, 1991, for the Great Depression; and *We Were the Salt of the Earth*, by Victor Howard, University of Regina, 1985, for the On-to-Ottawa Trek.

Acknowledgments

MY SINCERE THANKS GO to Marlyn Horsdal, for her usual editorial diligence and helpful suggestions, as well as the entire staff at TouchWood Editions whose talented efforts shine in the presentation of this book and its predecessors. And endless thanks to Jaye, for her endless support.

OTHER WORKS BY BILL GALLAHER

The Journey	The Promise	Deadly Innocent	A Man Called Moses
978-1-894898-99-7	978-1-894898-83-6	978-1-894898-11-9	978-1-894898-04-1
$18.95	$18.95	$18.95	$18.95

"To experience Bill Gallaher is to participate in past tales that have, in their telling, moved into the present. He is able to open our senses to the essence of Canada and the lives of those whose sojourns have made this land."
—M. Stevens, Smith Hill Productions

". . . rich in detail . . . [Gallaher's] writing brings to life . . . experiences that can scarcely be images in the 21st century . . . a highly readable account of one of the most interesting, and most important, chapters in BC's history."
—*Times Colonist*

"I decided to read just a couple of pages before sleeping. At 2:00 A.M. I was still sitting bolt upright, biting my fingernails as the book drew me toward its shocking twist ending."
—*BC History Magazine*